IN EVERY WAY

IN EVERY WAY

a novel

NIC BROWN

COUNTERPOINT
BERKELEY

Library of Congress Cataloging-in-Publication Data

Brown, Nic, 1977-
In Every Way : A Novel / Nic Brown.
pages ; cm
ISBN 978-1-61902-459-5 (hardcover)
1. Women college students--Fiction. 2. Mothers and daughters--Fiction. 3. Domestic fiction. I. Title.

PS3602.R7224215 2015
813'.6--dc23

2014034099

ISBN 978-1-61902-459-5

Cover design by Kara Davison Faceout Studio
Interior Design by Megan Jones Design

COUNTERPOINT
2560 Ninth Street, Suite 318
Berkeley, CA 94710
www.counterpointpress.com

Printed in the United States of America
Distributed by Publishers Group West

10 9 8 7 6 5 4 3 2

For my mom

ONE

CHAPTER 1

MARIA IS FOUR minutes late to Life Drawing. It's the first time in two weeks she has even attended the class. The professor has been told that this is because Maria is not comfortable drawing the nude male model—a pale little specimen with a limp ponytail and an overabundance of moles—but that is a lie. Maria is no prude. Truth is, Maria's been avoiding her ex-boyfriend, Jack, and her own mother, both of whom are enrolled in the class.

Maria is nineteen. Notes in ballpoint pen tattoo her hands. A thick veil of bangs hangs just below her eyes. Usually she would keep her eyes there hidden, cast down upon her dirty red Keds, but today she's tingling with a rush of rare confidence. In her portfolio are six charcoal drawings of herself wearing nothing but a Hello Kitty mask. They vibe from her bag like hot-wired batteries of possession. So she brushes aside her bangs and steps into the studio as the eyes of her classmates rise.

At the long, paint-spattered drafting table where Maria usually sits, her mother and Jack are seated together.

"Hey," Jack says.

"Hey," Maria says.

These terrifying words are the first they've spoken in weeks.

Jack wears a Detroit Tigers baseball hat askew atop a frozen explosion of teased blond hair. He's all sinew and angles. He says that he was born full-grown, that he's going to wang chung. That he has tapped into the source. Maria doesn't always know what he means, but she knows he must be right because he looks so cool that it makes her chest feel hollow when she looks at him. Thing is, Jack hates stressing out and he has to make it stop. Maria knows this because he told her so the last time they spoke. He said, "If this is going to make me feel stressed out, then I have to make it stop."

"You mean us?" Maria said.

"I guess."

The reason Jack was stressed out is because he got Maria pregnant.

But today, on this soft March morning, Jack doesn't look stressed out. He smiles. The light shines through the wide black plug in his earlobe. Maria remembers the night he placed her finger in that hole. "You're inside me," he'd said, "but you aren't even touching me."

Jack pulls up a stool and motions for Maria to sit. For a moment she considers not doing so, but cannot see any other option. The room is full, there are no seats left, and she does not have the fortitude to turn and walk out of the class. She tells herself to show no fear. And she sits.

"I've been reading *The Three Musketeers*," Jack says. "Total mind fuck, m'lady. God your mom was right."

"M'lady?" Maria says. Jack has a short list of favored lingo, but this—m'lady—is one she has yet to hear. It is, to Maria, the sound of two weeks apart.

"Dumas style," Jack says, in proud explanation.

"Gross," Maria says, the very name of the author reviving years of oversaturation. Her mother, an English professor, is what they call the leading Alexandre Dumas scholar in America. Not the world. Claude Schopp in Paris has the world. But her mother has the States. Or did.

Now she's retired and ten months into life with stage four breast cancer. Both of the diseased breasts were removed months ago, but the cancer has spread to places that cannot be cut off. Since the operation, Maria's mother has had her daughter's name tattooed onto her wrist. She has visited her old college roommate three times. She has created a Facebook profile. She has enrolled in Maria's section of Life Drawing. She says she has never before been this alive.

Despite Maria's lack of interest in Dumas, Jack's still worked up. He says, "But it's good. Seriously. I had no idea. It's all about fighting and getting pussy."

"Jack," says Maria's mother. At the drafting table beside him she sighs.

Jack lightly punches Maria's mother on the shoulder and she laughs girlishly. A laugh that never before existed. A laugh that has appeared only since her sickness, like some spark sent up from a slowly burning house.

JACK FIRST APPEARED to Maria on a friend's porch arguing about the drummer for Wilco. He blew his bubble gum into an enormous orb and then popped it with a lit cigarette. Eleven weeks later Maria took a pregnancy test in the bathroom of the Carrboro Harris Teeter. Through a sheen of her own urine, a red cross appeared like a message delivered from God. She considers it a testament to her mother's judicial personality—one that imbued the house with frank discussions of conception and religion from the earliest ages memorable—that Maria's first instinct was to go home.

At the kitchen table, her mother was brushing loose hair from her scalp, collecting the limp gray strands in a stainless steel mixing bowl.

Maria said, "I'm totally screwed."

"Who isn't?" her mother said, twirling her hair like spaghetti.

"I'm pregnant," Maria said.

Maria's mother set her hairbrush on the table. She had not yet thinned the left side of her scalp, and it was significantly more full of hair than the other. Maria considered the fact that so many of those strands were already dead, just hanging on to their few surviving neighbors like some weave made from her mother's own locks.

"Well shit," her mother said.

Sitting in her old chair at the table, her own initials carved into the food-stained oak before her, Maria said, "It's like three weeks since I missed my period. So it's too late for the morning-after pill or anything."

"Now just a minute," her mother said. "What exactly do you want?"

"Not a baby," Maria said. She chuckled. She started to cry.

"Seems you already have one of those," her mother said.

"It's just a blob."

Maria's mother shrugged. She lifted a handful of hair from the bowl, then dropped it back in. "It Jack's?" she said.

Maria nodded, dragging the back of her index finger across her now running nose. She then instinctively wiped it under the table, only to discover the harsh topography of a miniature inverted mountain range built from the petrified chewing gum of her own childhood.

"He's a good guy," her mother said. "People wait their whole lives for that."

"What are you saying?" Maria said.

"When you're dying," her mother said, "you just start to think about babies. You see the whole world through hippie glasses."

The doctor had said her mother could expect another six months. Maria did the math. There would be no overlap, even if having a child were anything more than some weird slumming fantasy.

"You suddenly pro-life?" Maria said.

"Yes," her mother said. "In like every way."

"ON THE WALL," the professor says to the class. "Hang 'em if you got 'em."

He says this every class before critique. He considers himself wacky. His name is Milton Rigby. He is elderly and the most celebrated professor in the department, yet still teaches intro classes by choice. Rumor has it he teaches for only one dollar a semester, but Maria has her doubts. It's all campus myth. But unlike most of the students who are now delicately removing drawings from their portfolios and pinning them to a long corkboard, Maria and her mother have known Rigby for decades. Maria has seen his paintings in the Museum of Modern Art. She thinks of him as a species of human perfection and aspires to his achievement. But it is not celebrity that Maria admires—it is his skill. She is embarrassed that her situation with Jack has kept her out of his class. She is ashamed that she has lied to him.

Jack makes no motion to hang any drawings. Instead, he lifts a thirty-two-ounce Bojangles iced tea from a Florida-shaped puddle on the desk and sucks at the straw until it gurgles. Maria wonders if the life growing inside her is already engineered for stupidity.

"So, m'lady," Jack says, and leans his head back until the Tigers hat falls to the floor. He spits a piece of ice high into the air and then catches it in his mouth as it falls. He gazes down the bridge of his nose at Maria and exhales dramatically, air hissing through his teeth. He motions at her stomach and says, "You OK?"

Because they have not spoken, Jack does not even know if the pregnancy is still a pregnancy. He does not know that Maria has done nothing about it, spoken about it with no one other than her sick mother. He does not know that she has cried almost every night, sometimes while knitting, sometimes while streaming *Masterpiece* off PBS, sometimes while comparing the rates for abortion in Chapel Hill, sometimes while reading the canned internet messaging of adoption services and teen pregnancy helplines. She feels like she has yet to even convince herself of the truth of the situation she's in. It is an indisputable fact that she is pregnant, but what exactly will that fact mean? This is the mystery filling her days.

"I don't know," Maria says. "I haven't done anything."

Jack nods, as if all is as expected. He retrieves his hat and spins it upon a finger.

Maria hangs her drawings. They are immaculate and precise and so much better than anything else in the class that Professor Rigby has, more than once, told the other students that compared with Maria's, their drawings all look like seismograph readouts. She has always excelled at the transformation of life into line and color. Youth for her was a continual preparation for art school. She started private lessons in fourth grade, spent two summers at North Carolina School of the Arts, attended Governor's School the previous June. During each summer vacation to Beaufort, a small town on the coast, she spent her days not sunbathing or surfing or volleyballing in the sand, but instead painting seascapes.

When Maria was in high school, Rigby told her several times that she should apply to Yale. It is where he went. He seemed to think it was obvious she should just go there too. Maria was embarrassed to even ask if he thought she might stand a real chance of admission, although she wanted to, good God she wanted to, she wanted to qualify for her dreams, because something like Yale is indeed what she dreamed of—a flight into a studio not in North Carolina, not populated with sorority girls lovely and soft and fine, but with others whose dreams like hers seemed in search of some cosmic travel agent. But when her mother grew sick, Maria knew that Yale was not going to be an option. Maria's father died when she was two, her grandparents passed away long ago, the University of North Carolina is in her hometown, and tuition is discounted for children of faculty. And so she is here. The decision was never even a decision.

A red bandana dangles from Jack's back left pocket as he leans in closely to inspect her drawings.

"Damn you're good," he says.

In each drawing, Maria appears at a three-quarter profile, Hello Kitty mask turned to the viewer, small bare breasts catching the light from her upturned desk lamp. Jack stares in silence for a moment, then says, "Hot dog, Sweetcakes. I miss you."

"You're a baby," Maria says, proud of the sudden magic worked by this rendering of her own body.

Jack removes a ballpoint pen from the front pocket of his red plaid shirt and gently takes Maria's forearm in hand. The nib tickles her flesh as he writes on it. When finished, a full sentence crawls across her skin. It reads *I carry you through the threshold and do my duty, happy ending Sleeping Beauty.*

It sounds remotely familiar but Maria cannot place it.

"That's what?" she says.

"Dumas," Jack says, then points at the quote and nods. He whispers, "I'm serious. Or like, the way I wish it was. I know I'm a failure."

"I hear Dumas?" Maria's mother says, stepping closer. She traces her finger along the words on Maria's forearm. Maria is embarrassed at the touch. Her mother laughs and says, "All my live brothers is locked down with high numbers."

"Damn," Jack says. "You're right."

"Care to let me in?" Maria says, as Jack and her mother share a smile. Maria resents even the briefest exchange between the two that she cannot follow and again feels the time apart from Jack emerge in this new and confusing sound bite. "What are you right about?"

"That's not Dumas," her mother says, looking Maria in the eye. She squeezes Maria's arm softly, as if testing for ripeness. "That's the Wu."

"What?" Maria says. She hears her mother speaking the confusing code of Jack.

"You getting into it?" Jack says.

"It's like taking my brain to the gym," Maria's mother says.

"The Wu-Tang Clan?" Maria says, invoking the name of one of Jack's favorites, a group of rappers that makes Maria wonder about the hordes of people who understand something about music that she apparently cannot. She cannot quite believe her mother is quoting the Wu-Tang Clan. But she is.

"What about it?" her mother says.

Jack shrugs and flips his thumb. "Yeah," he says, "I just dumped some on her iPod."

AFTER DINNER, MARIA goes to Rite Aid and to Whole Foods. She picks up her mother's prescriptions, fish oil, a gallon of milk, four bananas, a seven-grain loaf, six eggs, kale, and quinoa. Maria's carefully negotiated guardianship of her '96 Volvo wagon is contingent upon these deliveries. Her mother no longer drives. Before delivery, Maria returns to her dorm. In the past two weeks, since she's known she was pregnant, she has delivered her mother's groceries late, after her mother is asleep, so as to avoid contact.

When Maria arrives in her dorm room, she finds Jack sitting at her desk. She calmly places the shopping bags on her bed.

"So you buddies with my mom now?" she says.

Jack removes one orange pill bottle from the Rite Aid bag. He squints at the label, then reads aloud: "Talwin." He smells the lid. "It work?"

"I don't know," Maria says.

Jack shakes two pills into his palm and swallows them with a mouthful of old coffee. Maria closely inspects the pill bottle. There is a warning about drinking alcohol. That one should not operate a motor vehicle. That women who are pregnant should not take it. She is suddenly afraid of the container, astonished to have found herself in any category that can now thus be poisoned.

"Seriously," she says, putting the bottle back into the bag. "Why's my mom listening to the Wu-Tang Clan?"

"Why not?" Jack says.

"She's sixty-three."

"She asked me what I was into."

"What are you into?" Maria says.

"That thing on your arm?" Jack says. "I'm serious as shit."

"You're immature," Maria says. "And irresponsible." She feels her words dissipate like so much breath into cold air. She has longed for Jack to appear to her like this, but now that she has him, she can think of nothing to say. In a desperate effort to connect, she conjures the Wu.

"Vivid thoughts," she says, "devils resort to trick knowledge. They kick garbage, lust for chicks and quick dollars."

"You rapping?" Jack says.

Maria nods. Yes, she is rapping.

"Come on," Jack says. "You don't even like them." He takes Maria's hand. "I know what you're saying, though. I do. Put on Hello Kitty. Seriously. No, I'm just kidding. But seriously, though. Yeah, put it on."

Maria lifts the Hello Kitty mask from its perch on her bedpost and places it on her cold face. Jack pops the elastic on the widest part of her skull.

"Now say something," he says. "No rapping. Say it in Maria."

"You're a piece of crap," Maria says.

Jack kisses her neck.

"I tell you to pull out," Maria says. "And you what? You don't pull out."

Jack pushes her onto the bed. Maria adjusts herself so that he may lie more comfortably atop her.

"I should put razorblades inside me so that your wiener shreds if you ever do me again," she says.

"I know," Jack says. "I know."

"You read my mom's books while I cry in Art History and everyone fucking stares at me," she says.

"I know," Jack says. "I know."

"I am so stupid," Maria says. She cries under her mask, thrilled and confused with desire. "This is so messed up."

"I know," Jack says.

"What am I going to do?" Maria says, running her hands inside Jack's shirt.

"I know," Jack says.

"I *asked* you," Maria says.

"Don't think about it," Jack says, kissing her neck. "We have time."

They make love for more than five minutes. Afterward, Jack says, "Jump in. The Talwin's perfect." He licks his lips and runs his fingertips across Maria's eyelids. She considers revealing that, unlike him, she actually read the label and cannot in fact take the drug even if she wanted to.

MARIA'S PHONE RINGS. It is close to 1:00 AM. Calls at this hour are not uncommon. With chemotherapy, her mother's sleep schedule has become erratic. But the phone has been silent since Maria told her mother she was pregnant. It is a pattern her mother repeats often, falling silent for days when confronted with decisions or complex family drama, trusting time as the best tool for perspective. The pregnancy has triggered the latest stretch of silence, but it has all been expected. Maria has been avoided, and has thus avoided back. This phone call now signals the resumption of normal relations.

"It was so good to see you today," her mother says. "I have to know what you did."

"Now's not a good time," Maria says. "Jack is here."

"He should know too," her mother says. "Have you been to a doctor?"

"I don't even know how to make an appointment," Maria says. The years of her life stretch away before her, definitively parentless and adult.

"What does Jack think?" her mother says.

Jack lies on the bed, ash falling from his cigarette onto the pillow. The cell phone is loud enough for him to hear Maria's mother's voice, tinny and bright and insistent.

"'Sup, Dr. M," he says.

"I don't know what he thinks," Maria says.

"Look," her mother says. "We've been talking about it. He says he'll do whatever you want."

"You've been talking about it?" Maria says.

Jack shrugs and exhales a spiraling ring of smoke.

"Then you tell me," Maria says. "Both of you. What do you want?"

"I want to have a thousand grandchildren," her mother says. "I want to go back to the beach. I want to live forever."

"I want whatever you want," Jack says.

Before falling asleep, Maria closes herself into the bathroom. She sits on the toilet and presses her fingertips into her stomach, kneading the flesh that Jack once swore felt exactly like biscuit dough. She imagines what it would feel like to be propped in bed, holding a sleeping baby. But there is no precedent. Maria has no nieces or nephews, no babysitting experience at all. It then occurs to her that the scene she has just conjured is set in the dorm room on the other side of the wall. But there are no family units available in Student Housing. Maria cannot even successfully imagine a space where holding her own child might seem possible.

THURSDAY'S LIFE DRAWING is the self-portrait. Maria stands a full-length mirror beside her easel. A wig of curls borrowed from her mother tumbles onto her shoulders. She shakes the prosthetic hair and imagines herself as a musketeer. She cannot conceive of successfully creating what the others here call a self-portrait. Every drawing of herself she has made, and there are many, looks like someone definitively not her. Only in a costume does her identity ever harden. Musketeer, Hello Kitty. In place of what should be her own image, these she lets stand in for herself.

Jack is working from a printout of a nude photo that Maria took of him in her dorm room. He is not ashamed. The photo is taped to his easel. Before class he smoked a joint that looked like a limp palm tree and swallowed another Talwin. He bobs his head to music no one can hear.

"Your proportions," her mother says. She spreads her fingers and places her hand on Jack's drawing, measuring the distance between shoulders. She then twists her hand to compare the torso, placing her thumb on the drawing of Jack's crotch.

"Weird," Maria says.

"Don't act like a child," Maria's mother says.

"You're thumbing my boyfriend's privates," Maria says.

"You her boyfriend again?" Maria's mother says.

Jack drapes his arm around Maria and lightly cups her rear end. Maria nuzzles into the lightning bolt tattooed on his neck. His pulse taps insistent and fast against her cheek and she considers the fact that both he and her mother are on the same drugs. Since Tuesday, Jack has ingested more than a dozen Talwins. Maria feels confident that by now he has so much of the stuff coursing through his veins that his own blood would be enough to poison their unborn child.

"She used to call her teddy bear her boyfriend," her mother says. "And she always put a diaper on him. I should have taken more pictures."

"Put diapers on me," Jack says.

Maria's mother smiles. One of the pigtails on her wig has come undone. Graphite is smeared across her forehead. Maria does not remember putting diapers on her teddy bear. She does not remember calling him her boyfriend. Her mother's brain is like a museum of Maria's childhood, its archives unexplored and now rotting.

THREE am. MARIA is Hello Kitty. Jack is doing the twist. Sam Cooke is on the stereo. Jack says he's the newest he's ever been, everything is the coolest it has ever been. Maria's phone rings.

"Sweetie," her mother says over the line. She sounds panicked. "You there? You get my pills, sweetie?"

Maria did not get the pills. She did not go to Whole Foods. She did not go to Rite Aid. She went back to her dorm room and lay naked in bed with Jack. Now Jack stands behind her and holds each of her protruding hipbones like handles. He twists her body with his as Sam Cooke sings *we're having a party*.

"It's this nerve thing," her mother says. "Oh God. It's my legs."

Maria swats at Jack and raises the Hello Kitty mask. "I got them," she says. "I totally forgot to drop them off. I'm so sorry."

In the parking lot, Maria leans into a cold wind. Old leaves stick to damp corners of banked concrete. Panicking with guilt, she tells herself that she must remain focused. The Rite Aid stays open all night. The prescription is in her pocket. She tries to envision her mother's imminent death, as if this meditation will calm her. But the scene is one she cannot conjure. Everything is inevitable, she tells herself. Everything will happen. But she cannot believe it.

The Volvo is not parked where she'd expected to find it. She looks frantically from side to side. She presses the panic button. In the corner of the parking lot, the car flashes and screams as a trio of passing students yelps in delight.

Maria drives slowly through the empty lot, shuffling oil change receipts and paper napkins from the glove box in a desperate search for a cigarette, which she knows she is not supposed to smoke, but what does it matter? She surprises herself by even taking the child's health into consideration. It is as if she has discovered a secret plot within her own brain, one covertly planning a safe transition into motherhood. She has the feeling that she should not indulge it. Her fingers locate a loose Parliament, and this is when her face smacks the dashboard. The car shudders. The engine ceases to run. The radio falls silent.

Maria raises her head to a cracked windshield, on the other side of which the hood now holds a loose grip on a concrete telephone pole. She drops the now broken cigarette and gingerly lifts a hand to her forehead. Her fingers come away dark with blood. The rearview reveals a small cut just below her widow's peak.

"I hit a telephone pole," she says into her phone, gasping.

"Where?" Jack says.

"The parking lot!"

Within minutes Jack appears, wearing a yellow fanny pack secured beneath the camel hair blazer that Maria bought at Goodwill. It is too small for his frame. He shivers in the light from the arc lamp.

"How fast were you going?" he says.

"One mile per hour?" Maria says.

"Will it start?"

"I don't know."

Jack looks closely into her eyes, then removes Maria's hand from her wound.

"You can't go to Rite Aid," he says.

"I'm fine."

"No, I mean, even if they're open, the pharmacy won't be. Give me the phone." He dials. "Dr. M? We can't find your pills. Maria's upset. But I have some stuff. And it's medicine in most states. OK?"

Maria has never heard Jack speak like this to anyone. Some inner leader has been unleashed. She has been her mother's caretaker for so long that she can almost feel a physical weight lift from her as Jack backs the Volvo away from the telephone pole. The grill falls off the car and wobbles slowly on the concrete as they pass it.

"I still have one," Jack says.

He opens his hand to reveal a pill, oval and yellow and small.

"If we give her just one, she'll know you've been taking them," Maria says.

"Then you take it," Jack says.

Maria does not know if Jack has read the label on the bottle yet or not, but she doubts it. And if a pregnant woman does take these pills, then what? Maria has knowingly avoided prescription drug warnings too many times to count. One of anything will not matter. And if it does matter, she thinks, maybe that's a good thing. She scrapes the pill off Jack's palm and swallows it dry. It lodges somewhere inside her neck, feeling ten times its actual size. She is scared it will become some time-release choking hazard, swelling to block all oxygen at a later hour. Silently she swallows again and again, willing it out of her throat.

A campus devoid of life. The lake. The streets of Maria's child-hood. Stenciled by the fingers of bare limbs, here and there a window still glows softly. They reach her mother's house. Almost every light is on. Long rectangles of pale yellow stretch across the lawn. The back door is unlocked. The kitchen wall holds an odd, semi-abstract portrait of Maria painted by Professor Rigby. The image embarrassed Maria as a child. It now seems profound. In an uncontrolled rush, she feels the desire for this object once her mother is no longer alive.

Jack says, "Dr. M?"

"In here," her mother calls. Her voice is labored and distant.

They find her in the bedroom wearing a bright pink robe. Each leg is propped on a pillow. An electric blanket is draped over them. Maria feels the presence of an invisible malicious magic. She does not under-stand the biology of this pain, why this disease should do anything other than make you cough and die.

"Mom," she says, and climbs on the bed. "I am so sorry." She lays an arm across her mother's chest, once so buxom; Maria is still sur-prised to find it flat. At her touch, Maria's mother flinches.

"What happened to your head?" her mother whispers.

"I banged it on my bedpost," Maria says, unsure of where she found this lie, knowing that it sounds even more illicit than the truth. "It's fine."

Jack unzips his fanny pack and says, "You smoke weed, Dr. M?" Maria's mother doesn't even open her eyes. It as if the pain in her legs, the disease, and the hour have all conspired to render anything they say impossible to shock. "Not in a long time," she says.

"Nothing better for pain," Jack says.

He produces a glass bong emblazoned with a yellow alien and places it on the nightstand. Maria's mother is in so much pain that she is beyond addressing the strangeness of this scene. Maria lets Jack maintain the direction. He lifts her mother's iPod and says, "This will help," then spins his fingers across it like he's casting a spell. The Wu-Tang Clan emerges quiet and insistent through the room's built-in speakers. Maria worries that even the soft bass line will hurt her mother's diseased nerves.

Her mother closes her eyes.

"Dr. M, open up," Jack says. "Go ahead."

"I don't know how. Do you know?" she says, turning to Maria.

"Sort of," Maria says.

"Help me."

"OK," Maria says. "Like this." She holds a lighter to the bong and inhales. "Here," she says, thick smoke curling out of her mouth.

"That's right," Jack says. "We're the three musketeers."

Maria's mother follows her lead. She coughs, smoke sputtering from her face. Tears stream from each eye. She leans her head on Maria's shoulder and shudders.

The music fills the air like fog. Verse after verse pumps into the room. Jack turns off the lamp, and in the new darkness, a cold light shimmers faintly from the skylight above. Maria's mother lies, eyes closed, on the pillow, silently moving her lips to the lyrics.

Wu-Tang Clan ain't nothing to fuck with, they sing. *Wu-Tang Clan ain't nothing to fuck with.*

"Yeah," Jack says. "Let it go, m'lady."

Her mother begins to sing aloud. "Wu-Tang Clan ain't nothing to fuck with," she says. "Wu-Tang Clan ain't nothing to fuck with."

"That's right," Jack says. "The Wu-Tang Clan *ain't* nothing to fuck with."

Maria lowers herself to the remaining edge of pillow. She closes her eyes. The music thumps through the mattress. The heat from the electric blanket warms the side of her thigh.

Jack begins to sing with her mother now. Together they sing, "Wu-Tang Clan ain't nothing to fuck with."

Maria feels left out. She cannot remember ever having sung anything other than "Happy Birthday" with anyone before, but now opens her mouth and raises her voice.

"Wu-Tang Clan ain't nothing to fuck with," they sing. "Wu Tang Clan ain't nothing to fuck with."

Their voices rise in volume, with each word growing more comfortable with the other. Maria feels her mother's hand crawl clammy and bashful atop her own. She opens her eyes. Framed in the skylight above are a handful of stars, radiant and distant and cold. The three of them chant to that unnamed constellation, emphatically telling those inevitable heavens exactly what should not be fucked with.

CHAPTER 2

SCHOOL IS OUT for summer. Maria is six months pregnant. Through the humid nights of June she sweats in her childhood bed, tucked beneath a thin orange quilt. In this house the air conditioning never runs: these days, Maria's mother is always cold.

A specter of steam rises from Maria's coffee cup and fogs the glass of the dining room window. Though the room is assigned for meals, Maria has not, in fact, dined in it since she was fifteen. For the past four years it has been her mother's office, the walnut table stretched to its grandest length. This was the vast and busy staging ground where her mother drafted her last book. And the table still holds notes, but they have not moved in months. The same five piles of paper have stood there since her mother's breasts were removed. The sheet of high-pound stock topping each was once bright white but has now grown yellow and dusty, and though Maria knows that their cursive notations are destined to never again engage with the mind from which they once sprung, she will not move them or even touch them. To do so would signify much more than the need for more table space.

But Maria is not there to look at her mother's old paperwork. She is waiting for the blue Lexus that is, at that moment, slowing to a stop at the curb. A young brunette emerges. Maria assumes this is Anne Vanstory, caseworker for the Children's Home Society of North

Carolina. Anne is in her midthirties, thin, and smart in a navy linen dress cinched around her waist by a leather belt. The wind flatters her by pressing the fabric close against her flesh. Maria has never met Anne, though the woman is not exactly a stranger. If you are a professional in Chapel Hill, if you go to fund-raisers at the Ackland Art Museum, if you shop at Southern Season, if you listen to bluegrass on the lawn of the Carolina Inn and get your coffee at Caffé Driade, Maria's mother knows you. And so it is with Anne Vanstory, who, in addition to being an adoption counselor, is a former student of her mother's.

Anne Vanstory appears representative of a whole race of women refined in a climate separate from Maria's. She wears a pearl necklace. Her large purse is of some perfect untanned leather. She is beautiful according to scientific proof, a gem polished by breeding.

Maria, on the other hand, is unbathed and clad in one of Jack's sweatshirts. It says CORROSION OF CONFORMITY and is torn along the left cuff. He gave it to her with great ceremony after staying up until sunrise on the night of his twentieth birthday, when Maria had said, "I'm cold," shivering in the front seat of his black Scirocco. Above her the sky had begun to pink up between the bare limbs of the maples lining the eastern edge of the Rainbow Soccer fields. They had parked there for the explicit purpose of seeing the sun rise. Jack said he had never before seen it happen. Maria had many times, though. At Camp Celo, a Quaker back-to-nature place where she worked as the horse counselor for the previous three summers, she rose before the sun almost every day.

"I'm cold too," Jack said, pulling the sweatshirt over his head. He handed it to her and said, "but with you, I'm happy to freeze to death."

His breath tumbled from his nose in two blossoms of steam and reminded Maria of the horses at camp, the old ones who would breathe on her neck as she bent to fill a bucket in the morning chill. The velvet of their noses. She misses those summers and their simple pleasures. She misses the other counselors too, whom she thought she would never befriend because they were all so different, religious and athletic and gregarious, but grew to love despite it all.

Now Maria does not have many friends. There are girls who listen to the same music, who drive jittery old cars and pick her up and take her to shows at the Cat's Cradle, who skateboard, who smoke and have an increasing array of tattoos. One calls herself Icy People and raps over drum machines at the Nightlight and the 506. Another, Jane, owns the brown Dodge Diplomat in which they most often cruise. When Maria first told these girls that she was pregnant, they all played it cool, said shit, said I had an abortion last May, said that was quick. Icy People hugged her, but Maria could smell fear. As she grew larger they stopped calling. How can you not drink! Jane asked once, incredulous. Maria does not enjoy sports, is not interested in Chapel Hill basketball, is not in any type of club or sorority. To her, Jack and his accouterments, sweatshirt included, are totems of team loyalty. But as Anne Vanstory ascends the three front steps, Maria feels this allegiance challenged. She lifts the sweatshirt over her head and tosses it into a shadowy corner.

At the door, Anne Vanstory says, "Maria?"

Maria slaps both hands on her swollen abdomen and smiles.

The living room is filled with blue leather chairs set upon an expansive Turkish carpet that camouflaged every dropped earring and paperclip of Maria's childhood.

"How far along are you?" Anne says.

"Six months," Maria says.

"You look great," she says. "You feel good? Good. Good. How'd you decide to get in touch?" She shuffles papers within her bag, withdrawing a yellow legal pad and short green pencil.

Anne sounds so comfortable, as if she's inquiring about the wallpaper. But this is not an easy question for Maria to answer. She had decided on abortion. Of course she had, she thinks. She cannot be a mother. Somehow, though, after sharing a house with cancer, Maria has found an incredible increase in tolerance for the protesters on the corner of Franklin Street outside Whole Foods who hold oversized poster boards picturing bloodied fetuses in forceps. These days, when Maria steps into sunlight so bright that it shines through her closed eyelids, she wonders if those rays are strong enough to penetrate her womb and reveal a rosy world of organs to her small hidden passenger. She doesn't know exactly how to answer.

"I'm nineteen," Maria says. "So. And the woman has the right and all that. But, I don't know. It's hard to explain. You know about my mom."

"I do," Anne says. "I'm so sorry."

"So, I don't know. I'm not religious or anything. And I don't even want to say I've been thinking about life, because that word just makes me think of all those weirdos outside Whole Foods with the signs, but, I don't know, I guess that's part of it."

"OK," Anne says, pausing to decode Anne's meaning. "OK. And, can I ask who's the father?"

"Jack Sveboda."

"Dr. Sveboda's son?" Anne says, naming Jack's father, a cardiac specialist at the university.

Maria nods and then, in a burst, chuckles. She is not sure why she is laughing, but then Anne starts too. It feels good to share any understanding with this woman, even if Maria is not sure what that understanding is.

"I can hear you!" Jack says from the hallway.

He enters the room and removes his hat. Maria is amazed at this, even the slightest condescension to convention, and is for a moment proud. Then a dog enters the room behind Jack and she is reminded that she is still mad at him.

The dog is a stringy border collie with eyes desperate for love and whom, before this morning, Maria had never seen. He cannot be even a full year old. Jack appeared with him only one hour before, unannounced.

"You think it's smart that I got her a dog?" Jack says. "It's so she'll have something to love, you know, for when after."

"It's smart if she wants the dog," Anne says.

"Damn!" Jack says, sitting softly beside Maria.

The dog is named Pinky. Jack appeared with him at breakfast, Pinky pulling him by a leash into the kitchen while Maria fried three eggs.

"The hell is that?" Maria had said.

"Your new dog," Jack said, restraining a determined grin of pride.

"No it isn't."

"After you pop that thing out," he said, "you're gonna need something cute to feed. It's science."

"Take him back."

"Shelter doesn't take returns."

"I'm pretty sure that's all they take," Maria said.

But despite herself, she understands both the logic and the irony of Jack's thinking: that an adoption will fix an adoption. The child will cry out to be loved and cared for, yet she has agreed not to respond. She is leaving that to the Children's Home Society of North Carolina. What will happen to any remaining urge to nurture? Who knows if it will even emerge, Maria thinks. She is not one to trust that it will happen. She has heard tell, yes, of biological love, of biological impulse, but doesn't she have enough biological matter to care for with her mother? She does not need a dog upon which to lavish any excess love.

Jack sits beside Maria and takes her hand.

"I love this beautiful woman right here," he says. "I don't want to freak you out. But listen. She's perfect. This is all my fault."

Anne nods, grinning as if she is not sure if he is joking or serious.

"M'lady," Jack says, and Anne cocks her head. Maria too is confused at the non sequitur, but Jack isn't talking to Anne anymore. He is addressing Maria's mother, who has appeared in the doorframe like a withered bundle of sticks in a bathrobe. Anne follows his gaze.

"Professor Matthews," she says.

"I *do* remember you," Maria's mother says. "You dated the boy with the big necklace."

"Chip King," Anne says. She laughs. "He did have a big necklace."

"What is man but a little soul holding up a corpse? You remember that?" Maria's mother says, sitting. "Anne took my Dante class." She opens one palm as if it might catch something falling from the ceiling, then shakes her head. "Christ. That's not Dante. It's . . ." She looks at what is left of her body and shrugs. "Place my grandchild with the royal family, Anne. Please."

Recently they've been hitting it hard. Chemo is streamed into her mother's veins twice a week by Dr. Jeanette, an oncologist whose office is housed in a hospital extension at the bottom of a hill behind the Harris Teeter off Highway 86. At her last appointment, Maria's mother told Dr. Jeanette he should just cut out everything other than her heart and brain. "You've got a lot of both," Dr. Jeanette said, and Maria's mother groaned. "Oh please," she said. "Go work for Hallmark."

Her mother cannot abide sentiment, yet Maria's situation softens her. She sits beside her daughter and places one cold hand upon Maria's belly. A sharp joint dashes nonchalant across her womb.

"God, it's always pointier than I expect," her mother says, and Jack rushes to place his hand atop hers.

"Is there anything more amazing?" Anne says.

The silence that answers is confirmation that there is not.

Maria does not know the baby's gender. She has asked the doctors to withhold the information, thinking it might keep attachment to a minimum. But what does gender matter, Maria wonders, when there is a little person pressing Maria's own flesh against that of her dying mother and her boyfriend? It is becoming increasingly clear to Maria that scientific knowledge is going to play no role in shaping her feelings about this child, a certainty both dangerous and enticing. She aspires not to indulge it at all.

Jack presses his nose against Maria's stomach. "Luke," he says, projecting directly into her flesh, "this is your father."

Maria pushes him away, embarrassed.

"OK," Anne says, removing from her leather bag one sheet of paper. Maria is sure she too is embarrassed and is using this paperwork as a distraction. Jack sits up, begrudgingly. "Let's look at your bill of rights."

The stationery is headed with the image of two minuscule baby footprints. Maria imagines the feet of her unborn child, curious if they are yet larger than those on the page.

"You have the right to receive this information, and all legal options related to relinquishment in an accurate, competent, and unbiased manner," Anne says. "You have the right to change the decision about relinquishment, and to choose to parent the child."

Jack squints at the paper and says, "Sprechen sie American?"

"Means you can change your mind," Maria's mother says.

"We gonna wanna?" Jack says.

"Some do," Anne says.

"We won't," Maria says. "We want you to give it to Philip and Nina."

Maria mother and Jack make no reaction to this—they already know about Maria's plans—but Anne raises her eyebrows and smiles, as if this, this is what she had been waiting for.

Philip and Nina. Maria found them on the internet. Family profiles are posted on all agency sites. Each has a photo of a prospective adopting couple with a short message from each. Almost all look like young student council members fresh out of church, their missives drawn heavily from verse. Maria cannot stomach the idea of her child growing up in a house filled with prayer. But as soon as she saw Philip and Nina, she knew she need no longer worry. She knew, in fact, that something magical was happening, something almost as mystic as conception. It was not because of what Philip and Nina wrote in their online message, nor what they look like that made her feel this way, though their appearance was indeed a point of interest—Nina is half Japanese and so beautiful it seems unfair; Philip is bearded, weathered, and striking—rather it was the fact that Maria recognized Philip's face. She knows who he is, she knows where he lives. And this she has told no one.

Maria's mother's old college roommate Karen lives in Beaufort, where Maria and her mother last vacationed in June. Beaufort is a small town on the coast known for its historic homes and Blackbeard's shipwrecks. Maria and her mother visit every year, sometimes more than once a season.

Maria spent most of her time this past summer sketching sailboats and passersby while seated at the end of a small public pier on a tidal creek. Almost every day, Philip would walk past with a rangy orange borzoi. She still has sketches of him saved within blue sketchbooks tied shut with ribbon. Maria did not know he was Philip then. She would have guessed that his name was something more continental. French, maybe. Claude. Gael. But she was curious about him. He was tall and thick, with a mess of dark hair tangled into a beard that seemed to grow up to his eyes. His wardrobe of loose linen and frayed oxford spoke to Maria of money and something distinctly cultured. At times he wore a knit maroon necktie. He was not exactly handsome, but this improved him in her eyes. Maria cannot remember what her first impressions were. They are colored now by the facts.

The appearance of Philip's face on the agency website astounded Maria less than she felt it should have. It was hard for her to believe, yes. She felt an awareness of some cosmic folly, yes. But nothing surprises Maria like it used to. The world has been filled with an excess of magic over these past few months. The edges of life sparkle and the shimmer of her days makes Maria increasingly numb. This, the appearance of a face she recognized while searching online for a family to adopt her unborn child, seemed like just another trick in the ongoing magic act of her life.

"Philip and Nina are one of our . . ." Anne says. She searches for the words. "Most complicated options."

"Meaning what?" Maria says.

Anne searches for more words. "Philip smokes," she says.

"I smoke," Jack says.

Anne looks at Maria. There is a moment of silence.

"OK," Anne says. "If we're sure already, that'll just make things easier."

She removes a dozen or so thin hardbound books from her bag. Maria has seen these sorts of things before. They are the type of photo albums you order online from uploaded files. Her mother makes one after each trip to Europe. Anne flips through them like an oversized deck of cards before selecting one and passing it to Maria.

Inside are eighteen pages of photographs of Philip and Nina, carefully selected to reveal nothing about where they live. But Maria can tell these are the live oaks of Beaufort, these are its sandy streets. They live in a white Victorian house. She thinks she has seen it before. It looks like so many others in Karen's neighborhood. They have and apparently love that one long-nosed and regal borzoi. They were married in what looks to Maria like Duke Chapel. They smile, but not always. Maria feels a deep unfairness at each photo of Nina. The woman is so graceful on film that Maria wonders at the worth of her own genes. She worries that any child of hers could never match the beauty of this family.

On the first page of the album is a letter typed in a font that approximates handwritten cursive. Maria feels certain that Philip and Nina do not like any font that attempts to mimic handwriting and that they have used it only to appeal to some adoption agency aesthetic. It feels like a secret she shares with them already.

Dear Birth Parent(s),

My husband, Philip, and I cannot begin to imagine all that you are facing right now, but what we do know is that you are a very strong and brave person (or persons).

After one devastating miscarriage and several years of trying to conceive, Philip and I have decided that adoption is the best option for us to start the family we so desire. If there is a child out there who needs us, we are ready to open our home and hearts to that little boy or girl. We also believe in open adoption and are excited about forming and maintaining a relationship with you, if this is something that you desire. We have placed this decision in your hands.

Philip and I have been dating since high school and have been married for fourteen years. We went to the same college and married the year we graduated. Education is very important to us. I have a law degree and Philip has a PhD. He is a professor. For several years I worked as a social worker, but am now a public defender. I love the work. We are natives of Mississippi but love calling North Carolina home.

We enjoy crafts and being outside. Our favorite television shows are Twin Peaks and The Cosby Show, though we do not in fact own a television; we plan on raising our child in a world of their own imagination.

We have one dog, an old and sweet borzoi named Ferdinand. He is very gentle and loves children, but does sometimes have bad breath. We brush his teeth as often as possible.

Here's a joke we like: how do you make a tissue dance? Put a little boogie in it. We're old-fashioned, but we like it that way.

Whether you choose us or another family, we wish you the best of luck. If you would like to get to know us better, please feel free to contact our adoption counselor, Anne Vanstory, at 1-919-555-0143.

Yours,
Nina and Philip

"Can you clarify what an open adoption is?" Maria says, handing the book to Jack. He and her mother begin to read it together.

"When you maintain contact with the adoptive parents," Anne says.

"I don't want that."

"We encourage it," Anne says. "Birth mothers, after birth, they want to see their kids. And even if you don't, with the internet, and Facebook, and God knows what. Even if you don't want to be found by the other party, it happens."

"We're going to do it closed or whatever the regular way is," Maria says. So much time has been spent making decisions that she feels she has run out of emotional real estate. This door, she feels, needs to close definitively.

"Do you make them write these just like this?" Jack says, holding the book open to the letter.

"There's a template," Anne says.

"That explains it," Maria's mother says, sighing in relief.

"To make this explicit," Anne says, turning back to Maria. "This is a closed adoption?"

"Yes," Maria says.

Anne makes a note. Maria's mother extends the photo album into the space before her, as if it might levitate.

"That's for you to keep," Anne says. "And that's what you'll get mailed to you, every year. A letter and some photos so you can track the child's progress."

"We get that even with a closed adoption?" Maria says.

Anne nods.

"Are adopted kids always screwed up?" Jack says. "Orphans and unwanteds?"

Anne's words emerge slowly. "If adopted children develop issues," she says, "it's not because of adoption. It's often in spite of adoption. We're going to put this child in the best household possible."

"Then why were you all weird about Philip and Nina?" Jack says.

"I wasn't."

"Yeah, but you were."

"Philip smokes," Anne says. "Like I said. And they're not religious. Most of their income is drawn from independent wealth. They're an unusual option for some people. Many people, actually. But if they weren't viable, we wouldn't have them in our organization."

"I smell fish," Jack says. "Do you smell fish?"

"Jack," says Maria's mother, and Maria is grateful for the attempt to calm him. She is concerned that Anne will be scared off by Jack's bluster.

The door opens and Pinky enters with a bra dangling from his jowls. The bra is new, not yet even worn, purchased at Roses to accommodate the rapid increase in Maria's breast size. One of the padded cups is torn apart in Pinky's jaws, the foam padding sprinkled in pink pieces across his muzzle. He lopes over to Anne, lifts his front paws into her lap, and there drops the bra.

"Jesus Christ," Maria says, rising from the couch. "No!"

Maria is mortified. But with convincing nonchalance, Anne rubs Pinky's head. Maria is filled with the sudden knowledge that Anne enters the houses of strangers every day. Strangers who do not want to keep their children. Maria has never even met another pregnant woman her age, let alone one planning an adoption. Surely Jack and a sickly border collie with bra innards scattered across his muzzle are a more common workplace sight to Anne than the bright abstract art on the walls of the country's leading Alexandre Dumas scholar.

Maria pulls Pinky off Anne's lap and pushes the shredded bra against his nose so firmly that she can feel him struggle for breath. She has never before had a dog and does not understand the logic of this move but has seen it enacted once by a neighbor and it feels right.

"Maria," her mother says. "Stop."

But Maria does not stop. Not only is she certain this needs to be done, she is frustrated at her mother's doubt about said fact. She wonders at hormonal instinct—if she would have been capable of this before she was pregnant, if there are now chemicals in her system sent from the fetus, preparing her for discipline, chemicals that her mother no longer has. There are times when Maria has felt unjustly deprived of her youth, and lately they've been increasing. The present moment is one of them. Maria is not above feeling sorry for herself. Where are her lost afternoons? Where are her petty arguments over what movies to see, what shows to attend? She is too busy with medicine and proto-motherhood to find them. So smell the bra, Maria thinks. My mom is dying and my boobs are getting weird and I have to pee almost always. And I'm nineteen years old. So smell this bra, and understand right now that you cannot make my life any harder.

Jack lifts Pinky by the scruff of his neck, something Maria has never actually witnessed done before. Silent and resigned, the dog dangles from Jack's grip, shifting his glance from side to side. Maria thinks it would be nice to be so resigned, to be so led. To be held in the air by someone trying to teach you the lesson that not everyone wants to be licked. He carries the dog out of the room, and Maria, dropping the bra into the trash, says, "I didn't ask for that dog."

"They can be a handful," Anne says, and gives Marie a two-page photocopy that outlines the five stages of grief.

"Actually, my mom's doctor already gave me one of these," Maria says.

Anne squints in confusion, then says, "Oh no, I'm so sorry." She looks at Maria like she shouldn't have to explain any further. But she does need to. "I don't mean . . . I mean, you're going to lose your child. It is a serious loss."

Maria nods with understanding, but as with so many of the truths she is told to accept these days, she does not in fact believe it.

THAT AFTERNOON MARIA finds Pinky asleep beside a bottle of
Dolophine. The bottle has been chewed open. Several pills remain
within the mangled orange canister, but others have fallen out upon
the rug. She is sure others are at that very moment releasing synthetic
morphine into Pinky's bloodstream.

She finds it surprisingly easy to lift the dog. It is as if his insides are
filled with nothing more than air and pills. She places him gently into
the backseat of the Volvo.

Heading north on Airport Road, Maria finds the Orange County
Animal Shelter on the left. The receptionist is young and blasé. Maria
wonders how many times a day the woman witnesses someone cry.

"He just ate my mom's medicine," Maria says, heaving Pinky onto
the couch in the entry.

"What kind?" the receptionist says.

"Dolophine."

"This isn't an emergency clinic."

"I don't want him back."

"Reginald," the receptionist says into a phone, and Reginald almost
immediately appears. He is a withered piece of humanity in blue scrubs
with a lined face sprinkled in gray whiskers. Lifting Pinky from the
couch, he says, "You eat too many goofballs, baby? OK OK OK."

As Reginald carries Pinky through a pair of orange swinging doors,
Maria is reminded of the last time her mother carried her to bed. She
was nine. She fell asleep on the couch watching *The Great Mouse
Detective* and awoke being lifted silently into her mother's arms.
Maria knew she was too old to be doted upon like this, but pretended
to be asleep anyway, savoring the pillow of her mother's shoulder as
they padded softly into the front hallway. But there Maria's mother

stopped. Maria opened an eye. Through the window, on the moonlit lawn, she saw a white dog hunched atop Sid, the neighbors' cat, with his mouth clamped calmly on Sid's neck. After a moment, the dog released his grip and strode slowly into the azaleas. Sid raised his head, looked both ways, and lay back down. Maria told herself he was going to be all right. She remained silent as her mother continued upstairs, sure her mother could feel her heart as it raced wildly within her chest. Only after she was tucked in and the door firmly shut did Maria run to her window. Below, Sid remained on the lawn, and as Maria watched, willing him to rise, her mother appeared in the moonlight. She carried a shovel glinting on her shoulder. Maria wondered what her mother was going to dig. But she wasn't going to dig anything. She raised the tool above her head and, with the sudden force of finality, let it fall upon the cat.

AFTER DINNER THAT evening, night falls easy around Maria for the first time in weeks. The home of her child is now known. Pinky is gone. Her mother is asleep. Maria sits in the small pool of light from the lamp on the kitchen table and flips slowly through the photo album of Philip and Nina. What good does it do her to dream of their house? She will not occupy its rooms. She tells herself to stop looking, but cannot. Their faces soothe her, smiling at her very decision to give her child away. She lingers over each page, thinking she recognizes a tree there, a corner. The waterfront of Beaufort in the background. Then her reverie is interrupted by the door. She raises her head. It is Jack, wiping his hair from his eyes, a leash in his hand as he enters through the back.

"I came to take him out," he says. "We're in this together, partner."

"I took him back," Maria says, closing the book. She is embarrassed to be seen dreaming over its pages.

"To jail?" Jack says.

"He ate Mom's medicine."

"Well I do too!"

"It's too much," Maria says.

"No," Jack says, grabbing the leash with both hands and pulling it taut before him. "No no no. You're gonna want him back." He loops the leash around the back of his neck and raises his face to the ceiling. He breathes a deep sigh.

"I don't need a dog," Maria says.

"What do you need?" Jack says, his eyes still pointed upward.

"You," she says.

Jack lowers his gaze and sets the leash gently on the counter. He circles the chopping block and kneels before Maria, pressing his face against her stomach. "Listen to me, little pollywog," he says into her flesh, over-pronouncing each word. "Your momma is a sweet, sweet thing."

Maria tangles her fingers into Jack's hair. She feels the warmth of safety and love tangled therein but is immediately suspicious of it. Is it Jack who is making her feel this way? She is unsure. It seems more likely she is just experiencing a reflex of affection triggered by something soft and warm. Perhaps he was right about Pinky after all, she thinks.

"You're part baby and part dog anyway," she says, and Jack raises his eyes and barks.

WHEN MARIA'S OWN father had a heart attack in the blue leather chair in their living room, she was two years and three months old.

She remembers neither him nor the event of his death. But she does remember when, at age four, she got out of bed after a nightmare about a fox and scampered down the hall to her mother's room. At the door she stopped. Within she heard what sounded like a sick animal, though she knew it was no such thing. She understood that these were the sounds of her mother's sadness. To return to her own bed, haunted there by that evil fox, was still more tempting and safe. She felt guilty, even then, at the fear of her own mother's pain and the decision to not enter the room and comfort her.

"Thank God I get these summers off," her mother would say to Maria from time to time. "My job is the best in the world." Even then Maria understood that she wasn't talking about her actual job, but rather the space around it—the hours it allowed her to devote to Maria. Her childhood was filled with joy and the opportunity for even more of it. Now Maria understands that she will come to know loss. This is not what looms largest in her thoughts of her mother, though. What she spends her nights thinking about is how her mother deserves as many days of happiness now as possible. These she is determined to provide.

CHAPTER 3

LATE AUGUST. SCHOOL has already begun, but Maria is no longer attending. As her classmates gather in fluorescent-lit classrooms and play the name game around circular seating, she sits on the edge of her bed, groaning in the dusty afternoon daylight. The yellow shag carpet is clenched between her toes. When the contraction ends she falls back upon the bed and pants.

Down the hallway she tiptoes. "Mom?" she whispers.

Her mother is frail, yellow, and attended to by a bearded nurse named Hank. She is still alive is what's amazing. There has been no change in weeks. Every few days, she tells Maria to drive her to the coast. "Let's go to Beaufort, just for dinner," she says, but Beaufort is four hours away and Maria's mother knows she would not, at this stage, even survive the car ride. Maria feels certain that her mother has willed herself to stay alive long enough so that she can meet her daughter's child and wonders why, if her mother could do that, why she cannot will herself to live forever.

"It time?" her mother says.

"I just had a real one," Maria says.

Hank—a man who wears several colorfully beaded bracelets—steps out of the room, his finest qualification an ability to disappear. Maria's mother places one papery hand on Maria's abdomen.

Blood has spilled in pools of blue and green under the surface of her mother's skin.

"Can you believe it?" her mother says.

"How can I not?" Maria says, looking at her stomach. Another contraction starts and the spaces between her breaths begin to shorten.

"Here it comes," her mother says.

Maria crumples to the floor. There is nothing else her body can fall upon that is not plugged in, piped, or brittle. Hank peers into the room, only to relax once he has confirmed that the groaning is not coming from his own patient.

"You OK?" her mother says.

"No," Maria says. She understands that this progression of events was always supposed to happen, but that does little to make any of it feel right. It seems possible that her body is breaking.

"OK. She's OK," her mother says to Hank.

Jack arrives seventeen minutes and one contraction later in khakis and a blue oxford, sleeves rolled up.

"Look at you," Maria's mother says.

"Like I just got a job at Kinko's," he says. "I know. But you gotta look like business if you want to do business." He sits beside Maria on the couch and gently pets her head. Maria bats his hand away.

"Relax," he says.

But Maria does not relax. Two nights pass without the gap closing to the four-minute window she has been instructed to wait for until going to the hospital. She has, since the beginning, been determined to have a natural childbirth and avoid the hospital as much as possible, but by the second night of labor, she begins to think this plan of action is folly. She is so tired that she starts to nod off in the moments between contractions, even if only for a few seconds at a time. She lays her head back and closes her eyes, the voices in the room passing like fog, until everything snaps into sharp focus as a new contraction begins.

"I'm glad you're not telling her to breathe," Maria's mother says, early in the third day of labor.

"She knows how to breathe," Jack says.

"Take me to the hospital," Maria says.

"I'll deliver that baby in the kitchen if I need to," Jack says. "Hank can do whatever it is he does if we need him. But you're perfectly safe here until it's time."

"It's time!" Maria says.

"Breathe," Jack says.

"Fuck you," Maria says.

"God I love you," Jack says.

During the third sleepless night, the gap finally closes. At the hospital, the pain is worse than anyone had been able to explain. Maria tells herself to expect a leg to fall off and the fact that one does not is the only thing that makes each contraction seem tolerable. When the baby finally emerges, Jack places the gasping, viscous child upon Maria's breast.

She has heard stories of birth mothers who refuse to hold their newborns for fear they might become attached. But Maria is not so afraid. She tells herself she can do it all. That she can love for a few days and that then she can let go. After all, hasn't she been touching the child for nine months already? So Maria now holds her child to her chest, sobbing. She is baffled by all that her body has endured. A pride absolute and different from any other she has ever known has settled upon her. She cries, but they are not tears of sadness. Never before has she cried from joy and exhaustion. So these are happy tears, she thinks, and then realizes that she does not yet know what sex the child is. In this moment, Maria uncodes how parents carry on through defect, deformity, and sickness. It doesn't matter what sex this child is, she thinks, or how it is, or why it is. It only matters that it is.

ANNE ARRIVES FOUR hours later, and Maria has the feeling that she's been taking babies from mothers all day long.

"It's a girl," Maria says.

"Isn't it, though!" Anne says, lifting the child from Jack's arms. "And what's this girl's name?"

"Bonacieux," Maria says.

"Bonacieux," Anne says.

It is the surname of Maria's mother's favorite Dumas character, the woman with whom D'Artagnan falls in love in *The Three Musketeers*. When Maria suggested it, Jack said, "God, you're smart." He has a hard time saying the name, however, and refers to the child mostly just as B. Maria has not yet told her mother of the name. It will be a surprise.

"When do you take her?" Maria says.

"Right now is *your* time," Anne says.

"I just need to bring her home to meet Mom," Maria says.

"You can't actually move her."

"I know."

"I mean the baby."

"You think she's going to steal something that's already hers?" Jack says.

"No, it's OK," Maria says, remembering this rule. "Mom will come here."

But Maria isn't sure her mother can come here. Her mother has not left the house in two weeks. To her surprise, though, after dinner Hank wheels her mother into the room. Maria is sure that there has been some computation about how many hours of life are lost with each minute it took to get here.

"She looks like Jack," her mother says, gazing at Bonacieux. "And it's a good thing he's so handsome."

When Maria's mother first met Jack, she told Maria that he was a loser and that it wasn't opinion, just empirical fact. She said he looked like a fool. Maria is jealous of the purity of her mother's mind now— she knows that her mother still believes these things about Jack but has reached a point where other things matter more.

Maria cannot tell if the child looks like Jack or not. It is as if there is a filter on her vision when she looks at the baby. Bonacieux looks like no one but herself, Maria thinks. She has blue-gray eyes, the same color as Jack's. Maria can see that. There is blond down on her head. Eyebrows so faint they are barely there. A bright red fig-sized birthmark on her stomach. But Maria can see no resemblance to either herself or Jack other than the most obvious traits of genus and race. Tracing back photos of her mother over time, Maria has always thought it all made sense—she always looked like the woman she one day became. Maria now realizes that this certainty works only in reverse. What this child will look like is a complete and total mystery.

Jack helps her mother stand. Maria has seen him do this more than a dozen times since the Fourth of July and wonders if this one will be the last. They have passed the window of life predicted by the doctors and are now in what her mother calls the Dakotas: a land of unknowns to which few have ever before traveled. Life in this territory could last for days, perhaps more. The doctor won't say how much more, but according to the websites featuring Mexican alternative treatment centers that her mother has been leaving on the screen of Maria's laptop, life could continue for months, years, or decades. This sickness could mean nothing.

Her mother struggles out of her wheelchair, rising almost one joint at a time. She holds on to Maria's bed and finally collapses beside her. The mattress barely shifts.

"Meet Bonacieux," Maria says.

The name settles like a balm upon her mother's face. She says nothing, but Maria can see the rightness of this name, the wisdom in its choice. Her mother takes Bonacieux and holds the child to her flat, scarred chest. Bonacieux cries, and as she does, Maria's mother nods gently as if in complete and utter agreement.

IN THE MORNING, Anne stands at the foot of the bed. For the fourth night, Maria has not slept for more than a few minutes at a time. During the hours between sunset and sunrise, she was tended to by a lactation consultant named Maud who helped her successfully breast-feed, a challenge that brought such unexpected pain that Maria now feels like her doctor should be held accountable for negligence. At first the nurses were surprised that Maria even wanted to try. But she has read the literature. She listens to the reportage on NPR. She is not going to deny her daughter the benefits of her own milk, even if it is only for a day. But now, her nipples are chafed and raw, and she is, for a moment, excited to have anyone take the child so that she can just close her eyes and rest. This thought fills her with immediate guilt, but she cannot deny its veracity.

Anne says, "You're giving Philip and Nina the most wonderful gift a person can give."

Maria lifts Bonacieux and the child's head droops onto Maria's chin. Maria gently takes a few strands of Bonacieux's soft down into her lips. She raises the child's chin, kisses her daughter on the lips, and holds her to her cheek, as if Maria's tears might mark her own daughter with some permanent scent that nine months in her womb could not. Bonacieux is a gift, she thinks. A gift for people who are ready to love her. But Maria already loves Bonacieux. She has been blindsided with love. The pride she felt after childbirth has only grown and somehow encompassed the child too, as if Bonacieux helped birth herself. Maria now feels with absolute certainty that she should keep the child. She knows that she should not, under any circumstances, pass this child to Anne. But there Anne stands, right there beside her in a gray dress that looks both perfectly casual and simultaneously more elegant than anything Maria has ever worn. And sixty pages of release forms have been signed. And there are Philip and Nina, beautiful both of them, birdlike Nina, somewhere, waiting in a house filled with baby things. And Maria has no baby things. She has no crib in which to place the child. She has not slept in almost five days. So she lifts the child into the air, terrified and confident that what she is doing is criminal, and delivers her daughter to Anne.

CHAPTER 4

I N THE REFLECTION of the mirror on Maria's white dresser, breast milk seeps in two small ovals through her thin gray sweatshirt. It has been three days. Three days that have passed with a magical ease, as if Maria has been stranded in some benevolent foreign land. The certainty of her own error has passed. She feels now that she has indeed done right by Bonacieux and wonders at the first stage listed on her photocopied stages of grief: denial. The steps beyond scare her and she hopes that denial, if that is what this is, can last forever.

It does not.

Two weeks and four days later, Maria stands inside the Orange County Animal Shelter. Behind a massive computer monitor a young woman clatters around a keyboard.

"Pinky, Pinky, Pinky," the woman says. "Border collie?"

"Yes," Maria says.

"I love that scarf."

It is Maria's mother's orange Hermès. She also wears her mother's wedding ring on her middle finger and a touch of Chanel No. 5 from a dusty bottle in the medicine cabinet. "I don't need that stuff," her mother has been saying. "Take it." Maria is willing herself to be good enough for these items, as if they might wear her in and not the other way around. She is not yet there. She feels them on her flesh like new bandages.

"OK," the woman finally says. "Pinky Pinkerton. Border collie." She twists her mouth as if tasting something bitter, then bares her teeth and inhales a hiss. "Processed. A few months back." At a glance she understands Maria's optimistic confusion. "Put to sleep," she says. "After two weeks, that's procedure. I'm so sorry. Was he yours?"

"Yes," Maria says. "Sort of."

"I'm sorry."

"Are there any other dogs I can see?"

"Yeah, of course. Second door on the left," the woman says, "and I really do love that scarf."

Maria opens the door to a mass of yelping life. A dozen dogs rise up on their hind legs and bounce, trying to reach her face with their tongues. Maria kneels, trying to locate just one head to pat, and they all pile atop her, licking any exposed flesh as if it has all been coated in gravy. Maria allows the weight of these beasts to roll her back onto the floor. They pant warm breath into her ears while nipping at each other in a battle over this human real estate. She purses her mouth shut against their lapping urgent tongues, but that is the only constraint. She lays her arms flat against the ground and, as they destroy the lauded scarf, she allows them as much access to her flesh as they want.

Later, inside the Volvo in the parking lot, Maria lights a cigarette. Pinky was just a dog, she tells herself. She removes the cigarette from her mouth and holds it above her forearm. She has memorized the pamphlet about grief. According to its progression, Maria is now due for anger. And she is indeed angry. She has been overwhelmed by a surprise onslaught of sorrow, confusion, and fury. She recalls stories from the news about recent mothers who have become suicidal after giving birth, of infanticide, of postpartum psychosis. And though

Maria is sure that she has not gone crazy, these accounts of new mothers becoming mentally unhinged now make a type of sense to her. At
dusk every day, Maria cannot help but cry. She knows it is coming,
like the eventual setting of the sun. There is no trigger needed, nothing but the hour. It brings with it a sadness mixed with anger, both
at circumstance and at nothing. Her sharpest rage is often nebulous
and confusing. She is ashamed and scared of these cyclical breaks, but
knows they have happened before and will happen again—to her and
countless others. The obviousness of it all infuriates her even further.
Though the cigarette still glows just inches from her arm, she does not
allow it to touch her flesh, although she is compelled to. She cannot
imagine a way to explain the wound to Jack and her mother.

Maria knows they speak about her when she's out of sight. Jack
and her mother grow closer by the day. They've been smoking more
weed, a ritual surprisingly less shocking to Maria than she might have
ever guessed. In a house like hers, the big news is not that her mother
is smoking weed with her boyfriend. It's that her mother is dying. It's
that Maria has just given birth.

Before she starts the engine, Maria acknowledges what this desire
for Pinky really is. It is an irresistible and obvious craving—like a tsu-
nami of psychic force, one that has been washing over her for days
now—for contact with her own child. She wants to see her, to hold
her, and to smell the down across her scalp. These urges first arose
with what seemed like innocuous questions—how was she eating, how
was her sleep, who has she started to look like. They then became
coupled with a growing sense of loss. Because although Maria had felt
confident in her plans to avoid the responsibility of mothering, in its
place she has found very little. The pride Maria felt in those moments

just after birth has been replaced with something like shame. There is no other way she can think of to ease this burden: she needs to know that her daughter is well.

THAT AFTERNOON MARIA drinks white wine on the porch with Jack. He wears a long gray T-shirt with the sleeves cut off. It flaps around his lanky frame like a frayed flag.

"Then let's find her," he says. They've been discussing Maria's desire to see her daughter, to gather some sort of information about her, to confirm that she is healthy and in a good home. To learn anything. To put something into the void.

"That's not what I'm saying," Maria says, even though that is exactly what she's been saying, in so many words. She is frustrated with her own increasing interest in the child, but is not necessarily surprised with it. It is Jack's concern for their daughter that has come as a shock. Maria is afraid to encourage it. She can imagine Jack showing up on her doorstep one day, just like he did with Pinky, this time holding their child. And what she finds most terrifying about this possibility is not what Jack would then do, but what she would. "I just want to see her," she says.

"Google her," Jack says.

"She's three weeks old. She's not online."

"Of course she is," Jack says, running his fingers up Maria's shin. "Don't tell me that's not why you named her something crazy."

"What's not why?"

"With a name like that, she's gonna be easy to find."

Maria has never considered that she probably could someday find her daughter, if only because of her name. She is so constantly surprised at the connections Jack makes. He seems simultaneously older and younger than she, both more intelligent and less. He lifts the hair at the back of her neck and kisses her there.

"But you can do that later," he says. "Now let's remind each other how we made that baby."

"I have *stiches*," Maria says, pushing him away.

"They told me they put in an extra daddy stitch," Jack says, and slaps his hands together.

Layers of gauze still line Maria's underwear. She cannot at this point imagine ever again allowing anyone access to her body. Maria understands that Jack does not have this problem. She knows he longs for her, but she cannot bring herself to address him in any way that might bring him such pleasure. She pushes him away again as he draws closer and his face drops like he's been told that he can't have a toy.

"What," he says. "A man has passionate desire for his lady. You want me to deny it? That I have passionate desire? I cannot tell a lie."

"In time," Maria says.

After Jack departs, Maria opens her computer. On the screen is a website about a Mexican clinic performing blood transfusions from guinea pigs. She might be a little drunk. She types "Bonacieux" into the search engine. Actresses in movie adaptations of *The Three Musketeers* appear. Maria can almost feel her mother's exasperation at these digital priorities. She adds "North Carolina" to the mix and then "Philip and Nina," and in less than two minutes, she's looking at a photoblog called *Isn't Bonny Bonny?*

It's not clear at first. Is this really her daughter? Maria cannot remember exactly what her daughter looks like. She opens her phone to the photos Jack took of the child in those first few hours, as Maria held her close to her chest, a small stocking cap stuck on her head, eyes squeezed shut, her face puffy and yellow. What does Bonacieux look like now? Maria does not know. In these photos, here for anyone to see, someone's child wears bright red socks knit to resemble high-top sneakers. Someone's child sleeps in a white basinet that looks like it was made even before the ancient house in which she now lives. Someone's child bathes in the depths of a chipped enamel sink deep enough for four babies, presided over by an antique silver spigot and a dirty russet brush. And then Maria knows that this is not just any child, but her own. Because she sees the child's parents, and they are Philip and Nina. Together they have taken Bonacieux to a dock, to the beach, and to a restaurant near Beaufort that Maria recognizes: the Sanitary Fish Market. Maria has slept in a T-shirt from that restaurant for years, its cotton now tissue-thin and translucent. It worked, she thinks. She has constructed a family that will traffic in the same seafood buffets of her own childhood, that will drive the same streets, know the same weather. And this, these photos here before her, they have suddenly allowed Maria to enter their house, to see the cracks that line their sink, enjoy the art on the walls of the nursery, and to look into the silvery-gray eyes of her child. She knows already it will not be enough. She wants to see it firsthand.

IN THE LIVING room, Maria's mother listens to Patti Smith, a copy of *The New York Times* held close to her face and a red rubber water bottle perched atop her head. "The head is like a limb in Africa," she says, lowering the paper to her lap. "They carry laundry, groceries. Children. But I can barely keep this on, and I'm just sitting here."

"You cold?" Maria says.

Her mother nods and the water bottle flops into her lap.

"Let's go to Beaufort," Maria says.

"Yes," her mother says. "Right now."

Maria knows her mother cannot read anything further into Maria's suggestion. She does not know that Bonacieux is there. But it doesn't matter, Maria thinks, because her mother wants to go there anyway. She's been talking about it for months, for the same reason Maria chose Philip and Nina to begin with—because she loves the place. The only thing keeping them in Chapel Hill has been treatment, and the most recent run of chemo has now ceased. They should go, Maria tells herself, not for her, not for the child, but for her mother. She tries to convince herself that this is the real reason she wants to leave. She can almost believe it.

"I'm serious," Maria says.

"Me too," her mother says. She sighs and balances the water bottle back on her head. "There are so many stupid people there, but God I love that place."

"Me too," Maria says.

"Let's do it. I'm getting better."

Maria's mother is not getting better. At least she shouldn't be. But Maria cannot completely disagree with her assessment. Her mother's hair has begun to reappear in a fine blond stubble. She has begun to eat. She has begun to walk. Hank no longer spends each day on deathwatch.

Maria sits beside her and takes part of the paper for herself. She will say no more about Beaufort tonight. Instead, she will sit with her mother and help her finish the crossword. Because this is how they make plans. An option is introduced, like a seed in soil, then left to germinate in silence. Over the next few days, Maria watches this one take root.

CHAPTER 5

SN'T BONNY BONNY? She is. Each day, Nina posts a new photo, and each day, Maria inspects it closely. Milkweed has been tucked between Bonacieux's toes. She hangs limply off Philip's chest in a brown BabyBjörn. Atop a pile of Nina's laundry the child naps and Maria longs for each piece of clothing beneath her, elegant and colorful and tailored. On the day that Nina posts a photo of a monarch butterfly perched atop Bonacieux's head, Jack arrives at Maria's house earlier than usual. He delivers breakfast every morning these days. It is his most reliable feature. Today he has with him two sesame bagels from Weaver Street Market—one for Maria and one for her mother. He runs his fingers through his bangs then snaps them in a sharp pop.

"We have to talk," he says.

"That's my least favorite way to start a conversation," Maria says, squeezing the bagel. Warm butter runs into her cuticles.

Jack snaps his fingers again.

"That's freaking me out," Maria says.

"I hate this!" Jack says.

"Hate what?" Maria says. Jack trades in hyperbole and drama. Even the most mundane of conversations will be peppered with yelps and declarations. She assumes he has been angered by the bagel.

He snaps. "When are you going to Beaufort?"

"I don't know," Maria says, surprised that he has indeed addressed a real topic. She looks him in the eye. "A few weeks? It's up to Mom."

"And for how long?"

"As long as she wants. She's . . ." Maria does not want to finish the sentence. She feels certain this will be their final trip together, the one that will end in death, but she is reluctant to name it as such. "You know where we'll be. It isn't far away."

Jack raises his hands in exasperation, then snaps with both of them.

"What," Maria says. "Say it." She can tell that something bigger than scheduling is at work on his mind.

Jack begins to shake his head slowly from side to side, then with increasing pace and vigor. As his face blurs, his lips begin to flop in a wet gurgle at each pivot. Then he snaps his fingers and stops.

"A man has needs!" he says.

"Go on," Maria says. She has heard this before, his lecture about biology. How he cannot simply provide, provide, provide. How he too has needs that he must satisfy. How he requires physical attention, what he calls basic animal trade. He wants sex, is what he wants, and Maria is still not ready to give it. "But you know I'm not ready for that yet," she says. "I'm sorry, I am. But you're going to have to be patient."

"It's not that," Jack says. "Not really."

"Oh shit," Maria says. She can tell now that Jack has something of consequence on his mind. "What?"

"I fucked up," Jack says.

Maria is afraid of the explanation. Jack's patience is not something that stands up well under duress. For weeks she has feared his breaking point and is certain now that he has reached it. She does not know if she can bear to hear how.

She closes her eyes and says, "What did you do?"

"Yeah, some stuff." He nods. "Yep."

"Is there someone else?" Maria says, voicing her greatest fear.

Jack continues to nod.

"Yes?" Maria says. "Are you actually saying yes?"

"I hate biology!" Jack says. "But it's there, all over me. In here." He points at his chest.

"So yes? The answer is yes? Are you kidding me?"

"I've been hanging out with Jennifer," he says.

Maria sighs. It is as she feared. She feels, in a span of seconds, older by years. She is aging more rapidly than normal these days. The hours have been passing in new ways, warping their route. Stopping. Skipping.

"Who the fuck is Jennifer?" she says.

"Rock-and-Roll Johnny from the 506's sister," Jack says.

"You mean Icy People?" Maria says. "Icy People?" It is her friend, the rapper.

Jack nods.

"Is this because I can't have sex?" Maria says. She starts to cry and hates that she is starting to cry. She feels sick to her stomach. She imagines Icy People talking about Jack with the other girls, smoking filterless Camels in Jane's Dodge Diplomat, telling them how big Jack's dick is, how bad he is in bed, how Maria has no idea.

"You understand that the flesh on my privates is torn and sewn together," Maria says. She tries to employ the same didactic tone of her second-grade teacher, Mrs. Turner, as if explaining volume. "Because I squeezed a human out of it. A human that you conceived."

Jack bites the air. "Everything's about B right now," he says. "The baby the baby the baby the baby the baby."

"Right now, that thing? The baby? And the fact that we gave it away? Yes. It is on my mind."

"I can't handle this stress," Jack says. "I wish I could. I hate it. I suck."

Maria has heard these excuses before. Jack does not deny his shortcomings. In fact, he embellishes them. He discusses them with gusto, as if their entry into conversation might just decrease their capacity for destruction.

"Just because you can admit you're horrible doesn't mean you aren't horrible," Maria says.

"I'm horrible," Jack says. "I am. I'm a horrible man who loves you."

Maria takes a deep breath and tells herself that Jack is trying to apologize. She cannot lose him. She thirsts for him like water. In this situation, with her mother sick and her stomach now not yet returned to form and what feels like a hole in her heart that could be filled only by the daughter she gave away, she feels the need to cling to Jack in whatever manner possible. She says, "I'm telling myself right now that anyone can make a mistake. I'm really trying to convince myself."

"Well, it's been like maybe five mistakes," he says.

The morning light has moved from soft to solid. A bright parallelogram of it now shines on the kitchen linoleum beneath Maria's feet. It makes the whole room glow an increasingly intense yellow. It is all too bright. Maria closes her eyes against it. She feels the need for Jack in her life now trumped by his selfish cruelty.

"Are you OK?" Jack says.

"Go," Maria says. But she does not want him to go; she wants him to stay, to beg forgiveness. He should know this, she thinks. She shouldn't have to explain. But of course he does not. He sighs a slow susurrant hiss. Maria does not open her eyes. They maintain this stalemate for one long moment until Jack steps to the door and opens it. Maria raises her eyelids. Through the window, she watches Jack walk up the driveway, stop at the recycling bin, and select from it a plastic Tide bottle. He spikes the bottle onto the concrete and it bounces high into the air. Jack then continues into the street and enters his dirty black Scirocco, but the bottle never returns to earth. Maria approaches the window. She looks up into the magnolia and at her neighbor's roof. But Maria cannot see the bottle anywhere. She is not surprised. On this October morning, in this sunlight, with this knowledge about Jack and Icy People, with her underwear lined with gauze and her mother bald and dying, the broken rules of physics cannot even begin to astonish her.

AFTER DARK, MARIA steps into the backyard and stares at the few small clouds above, their edges lit by a moon she cannot see. She walks into the driveway and slides herself into the small space under the Volvo. There, atop an oil stain, she feels both safe and dangerous. It is the fact that she should not be here, that no human should, that attracts her to this odd space. She has reached a point in life where new zones of refuge are required. She understands this is the action of a crazy person. But by lying here, she is giving herself the opportunity to try that role on for size. Here she is, so she must be crazy. She is not sure if she is convinced.

Maria remains under the Volvo for what feels like a very long time, though she is not sure it actually has been—she is wholly distrustful of any measurement of time these days—then emerges and enters the yard of the Copelands, who live next door. The house is dark. They are rarely at home. Mr. Copeland services a series of manufacturing plants throughout Virginia and the Carolinas and has a house in each state. Maria lifts from their hot tub the stiff blue cover, its vinyl surface slimy, and flops it onto the patio. The prospect of cold water has always held some perverse allure for her, if only for its ability to shock the system. So she removes her clothes, piling them at her feet, and slides naked into the flat water. As her heart races in the chill, she reveals her face to the mysterious glowing sky, resting her head on the cold plastic lip.

She imagines Bonacieux at that moment and wonders if she is longing for Maria's milk, her arms, or her love. She feels certain the child is not. Bonacieux is in a beautiful home with beautiful people ready to love her. But parental love, Maria knows, is not enough to safeguard a child from life. She wonders if Bonacieux is going to grow up lonely and betrayed. She wonders if maybe she should have had an abortion. She knows she is overreacting and courting melodrama, but she cannot deny her despair.

"Maria?" says a man.

She flinches, each fingertip tingling with terror. On the porch behind her stands Mr. Copeland, the owner of this house, fidgeting with an unlit flashlight.

Maria folds her arms across her chest. Mr. Copeland remains still, as if confronting a wild animal, and Maria is aware that she is, at this moment, scaring him.

"I'm sorry," Maria says. "I didn't know you were home."

Mr. Copeland shifts the flashlight from one hand to the other as Maria splashes out of the hot tub. He averts his gaze as she yanks up her shorts. She buttons her shirt into the wrong buttonholes.

"I'm so sorry," she says, lifting the hot tub cover from the ground. She struggles to place it atop the tub. "I was just . . ."

"I'll get that," Mr. Copeland says.

"I'm sorry," Maria says. "I'm just, just feeling a little crazy."

"I understand," Mr. Copeland says, calmly, as if soothing a skittish dog. "You just let us know if you need anything, OK? We're here for you, OK? No one is made for all this."

It frightens Maria that Mr. Copeland is so understanding. She feels like her actions have been predetermined, as if she is living a script everyone but she has read.

"I'm so sorry," she says.

The kitchen is dark and filled with the sharp tang of sour trash that Maria has forgotten to remove. She stands before the oven in a dim region of light cast by the halogen streetlamp. A glimmering puddle collects around her feet, expanding slowly across the worn linoleum. She wonders if Mr. Copeland knows she is doing this very thing. If her mother knows. If Jack knows. If Anne Vanstory knows. If she is the only one who does know what to expect.

CHAPTER 6

IT IS HALLOWEEN. Southeast of New Bern, Highway 70 cuts through a tunnel of longleaf pines grown so closely together that they resemble cliffs of solid green. Maria's arm is hooked out the window, her fingers drumming along to Little Richard. The silver Volvo is so coated in sandy grit that her flesh rises in goose bumps at each tap of her fingers. Within the cocoon of a red plaid blanket, her mother sleeps soundly in the passenger seat, even though the temperature today is a humid seventy-eight degrees. They are driving east across North Carolina, down out of the Piedmont and into the coastal plane, past Smithfield, Goldsboro, over the Neuse River in Kinston, now through the Croatan National Forest, toward the end of the continent, the Carolina coast, destination Beaufort.

Maria sings along in a whisper. "Tutti frutti," she says. "Alutti." She need not sing quietly, though. Almost nothing wakes her mother.

A road sign warns of bears, and within six miles of it, an old Ford Country Squire with faux wood paneling is stopped on the side of the highway, its hood crumpled into a small alpine range. On the wide gravel shoulder, one man and a small girl in a tangerine dress stand before a large bear lying on its side.

"Mom," Maria says, but there is no response.

The bear is black with a tan muzzle and three distinct white spots on its forehead. Maria slows almost to a stop as they roll up alongside the animal. As she does so, the man gingerly pokes the bear with a stick, and Maria steps on the gas, suddenly afraid the bear might at that very moment awake.

One hour and twenty minutes later she enters the corridor of strip malls west of Morehead City, a horror she seems to never recall until she encounters it once again in the flesh. Traffic here is slow, chopped up by stoplights. The cars surrounding them increase in luxury the nearer they come to the coast. By the time they reach Morehead City proper, the cars are almost all SUVs made by Lexus, Infiniti, and Cadillac. Maria begins to fear that they have made a mistake leaving Chapel Hill, that they have remembered this region incorrectly. But then, soon after they pass a thirty-foot-tall inflatable penguin standing in front of the UNC Institute of Marine Sciences, the strip malls begin to recede, replaced instead by small, tin-roofed houses painted turquoise, pink, and gray. White latticework surrounds their foundations. Gingerbread lace rots on the dormers. As the landscape of her memories returns, Maria's fears abate.

The Sanitary Fish Market stands among boat slips on the Morehead City waterfront, lorded over by a sculpture of King Neptune holding an invisible scepter, long ago vanished from his cracked wooden hand. Two young girls walk without sunglasses through bright sunlight, their brows so furrowed by the glare that they both appear angry. Their father follows in khaki shorts and a T-shirt emblazoned with a jumping marlin. Maria remembers walking here so often with her mother, jealous of the tanned flesh of her coastal peers. She tells herself they will die of cancer long before she does, but then again, her mother is as pale as she.

On the shore beside the bridge over the Newport River stand two rounded warehouses tipped with tiny galvanized sheds. They rise like a pair of huge industrial bosoms. Maria's mother always called this place the boob factory, and Maria is glad her mother is now asleep so that they are not forced to make the joke today, dangerous with all of its pitfall connotations. They pass Radio Island Marina at the base of the bridge and approach the drawbridge that spans the last stretch of water into Beaufort. A green North Carolina state sign announces the town and its founding year: 1709.

With miles of strip malls behind her, crossing the drawbridge feels like rising to the surface. Maria can now breathe. Nature reasserts its supremacy. Marshes open on either side. Gulls swoop in low. The air is briny through the window. Though Beaufort is not an island, the bridge is the only access point of which Maria knows. Hurricanes have cut into so much land north of town that, depending on the map and tides, Beaufort is basically more island than peninsula. It feels that way. This isolation is part of what Maria loves.

They pass Big Daddy Wesley's, a convenience store whose windows advertise bloodworms, night crawlers, cut minnows, cigar minnows, ballyhoo, the coldest beer in town, cigarettes, and bail bonds. She turns right on Live Oak Street, which is cracked and shot through with tall, rangy weeds. Things are lush and confused here, rich, run-down, immaculate, decomposing. Little feels precious, though it seems it all should be. The houses are as ancient as American homes can be. Mansions stand beside shotgun houses that are little more than shacks. Some are immaculately restored beside others that look prepared to crumble. Flags flutter on poles anchored to porch columns. American flags, North Carolina flags, Beaufort flags, blue UNC banners. Hand-painted shields beside door-ways announce the year each house was built and by whom. J Sharp House 1780, Alexander House 1852, The Chaplain House 1817, The Philip Knowe 1828. In each of these, Maria has imagined herself living a simple, solitary existence. She has no children, no parents, no spouse at all in these dreams. But now, seeing these houses anew, she can no longer believe in her fantasies. They are the daydreams dreamed only by youth, a designation that Maria feels no longer applies to her. A life lived in any of these houses, no matter how lovely, Maria now feels certain, will surely be complicated by birth and love and death. Her conviction seems confirmed by the prevalence of toys in yards, by tandem bikes, and by the ubiquitous sneaking mold, because anything painted white in this ocean-humid town—siding, columns, fencing—is bled through with a faint network of steadily creeping mildew.

And then, up ahead, where the street narrows to a bright blue win-dow, Taylor's Creek flows into Beaufort Inlet. Here the continent ends.

The moment they turn onto Front Street the wind shocks Maria by lifting her bangs and shaking them furiously. Like it always does, the air has gathered strength across the Atlantic and there's nothing left to stop it other than a double-decker tour bus crawling south and three couples holding hands. The gnarled trees all bend in the same direction—away from the water. Grand houses face the inlet with huge porches that sprout columns two stories high. Each house has a wid-ow's walk, a gated square on the roof like a dark crown from which, it is said, the wives of sailors could watch for their husbands' return. Maria used to imagine her mother on one—she now pictures herself.

To Maria's right flows Taylor's Creek, which is not a creek at all, but an inlet closed in by Carrot Island, one of the last tiny shards of land standing between Beaufort and the Atlantic. She can do without the beach, only a few miles away—its crowds and their ensuing expectations of festival hilarity repel Maria like a foul smell. This snaking path of salt water is her coast. On the island, only a hundred yards away, three wild horses graze high grass atop a low dune. Between them and Maria, a dolphin shows its back. The riches of the world here seem almost too exposed. Maria is concerned for the safety of these animals, amazed that they can live like this right out in the open and not behind electrical fencing. This, she thinks, is how she felt when first seeing infants in public, after giving birth. They all seemed too fragile for outdoor travel. She is glad when the dolphin returns to depths unseen.

They park two blocks from the inlet in front of a house she knows well, a three-storied Victorian painted Carolina blue with white trim. The front porch wraps three sides of the house and stretches so wide on the western end that the ground floor there is almost twice as broad as the level above it. Two rocking chairs sit empty on the porch beside a round wicker table holding a potted purple creeper, its vines dangling to the blue floorboards. Feathery ferns sway from the eaves. On the top step stands Karen Balcomb, smoking a cigarette.

Karen was Maria's mother's roommate at Saint Mary's boarding school in Raleigh and then again at Barnard. She is divorced, tall, thin, topped by a curly mushroom cap of dark hair, and utterly committed to Maria and her mother.

Maria wonders at the bond between her mother and Karen, one she knows she has already missed her opportunity to replicate for herself by opting to not have a roommate when she lived in the dorm at UNC, by opting to then give birth to a child, by deciding to then drop out of school altogether. The possibility of making a true friend, one who imprints for life like Karen, now seems even more remote than before. Maria will go back to school, this she knows, but she does not want it to be in Chapel Hill. In the last few weeks, overwhelmed by a desire to escape any town occupied by both Jack and Icy People, Maria has submitted a transfer application to Yale. It is a dream escape for when her mother leaves this world, a place she wants to attend so badly that she tries to keep herself from thinking about it too much, lest her hopes rise to a level from which they might never safely descend. Maria knows her chances of admission are slim at best and feels like she might not have even finished the application correctly. Her essay was about cancer, conception, and drawing self-portraits. She is afraid it is only crazy.

Maria steps out of the wheezing Volvo, her mother still asleep in the passenger seat. She waves to Karen before retrieving her backpack and pillow from the backseat. Karen crushes her cigarette into an ashtray, steps into the yard, and says, "Can I help?"

Maria raises her small load, as if to say I got it, and as she does, a swarm of white feathers appears around her legs. In the breeze they skid across Karen's lawn. Maria looks down. The pillow has sprung a leak. Maria grabs at it and a new burst of feathers shoots out in a small, slow explosion. This is the pillow Maria has slept on since fifth grade, that her mother insisted she travel to summer camp with. Her mother has slept beside her on this pillow. Jack has slept with his head on this pillow. Maria had this pillow in the hospital during labor. Bonacieux has even cried here, restless, while her first day shimmered cold and bright around her. A corner is now torn. Its innards have found the light.

"Come here," Karen says. "Come here." Maria begins to cry.

It has been only two weeks since Jack told Maria about Icy People, who according to Facebook has recently released three singles on her MySpace page, which Maria has since examined closely. To Maria's dismay, one of the new songs, a theme song of sorts titled simply "Icy People," is excellent. Its chorus—"Icy People got things and stuff"— will not cease playing within Maria's mind.

In Karen's arms, Maria feels a rush to tell her about Icy People, Jack, and Bonacieux. She does not know what her mother has already shared. But Maria knows it will all emerge in time. Karen eases information out of people by making them feel like nothing they say might shock. "I'm sorry," is all Maria says for now. She feels that Karen already understands it all anyway.

Karen's house is furnished with marble-topped dressers, mirrors so large they make Maria nervous about their hanging devices, antique cabinets filled with porcelain plates, portraits of ancient bearded men staring out from fields of darkness, and glass coffee tables standing at attention in seemingly almost every room. Bookshelves hold large-format catalogs from the art museums of other continents, hardback Junior League cookbooks, and John Irvings and John Grishams and John Updikes. In the living room, a pair of red reading glasses rests in the spine of an open *Town & Country*. An iPad glimmers on the table beside it. Maria feels a longing to be in the very room she is now in. The physical act of being there in the moment is not good enough. She sinks into the white leather couch and wishes she were more than just a visitor.

It is part of Karen's design, this desire to belong. She cultivates guests, always convincing them to stay longer than they had planned. Maria's mother says this is to keep her from getting lonely. Karen's ex-husband, a trial lawyer, left years ago but moved only a few blocks away. His proximity is only an amplification of his removal. Maria feels like Karen needs to leave Beaufort to start her life anew but is afraid that if she does so, she and her mother will no longer have this waterfront escape. Nor will Karen need them as much. Selfishly, Maria hopes Karen will never leave. She does not want the balance of dependence to change.

A young man dressed as a skeleton enters the room, blowing listlessly through a Twizzler.

"Boo," he says.

"Boo," Maria says.

This is Christopherson, Karen's fifteen-year-old. Maria has known him since he was born. He is now, for the first time, obviously not a child. There it is again, Maria thinks, that cosmic clock that refuses to adhere to standard measure. It was so long ago that she was his age, so much longer than the four years that actually separate them. It was not long ago at all, though, that Maria was in high school with boys his age. She is embarrassed at the swell of nerves now conjured by his sudden adolescent presence. But Maria too has changed since they last met. Her stomach has still not returned to its original shape, but it almost has. She feels it's an improvement. The angles on her body, for so long too acute in her mind, have now been softened by the process of motherhood. She questions if her breasts might remain permanently larger. Her skin is a new wardrobe. She is mysterious within it. She watches Christopherson admire it.

"Wanna trick-or-treat?" Christopherson says.

"Is that a metaphor?" Maria says.

"What."

"Never mind. Aren't we a little old?"

"Who cares. I want candy."

Maria is not thinking about candy but says, "Me too," and Christopherson blows through his Twizzler again, raising it like a trumpet into the living room airspace.

Maria does not know the address of the house in which her daughter lives, but she feels certain it is near. The whole neighborhood is little more than a dozen blocks square. Go ahead and walk these streets with Christopherson, she thinks, eat the candy of the generous neighbors and enjoy this warm October evening. She will celebrate a holiday in a town that she loves, that she has missed, and if, along the way, she finds the house in which her child lives, so be it.

She does not have a costume but that afternoon makes do. Karen retrieves an old white bedsheet from the attic, and with the removal of two small pieces, it happens: Maria becomes a ghost.

CHAPTER 7

THE SUN HAS set. From behind the old sheet, in her own private cloud of mothballs and fabric softener, Maria can view the neighbors' yard where dry ice swirls around a ten-foot mechanized reaper whose scythe slowly slices back and forth through the counterfeit fog.

"Don't go into the graveyard," Karen says. On the top step she is backlit by the porch light, Maria's mother beside her wearing a floppy witch hat at a rakish tilt. She looks radiant and ecstatic, and at this moment Maria feels the rightness of their journey to Beaufort. Already life has become magical and exotic. Her mother looks nothing if not alive. "Or anything else stupid," Karen says.

Christopherson gestures to Maria. As if, he seems to say, with her?

The neighborhood teems with more costumed children than Maria has ever seen in one place at one time. It seems like every family from a hundred-mile radius has driven in for the night. Jarheads from Camp Lejeune lead sunburnt children from door to door. Black kids from the county giggle with nervous glee inside plastic costumes. Neighborhood children goof with each other, recognizing friends from across the street, even behind masks.

Christopherson leads Maria west, away from the crowds, in the direction of the drawbridge. Low-limbed live oaks shade the streetlights, Spanish moss hanging from a few like hair that has just shaken loose. The streets smell vegetal and decaying, like the depths of a forest. Two lost princesses clutch empty Harris Teeter bags that rustle in the breeze. One Spider-Man trips on the sidewalk. An elephant cries until placed on his father's shoulders.

At each address, Maria looks for the double floor of columned porches, the magnolia, the stallion weather vane she has seen in Philip and Nina's photos. And each house is almost right. Does she want it to appear? She does not know exactly. She feels relief when they finish walking past a block of houses where she recognizes none as Philip and Nina's. But nevertheless, at the next block she begins again to look.

As Maria follows Christopherson in a whisper of footsteps, she turns her whole body from side to side to better see the passing homes through the holes in her sheet. The going is slow. They stop at one house where the owners hand out full-sized Snickers bars. At another a young couple dispenses apples, yet none of the children seem disappointed. Soon Christopherson starts skipping houses, even those clearly decorated to attract passing trick-or-treaters. They depart the tight bundle of columned homes and approach the edge of the Old Burying Ground, the very graveyard of which they were just warned. Like the proof to some theorem of adolescence, Christopherson has led her directly here.

The graveyard is shrouded in the limbs of craggy live oaks. It dates from the 1700s. A girl is buried in a rum barrel here. A British officer who was interred standing up. Someone with the cannon of his ship as part of his grave marker. There is no one who Maria has known whose bones rest in this sandy soil; still, it is one of her favorite places to visit. She has walked its poorly marked paths countless times, but never after dark. A wrought-iron fence encloses the yard, cracks in its concrete base yielding sandy weeds. A thick chain casually loops the gate shut, but this closing is only symbolic. There is a gap wide enough for all to pass through and many already have. Shadows move along the graveyard's far edges.

"You like being scared?" Christopherson says.

"It usually makes me feel like I'm going to die," Maria says, "and I don't want to die. So, no."

"Then I'll just tell you. It's awesome. My friends all lie down on the graves here. And as you walk by they sit up."

"And?" Maria says. She is both charmed and suspicious of Christopherson's teenage enthusiasm.

"And nothing. That's the thing. They just sit up and then lay back down. It's awesome."

He ducks under the chain and steps through the gap in the fence. From within he then beckons, waving palmfuls of humid air urgently toward himself. Maria follows. What else is she going to do? She is not going to return to Karen and tell on him, nor is she going to reprimand him herself. She fears what might happen if caught, but who is going to catch them? And what are they even doing?

The gravestones that she passes are so old that the years lived by those memorialized are illegible. Several graves stand above ground, enclosed by a blanket of brick pebbled with seashells. As they walk by each grave along the sandy path, a teenager dressed as a skeleton sits upright, only to then lie back down once they pass.

"Cool, huh?" Christopherson says.

Maria cannot help but answer yes. As the teenagers of Beaufort rise and recline in silence at her transit, the sorrows of her time in Chapel

Hill ease. Even here, surrounded by reminders of death, the very specter that has haunted the last year and a half of her life, the cure of geography works. She cannot explain the magic of this stupid act, lest it be some halfhearted symbol of a resurrection in which she does not believe. "It is," she says. "It is."

"You've had a shitty year, right?" Christopherson says, as they pass through a grove of gravestones so old and sunken they seem merely stubs of stone peeking out of the earth, as if they might, at any moment, close their granite eyes and disappear forever. There is a measure of privacy in this ancient corner of the yard, the teenage ghouls more tightly populating the extravagant and grand markers elsewhere, and Maria appreciates both Christopherson's interest in her and his discretion in waiting till now to reveal it.

"I guess," Maria says. She is glad he already knows. She prefers the knowledge to precede her.

"Well," he says, choosing his words carefully. Maria understands he is forging new conversational ground here, that he has, in all likelihood, rarely before discussed an epoch of such consequence in anyone's life, let alone anyone even remotely near his age. "I'm glad that this isn't shitty."

"Thank you," Maria says, touched by his meager offering.

The graveyard adventure ends quickly. The last of the phantom teens behind them, they exit the yard in silence. Maria understands Christopherson had no true business in this graveyard, only that he wanted to impress Maria with the performance. And she was indeed impressed. More importantly, she feels she has been transported. Nothing about this evening resembles the days she has been living. Of this she is glad.

They move parallel to the water, stopping at more houses now, gathering more fruit and handmade candy. Still Maria watches for Philip and Nina's house, but with each that is not theirs, Maria begins to feel that perhaps she has guessed incorrectly. Maybe Philip and Nina live in a different town, one nearby, one she has no knowledge of. Perhaps Philip only walked his dog here. As she scans the street, Christopherson leads her toward a large blue house, one of the oldest on the block. Its shield reads WHEELER EDWARDS 1714.

"This's my dad's house," Christopherson says, defeated, shuffling up the walk. Maria can tell he's embarrassed to have to hew to parental authority in her presence. "I promised him I'd stop by."

Though she vacations for weeks at a time only blocks away, Maria has not seen Christopherson's father in years. When he opens the door, she is stunned by how handsome he is. His hair is gray and his face has thinned with the years, but it is definitely an improvement. It is new for her to see someone's parent as a person and not just a position, let alone someone who is handsome, and she wonders if it is the bearing of a child that has given her a newfound appreciation for a generation who has already done so.

"Hey there!" he says, elated to see his son. "Alright. Skeleton man."

"Hey, Dad," Christopherson says.

"You guys been looking at all the weirdos in the graveyard?"

"Yeah. Dad, you remember Maria."

"Hey, Mr. Jessee," Maria says. She extends a hand from within the sheet and waves.

"Maria!" he says. "You look pale."

Maria laughs courteously but does not reveal her face. She is afraid she is blushing and opts to keep herself well hidden.

After they return to the street, Maria surrenders the last of her hope. She will not find her daughter tonight. It is probably for the best, she thinks, as they make their way west. The children have begun to pack up and go home, their bedtimes quickly approaching. The volume of screaming has slowly decreased. Christopherson circles back toward his mother's house.

"You see your dad much?" she says.

"Yeah," Christopherson says. "He takes me out on the boat."

Maria wonders what it is like to have a father. In her own life she has never truly felt the absence. Maybe she simply doesn't know what she's missing. Perhaps, she thinks, it is not that she has missed anything, but rather that a second parent is just insurance against the other. For Maria, to whom her mother has been everything, the approaching loss of that person spells absolute family destruction. She ponders the arithmetic of parental population while unwrapping a mystery-flavored Dum Dum, its wrapper printed with purple question marks, and that is when she sees it: the very house for which she has been hunting. A chill runs through her, despite the late October heat. It is enough like the photos for her to recognize it, but film could never capture its true splendor. The grounds are filled with nappy grass across a wide lawn dotted with azaleas and rosebushes. The house is both more grand and more run-down than she expected. Maria has envisioned her child on this very lawn, the one Christopherson is now crossing. She rushes behind him, hidden and shushing within her white sheet. The mailbox reads PRICE. Their last name. Maria never missed it, but now that she knows it, the family seems material. She realizes that, before now, she has not known her daughter's full name. Bonacieux Price. It sounds right, she thinks, relieved.

At the stoop, before Christopherson can even knock, the door opens
and Nina appears dressed as a tube of Aim. Even in the guise of toothpaste, she is more beautiful than in film, avian and fragile and fine.

"Aren't you like twenty by now?" Nina says.

"Trick-or-*treat*!" Christopherson says.

Maria approaches slowly and in dread. She is pleased that
Christopherson knows the Prices but hopes it does not lead to conversation. What could she say that would not betray her? Again she is
thankful for her costume, redolent of softener and dust.

Rolling her eyes, Nina extends a bowl of saltwater taffy. Behind
her, at the end of a small hallway, a blue baby seat sits on a worn
hardwood floor. It is empty, and for a moment Maria is both disappointed and relieved. Then, across the doorway, Philip passes. He
wears a pair of glasses from which bloodshot eyes dangle on springs,
bouncing slowly above a tightly wrapped bundle held close to his
chest. He approaches the door and reveals what is so tightly wrapped.
It is Bonacieux.

What the days have so quickly wrought. The child's left eye is
bruised black and a Band-Aid spans the bridge of her nose. Maria's
mouth opens in pure primal terror and she is glad to be wearing a sheet
to hide her betrayal of bald emotion.

"Our little welterweight," Philip says, and Christopherson begins
to laugh.

Maria is left out on some joke here, overwhelmed by the fact that
her child has been damaged. Nina pulls more of the blanket away,
revealing small boxing gloves taped onto each of Bonacieux's hands.
And then Maria gets it: this is a costume. Her daughter is dressed as a
boxer. The child, eyes still closed, raises one gloved hand to her face.

Maria is startled by the paths her mind so readily took. Philip takes Bonacieux's hand and with it lightly punches Christopherson on the nose. He feigns a knockout, swinging both skeleton arms for balance.

As Maria stares at her daughter's soft face, her breasts begin to swell. She backs up a few steps, scared of the biological magic at work here. She is not even sure at first of what it is, but it soon begins to make sense: her milk is starting to flow again. She feels betrayed by this production of her own body, triggered by nothing more than an image.

Philip and Nina have ignored Maria until this point, but now they turn to her, and Philip says, "TKO!"

Maria says nothing. They don't seem to expect her to. She is just another trick-or-treater. They've already had hundreds.

"Y'all be safe," Nina says. "And tell your mother we said hi."

"Alright," Christopherson says.

Maria raises one hand within her sheet, where it cannot be seen, and waves, secretly, to her daughter. She backs slowly down the sidewalk, passing a tall azalea as a crowd of other teenagers flow down the walkway, keeping her eyes on her daughter until she loses sight in the mob of trick-or-treaters. Maria feels a confused energy she does not know how to expend. She has a desire for a cigarette, a drink. A drug.

"You OK?" Christopherson says.

"I need to go," Maria says.

"Home?"

"Not home. Just not trick-or-treating. I think I want to do something crazy."

"Alright," Christopherson says, grinning. "Let's."

A block removed from Philip and Nina's house, Maria can now recognize the excellence of the boxing costume. It's a relief is what it

is. She feels like she has proven her achievement. Her daughter lives
in town that Maria loves in a beautiful old house with a woman who
dresses up in a homemade toothpaste costume and a man whom she
has admired from afar. Her child is with the right family, her ex-boyfriend is in a different town, and she is at the edge of the continent
carrying a pillowcase filled with candy.

CHRISTOPHERSON STOPS BEFORE a huge, dilapidated house that
looks like it has been constructed explicitly for the set of a horror film.
It is clearly uninhabited. Pieces of siding hang at odd angles from the
facade. Plywood covers each window. Dark gables serrate the roofline.
The largest magnolia Maria has ever seen takes up most of the front
yard and has sprouted branches directly into the second-story balcony.

Maria is surprised this place isn't crawling with delinquents. She
guesses they are all still practicing phantom sit-ups in the graveyard
and is glad of it. Christopherson takes Maria's elbow and leads her
across the yard, dead magnolia leaves crunching beneath their feet. He
pushes the front door open and crosses the room behind the flickering
flame of a black Bic lighter. On the mantle is a half-burnt votive candle
that he carefully lights.

The room was once grand. Now Maria can see at least one hole
in the floor; who knows how many others are hidden in the darkness.
An ornate mantel stretches over a fireplace from which logs, recently
burnt, have tumbled onto the floor. The walls are mildewed and, once
probably white, are now a filthy ochre. A cut-glass chandelier glimmers at the end of a kinky chain. And over the mantel, flickering in
the candlelight, is a red octopus, spray-painted onto the wall, its arms
stretched across the room, onto the ceiling and adjoining walls, binding

the space together in a web of limbs as if they are all that maintain the room's integrity.

"Whose house is this?" Maria says.

"No one," Christopherson says.

"You paint this?"

Christopherson nods.

Maria is impressed. The image is excellent in a careless way she could never execute.

"Here," Christopherson says, and lifts from his pillowcase a canister of gold spray paint. "Knock yourself out."

The can is cold and surprisingly heavy. Maria has not drawn or painted a single image since well before she gave birth. She has never used spray paint. Before a region of wall free of octopus legs, she points the can and presses the nozzle. A weak spittle of paint sputters onto her knuckles.

"You have to shake it," Christopherson says.

Maria shakes it. She makes one gold dot on the wall. Then another and another. At first this was only a test. Here is the paint, this is how it comes out. But she keeps making dots, and pretty soon they add up. They are becoming something, a sort of upside-down broken eggshell. She connects them until they form the outline of a cartoon ghost. Where this came from, she does not know exactly. Jack liked to play an old tabletop Pac-Man in the back of a bar in Carrboro, and she guesses this painting is some psychic regurgitation of those graphics, a video-game hieroglyph of a man she is trying to forget. She cannot claim to understand the odd firings of her brain. She paints a thought bubble above the ghost and, in slow cursive therein, writes WHAT AM I DOING?

"What *are* you doing?" Christopherson says.

"I don't know," Maria says, stepping back, paint fumes searing her throat. Gold paint creeps down the wall and collects into a thickening bead along the baseboard. She coughs. "This stuff gonna make me pass out?"

"Not unless you spray it in a bag and put it over your face. Which can be fun. Ever make yourself faint?"

"That sounds like a terrible idea."

"Not with the bag. I mean, just with breathing. It's not even drugs or anything," Christopherson says. "Here. Watch."

Christopherson squats against a wall under two octopus tentacles. They reach toward him as if trying to pull him up. "Count my breaths for me," he says. "To thirty."

As Maria counts, Christopherson inhales and exhales in a rapid and violent sequence, then rises wide-eyed and expectant. He points at his chest and says, "Press!"

Maria tries to remember his simple command: press? Why she should, she is not sure, but she places her hands on Christopherson's bony sternum and pushes. He exhales in a rush and then drops to the floor. Unconscious, he lays crumpled against the warped baseboard. Maria is terrified.

"Christopherson!" she says.

He is out for one, maybe two heartbeats, before he opens his eyes beatific.

"Hot dog," he says.

"What the hell!" Maria says. "You OK?"

"I just had the best dream."

"Just now?"

He nods silently and softly, as if to say of course, and sits up.

"You dream?" she says. She does not understand the course of this miniature mental journey.

"They're like even more than dreams," he says. "They're visions." He rises from the floor. "Here," he whispers. He gently pushes Maria against the wall, pieces of it crumbling around her feet. "Try it. Squat."

Maria is not sure she wants to reenact Christopherson's sudden psychic departure, but what else has she come here for? She is terrified but curious about anything that might transcend the plane on which her days have been skidding along. She starts to inhale and exhale rapidly, mimicking what Christopherson has just done. He counts each breath aloud, excited for her, and as he does, Maria begins to grow less scared. The night has become overstuffed. The set pieces of some drama have been gathered around her here, but she does not know what scene to act out. She longs to flee to the wings. Here is an escape, however brief it may be. Christopherson continues his count, and when he reaches thirty, Maria stands, already so lightheaded and dizzy she can feel herself losing control. Christopherson presses his forearms across her chest.

"Now exhale," he says, and pushes.

Maria finds herself naked in a room with Jack, Christopherson, and Philip. Even as it happens she knows it is only a dream. One of them takes her in his arms, but she cannot tell who. She can't believe she's dreaming about group sex. It seems both silly and inevitable. She wants them all at once, feels a businesslike requirement for it. "I'm going to need you," she calls out to no one in particular. "Get over yourselves. Do it." She feels lurid and wild, yet still obvious and predictable.

When she opens her eyes, Christopherson is standing above her. Her head feels soft and numb, her tongue swollen.

"My God," she says.

"See?"

"How long was I out?"

"Two seconds?"

Maria reaches out to Christopherson and pulls him down, onto his knees. She is still rushing on her dream. He pushes his tongue far into her mouth. One hand rises to her breast, still swollen with milk, and Maria lowers his arm. She wonders if he's ever done this with anyone before. "This can't happen," she says, but it is still happening. It is more dangerous than anything she has seen in her dreams. She feels only young.

CHAPTER 8

MARIA FINDS A tandem bicycle in the back of Karen's storage shed. The seats are cracked and dusty. There is a clatter of metal on metal as she pulls it into the light, its various mechanisms long ago loosened and rusted. But it rolls. She puts air in the tires with a foot pump. She is embarrassed at the prospect of riding this thing by herself, its second seat empty, but she wants at least a bit of speed for the trip she is going to take. In the basket affixed to the handlebars, she places a white canvas tote bag monogrammed with Karen's initials. She folds the bag over on itself, self-conscious about being seen with anything monogrammed. Inside it are three Mirado Black Warrior pencils, a blue sketchpad, and a towel.

Four days have now passed since she made out with Christopherson in the abandoned house. Since then, Maria has kept her distance, a task that has been surprisingly easy. With a friend, Christopherson runs a little lawn care service, and this time of year they are fully employed, blowing leaves out of neighborhood yards into tall, tidy piles at the foot of the curb. He is almost always out of the house. Maria has heard him talk about her with his partner in the yard, though, mixing oil and gas for their leaf blowers, using the words *Chapel Hill* as some type of teenage totem. She has witnessed these words work their magic before, conjuring the specter of college before wide high school eyes.

But even though Maria has avoided Christopherson just enough to let him know that any romance between the two cannot progress, she does not regret what happened on the dusty floor of that dark abandoned house. She has thought about it many times since, each time gaining a confidence and a rush of feeling wanted. She is aware of a need to be wanted.

But Christopherson has not given up. Last night he passed a note under Maria's door, but she did not find it until morning. It was a drawing of a cartoon ghost with an empty thought bubble floating above it. Underneath was written: HEY GHOST—WHAT ARE YOU DOING? Maria folded the note, like it was a piece of artwork by a child, and carefully placed it into her address book.

With Karen helping care for her mother, Maria now feels untethered. Not pregnant, not required to be near her mother's bedside, confident about the home of her daughter, she is once again a young woman with time on her hands. Her void of responsibility seems more profound than a mere reprieve from the chores of life, as if it is the emptiness of age, earned. She wonders if this is what it feels like to be retired. She feels like she might have earned this time, at least for now. This day.

Squeaking at each push, she pedals onto Federal Street, a short tunnel of arcing chestnut limbs interspersed with a dense network of honey locust and crape myrtle. Though the bike emits a constant rattle, she aspires to be inconspicuous. She can just see the driveway of Philip and Nina's house, where twice in the past four days she has glimpsed her daughter, both times exiting a small blue Mercedes, not modern, perhaps from the 1980s. She rattles even closer. This morning the driveway is quiet. Empty. There will not be another sighting today.

Maria is not disappointed, though, only more determined. She will return again, maybe tomorrow, maybe later that same day, because the urge to see Bonacieux has increased not only with each glimpse Maria has caught of her, but even with each failed attempt. It is a growing thirst, and she knows now where the well is to sate it.

So she pedals on, continuing toward the water. She does not care that a few people have turned to watch. It is enough to have a means of escape, particularly today, after an earlier conversation with her mother—a conversation that she is happy to leave behind.

From her bed, her mother had said, apropos of nothing, "Do you miss Jack?"

"Less than I thought," Maria said. But she was lying. Her heart, she is afraid, has undergone a physical transformation in the wake of Jack's break. He has injured it. Of this she is certain. Because sometimes when she thinks about him, it feels like it hurts for blood to pump through it.

Her mother had turned to the window to watch Christopherson, in shorts and cowboy boots, push a quiet lawn mower across the neighbor's front yard. The low whir of its little engine filled the space.

Then she said, "I do."

"You do what?" Maria said, having lost herself in the memory of Christopherson's flesh.

"I miss Jack."

Maria was shocked. Is shocked, still. She thinks the damage inflicted by Jack on her heart should trump any lasting desire on the part of her mother to smoke weed with him or listen to his Wu-Tang files.

"He made me feel young," her mother had said. "I'm already sick of Karen's old-person shit. I can't watch *Antiques Roadshow*."

"Well, you're not young," Maria said, "and *Antiques Roadshow* is rad."

Maria now feels guilty and wonders if it was worth picking this fight with her mother, or any. There is so little time left. They have chosen Beaufort for her mother's final days—why can Maria not fill them with pleasure? She will die, she will die, she will die. Maria tells herself this in order to believe, because in truth, she cannot.

Maria parks the heavy bike at a small gazebo on the waterfront across the street from the post office. Beside it, a short and deserted public pier extends into Taylor's Creek. It is her favorite place to access the water. She is not interested in crossing the bridge to Atlantic Beach. Even on quiet days, the shore there is overrun with people hustling for position. Damp swimsuited couples walking hand in hand make Maria feel self-conscious, pale, and out of shape. She prefers instead this dead-end bridge to nowhere. It might be built on nothing more than the bank of a tidal creek, but it feels like it is hers and hers alone. It is also the spot from which Maria first saw Philip the summer before, and though she has yet to see him in public since arriving in Beaufort, she cannot deny that she is hoping he might again appear here.

She lifts the tote bag from the bike's basket and removes the large towel and blue sketchpad. Other than the golden ghost she spray-painted onto the wall of the abandoned house with Christopherson the other night, Maria has still not drawn a single image since well before Bonacieux's birth. But the urge has begun to return. With the sketch-pad, she walks to the edge of the pier, folds the towel in thirds, and sits.

Her feet swing only a few feet above the high tide. Sailboats are anchored nearby in the creek. More horses graze on Carrot Island, close enough that she can see their ears twitch at the scream of a gull.

She unties the ribbon on the sketchpad, and from its first pages tumble three brittle four-leaf clovers, like secret messages sent from Maria's past. She found them with Jack months ago; they were growing around a gas pump in south Durham. "Radiation magic," Jack had said. "Exxon lucky charms!" Two evade her fingers and drift onto the water below, but the third she catches, and as she does, it crumbles into dry green shards in her palm.

Though it is early November, the sunshine is still bright and warm. Maria sketches a sailboat, clumsy with her first lines, but as the image slowly emerges, it does so with increasing authority. She is empowered by this reminder of her skill. She removes the old Brooks Brothers oxford she found hanging in the closet and slips off her shorts. Beneath she wears a black one-piece. The water will be frigid, she knows, but she is not afraid.

Off the pier she dives. Going under is an electric shock. She emerges, gasping for warmth, thrilled and buzzing with life. Three tanned men in an open-hull fishing boat turn in unison and, one by one, wave, as if they can hear the very frequency of her psyche. Maria does not wave back, but is not unappreciative of their attention. She feels herself emerging anew in Beaufort these days, though it is not a return to form; it is a new Maria who has begun to surface. It is a woman yet to be identified. She climbs a ladder of two-by-fours nailed to the pier, each slat grown over in oysters sharp enough to slice open a careless shivering foot, then lies on her back on the warm wood. People on the sidewalk pass intermittently, appearing upside down in her inverted view. They are not interested in her. In Chapel Hill, no matter how sunny the day might be, a person lying on the ground would bring traffic to a halt. Here, in the logic of a place where bodies are expected to submit to gravity and expose themselves to light, she is not even worth a second glance. After long minutes of this, it begins to feel as if she is in a different place altogether, one removed from Beaufort, one where she is simply observing from a distance, remote and unattainable. And so, when a dog clatters onto the pier and begins to tick his claws across its boards as he approaches her, it comes as a shock.

"Hey, doggy," she says, and then she sees its owner—a tall man in a wrinkled white shirt pushing a blue baby stroller. She had not recognized the dog, not from her inverted perspective, but this man she cannot miss. He has a lazy shuffle, and although the sun has backlit him into nothing but a featureless silhouette, Maria knows him at once. She catches her breath. It is Philip. He kicks the head of a dandelion, and its seeds explode into the breeze.

"Ferdinand!" Philip says, but the dog continues his advance. His pointy face growing larger with each step that he takes toward Maria. "Ferdinand!" he says again, "Hey!" But the dog doesn't stop until he's reached Maria's face. She has read that dogs are now trained to sniff out cancer cells in humans, and as his whiskers tickle Maria's forehead, she is certain that he can smell the molecular relation between her and the new child now living in his house.

"Hi, Ferdinand," she says, and the dog delivers one wet lick to her forehead. She considers the fate of Pinky. She understands that his death was of her own design, that it made sense at the time. She is wary of the shifting ground beneath her, what makes sense one day, only to seem unthinkable the next. Through the space between Ferdinand's legs, she cranes for a glimpse into the baby carriage. "Stay here, doggy," she whispers. "Stay."

Philip starts down the pier. At his approach, Maria feels his foot-steps shudder through the wood beneath her.

"Sorry," he says, wheeling the stroller to a stop. "He's always looking for friends."

"That's OK," Maria says, sitting up. There is a small bundle in the stroller, immobile. A nose.

Philip affixes a green leash to Ferdinand's collar and says, "Sorry," again, then, "Come on," and starts back. Ferdinand's claws tick atop the planks behind him.

He is older than she is. He has a job, money, a career; he owns a house. He knows things that she does not, but still, Maria feels he is someone she could know, someone with whom she could talk and, within minutes, find common ground. He is, after all, pushing her sleeping child down the sidewalk. She admires his taste in home and wife. If he lived in Chapel Hill, she is sure his circle would cross with her own and her mother's. He does not seem interested in being cool. He is beyond that. Philip is a grown-up. He is the opposite of Jack. Maria feels certain that she could step into his life and all involved would be happy to have her there. But with him she will never have the chance. A few words, a lick from his dog, a glimpse of Bonacieux's nose—this is all she can aspire to. She must be satisfied knowing that Bonacieux is with someone with whom she too would like to spend time. It is a gratification, but one not even close to complete.

THAT EVENING, MARIA opens her mother's Facebook account. Months ago, during the first weeks of pregnancy, she erased her own profile, happy to jettison its social pressure, but from time to time, she likes to look for photos of Jack. The first thing she does tonight, though, is search for Philip Price. Neither he nor Nina are here. Maria respects them for their privacy. It is in keeping with her opinion of them as travelers in a separate, heightened social sphere. So she turns to her usual search for Jack, which is, as always, a disappointment. He posts images of Ray Davies, Scooby-Doo, Dukakis, and Bob Dylan, but nothing of himself. It is the same high-low mishmash that defines his own identity. Maria can infer nothing from it. But after her conversation with her mother that afternoon, Maria has now started to wonder if her mother and Jack have been in touch.

They have. She finds one message that her mother sent to Jack dated three days prior. It reads, *I don't need any weed. What I need is for you to leave Maria alone because you've broken her heart and acted like a fool. I'm disgusted and disappointed with you and don't want to hear from you again.*

Maria has never played a sport, but she had two friends on the JV volleyball team at East Chapel Hill High. Those girls fought for each other, cried at almost every game, and cheered until their throats were raw. Maria wondered what it was like to be on a team so steeped in tribal loyalty. But now, while reading her mother's message, she understands. It is a rising feeling. An increase in trust. A magical rise in strength that makes her long to do her mother right.

She understands that the message does not negate what her mother had said that morning about missing Jack. He makes people feel opposite emotions all the time. This Maria knows well. No matter how much he offends, it is always part and parcel of what it is that attracts.

She closes the computer, ashamed of having snooped. It is something Jack would have done without regret, she thinks. The fact both impresses and disgusts her.

ON THE AFTERNOON of their fifth day at the coast, while Maria drinks a sweaty peach daiquiri with her mother on Karen's screened back porch, her mother says, "I know you don't want to talk about it, but have you even heard from that jerk?"

"Who?" Maria says.

"You know."

"Ugh," Maria says. "His name even sounds like jerk."

"He'll come crawling back."

"Truth is," Maria says, "just being here, out of town, helps."

"Let's stay," her mother says.

"In Beaufort?"

"I'd rather be sick here than in Chapel Hill."

"Maybe," Maria says, as if it's even really up to her. What does she have to return to? She'll stay where her mother wants her to.

"THERE'S ALWAYS SOMETHING on the neighborhood Listserv," Karen says, later that evening at dinner. They've been discussing what Maria might occupy her time with if they do stay in Beaufort, which, Maria understands, is indeed what is going to happen. She can hear it in her mother's voice. And Maria will not return to Chapel Hill without her. Not now. Each day at this point is too precious.

"It's mostly a forum for racism and paranoia," Karen says. "I mean, they always write about stray dogs and black people just out to take a walk, but they have odd jobs listed too. I love reading it. We can find you something."

Maria has enjoyed indulging herself in Beaufort, reminding herself that she is young. Drawing, riding her bike, reading local newspapers over coffee—the minutiae of her hours have satisfied her for the most part, not to mention her increasing surveillance of the Price house. So her life here has not been empty. But it is not her own time that she is most concerned with. She understands that any occupation she finds will make her time feel less like a deathwatch and more like a life. And so she says, "Alright, let's find me something."

Karen retrieves her iPad and relates to Maria a stream of employment possibilities. There are two administrative assistant positions at Duke Marine Lab, one waiting tables at the Beaufort Grocery, an internship at the North Carolina Maritime Museum, a shelving position at the public library, and a job as a basketball and kickball scorekeeper for the Carteret County Rec Center.

Over the next three days, Maria diligently follows up on all but the scorekeeping. But she has no administration experience, no college degree, no work experience at all other than summers at Whole Foods. Even the waitress position is too competitive.

"I can't even wait tables," she says to Karen, one morning at breakfast. They are on the porch, eating yogurt and raspberries picked from a bush in the back. Her mother is still asleep. The sunlight is just hitting the tops of trees, lighting them as if candles in celebration of this day's birth.

"You don't have to do anything, you know," Karen says.

"There anything on Craigslist?" Maria says.

"It's all working at Best Buy or the DMV or murdering people," Karen says.

"What about babysitting?" she says, but she is not asking this question in innocence. The constant consideration of her mother's mortality has given her the urge to take risks. With each lap she has taken past the Price house, an electrifying idea has pulsed stronger and stronger: Why not be with her daughter, just for the time she is here? Wouldn't it be the most natural fit of all?

Karen seems concerned. She says, "Couldn't that be . . . ?"

"Yeah," Maria says, removing the need for Karen to finish explaining her logic. Maria understands. Karen thinks it would be too difficult, what with having just given up her own child. "I could do it, though," she says. "If it was a family I liked. I'd be good at it."

What she means, of course, is if it was the Prices. If it was the family whose child she bore. If it was the family whose house she pedals past day in and day out, longing for a single glimpse of the flesh of her flesh. Karen raises her eyebrows, as if to say, you sure?

"Seriously," Maria says. "I have to do something or I'll go insane."

"Well there're a bunch, actually," Karen says, tapping dully at her iPad. "I didn't mention them, because. You know. But yeah, let's see." She reels off a dozen jobs, mostly one-offs for date night, some for longer. Some are full time. Most are within blocks. And one is for Philip and Nina.

Maria closes herself into the bathroom. She runs the water. She leans close to the antique mirror and blows up at her bangs, revealing her eyes for just an instant before the curtain of hair falls back into place. She feels the same detached wonder that she did at her discovery of Philip's photo online. All I have to do is quit, she tells herself. All I have to do is go home.

CHAPTER 9

MARIA STANDS BESIDE the large enameled sink in which she has seen photos of her daughter bathing. Philip leans on the chopping block, smoking, flicking ash into a coffee cup. The sharp tang of mint leaves fills the corner of the room, blending with garlic from a hanging basket in which green stalks reach through the weave. Ferdinand, the borzoi, floats in and out of the room, directed by some unknowable task, stopping only to sniff Maria's shoelaces. Two open bottles of Syrah stand beside the sink, both missing corks. The room is abundant. Overripe pears fill a cracked wooden bowl on the counter. From a fireplace in the brick wall a black stain of soot stretches to the ceiling in the very shape of a flame, like some shadow of its maker. Maria wonders at what blaze, or how many, ever burnt that strongly.

Through the open window the sound of a lawn mower enters the room, buzzing in waves. It is Christopherson mowing. It was he who brought Maria here, walking her the five blocks while pushing his mower beside her. They barely spoke except for him to say, "They're cool," as they came within view of the house.

In the kitchen, Philip says, "I know you. The pier." He points south.

"Right," Maria says, pleased to have it mentioned. She has not yet decided if she should admit to even knowing who he is. It is as if the introduction of one secret into her fiber has undermined her ability to handle any surrounding truths.

"Knew I knew you," he says, and pours a glass of sparkling water. "I've seen you around. Sorry about the dog."

Nina and Bonacieux are not home. Maria finds it odd that her interview is taking place without them. She does not ask where they are, though Philip seems unperturbed by their absence. Does Nina trust Philip to make all decisions? Or is this some rogue move on his part? Maria feels it is neither, in fact, but rather just the makeshift progress of a family with a newborn, an attempt to get things done.

"I've never watched a baby before," Maria says. "Or really done much of any babysitting. But Karen can vouch for me. And I do have this list of references." She brandishes a list of professors and former Whole Foods coworkers, names and email addresses handwritten onto a sheet of yellow legal paper. She knows she is not selling herself well but feels an aversion to casting herself as anything other than the novice that she is.

Philip waves his hand, as if the air around his face needs to go away. "I can just tell that you're right," he says.

"Really?" Maria says. Her cheeks become warm and she is thankful for the shadows in which she stands.

Philip plucks the stem from a fig. "Karen said you . . . You're her friend's daughter?"

"My mom and Karen were in college together," Maria says. "And high school actually. Roommates." It is not any sort of explanation, though. She feels the continued need for truth, as much of it as she can tell. She wants to shock him with veracity if she can right now, to enact some litmus test to see if she can't ruin this right away if it is indeed supposed to be ruined. "My mom's pretty far along with cancer right now, and I just had a baby girl that I gave up for adoption," Maria says. She rushes on the high of revelation, like she has just inhaled these truths rather than blurted them out. She feels radioactive and hot, lit from within by the dangers of a complicated life.

"Wow," Philip says, stunned. "I'm sorry to hear that, I really am."

"Thank you," Maria says. She has learned that this and nothing more is the best response.

He is quiet for a moment longer. Maria knows what he is considering, the almost unbelievable synchronicity of adoptions. And unbelievable it is, in fact. She almost feels like daring him to probe more deeply, to discover all of what she is hiding here and now. It is like the pressure of something has almost risen to the surface. She can sense the satisfaction of release.

"You know," Philip says, "Bonny was adopted."

And at that, Maria does not allow any pressure to blow off. She hears her daughter's name and knows she will keep her secret forever, or at least until a later date, a time at which it will be, of course, even more shocking than it might have been now. She says, "Wow," and can think of nothing else that might cut the tension except for a heinous joke. "What if she's mine?" she says, smiling wildly.

Philip laughs. It is ridiculous. Maria laughs with him, relieved that it has played out thus.

"So," Maria says, now desperate to change the subject, "you profess?" She remembers from the letter that Anne Vanstory shared with them that he is a professor, but once she asks, she realizes that she must be careful. This is not otherwise information she should know.

"I do," Philip says, seemingly unaware of her slip. He laughs again, this time at her joke. It is her mother's, who always turns her title into a verb. "History."

"Where?" she says, happy to ask a question she does not, in fact, already know the answer to.

"Duke. But I'm on sabbatical, which is what we're doing down here. That's when you have time off."

"I know what it is," she says. "My mom's a professor."

"Where?"

"Carolina," Maria says, suddenly afraid that the proximity of the two schools—only twelve miles apart—is too close, that he will surely know her.

"In what?" he says, and Maria is overcome with relief.

"English."

"What's her name?"

For a moment Maria considers lying, but she cannot multiply her deceit. In this town, surely Philip and her mother will meet. "Eliza Matthews," she says. It is her mother's real name.

He shakes his head, not recognizing it. "I don't know why I asked," he says. "A different department is like a different country."

She has heard her mother say as much before, and today Maria is glad of it. She wants as few crossed paths as possible at this juncture in her life. It is her aspiration to have seemed to appear out of the ether to Philip and Nina. She feels certain that this is all that can keep her safe, though the truth is, she does not know what risks exactly she might be running. The dangers of contact with the adoptive parents were never expressed. Perhaps there are none. Perhaps it is fine for her to be here.

"You writing a book?" Maria says, knowing that this is the excuse behind most sabbaticals, though clearly it was also timed to coincide with Bonacieux's adoption.

"I was," Philip says.

"About what?" Maria says, again grateful for her ignorance.

"Blackbeard."

The image of this pirate, a cartoon really, with burning braids in his beard and double revolvers in hand, appears everywhere in Beaufort—on billboards, storefronts, boat hulls, and almost every piece of civic marketing. Maria is disappointed that this is who Philip spends his days writing about. It seems childish and commercial. She is not even clear on the pirate's local significance—he is supposed to have sunken his ship in the harbor here, she thinks, or maybe there is hidden treasure. "He even real?" she says.

"He lived right here!" Philip says.

"Well, I've seen the signs."

"Yeah, but I mean here," Philip says, pointing at the floor. "Here."

"In this house?"

"Yep," Philip says, and gestures toward the stairs. They are bare pine, stained and nicked and bowed across the middle. He climbs halfway to the second floor. "That," he says, pointing toward a stain spreading across three steps.

"Come on," Maria says.

"Story is that a man was stabbed here. Been sleeping with one of Blackbeard's wives. Or something."

"You're not sure?"

"Truth is, I don't care about Blackbeard," he says. "Not anymore."

Maria feels justified in her earlier disappointment. Even Philip has learned that he is better than this. "Why not?"

"Mostly because I have baby on the brain."

Maria laughs and follows him into the front hallway. As they pass the stairs, she says, "But is the story about the dead guy true?"

"I don't know," Philip says. "There're so many. One that everyone believes is that there's hidden treasure."

"Is there?" Maria says.

"If it is, it's hidden," Philip says. He points through an open window at the long green yard where Christopherson has stopped to adjust the mower blades. The land stretches downward for hundreds of feet until it reaches the water. "Blackbeard used to tie his boat up here. Onto the porch."

"With a long rope," Maria says.

"The water used to come up right here," Philip says. Maria can tell he's told the story many times. She likes the feeling of being cast into one of his usual spells. "They dredged the sound in fifty-three. Had the opposite effect of receding shorelines. Like I said. These stories, there are a ton of them."

In the morning light, he moves slowly throughout the house. He is all rough elegance and indifference. His blue oxford is frayed along the collar. He does not wear socks. Maria cannot help but think of how different he is from Jack. She wonders at Jack's genetic heritage, marked forever in little Bonacieux's cells, and how it will react as the child ages alongside a man so different from her father. Maria is pleased with the prospect.

"Here are the bones I dug up from the backyard," he says, pointing at a mound of debris on the mantel. "Here is the laundry room."

He is open to her. He almost does not even notice her. There is an immediate familiarity. Maria is pleased with the certainty that he already likes her.

The kitchen door opens and footsteps sound lightly. Maria turns to the hallway and sees Nina shuffling awkwardly through the darkness. Bundled against autumns' first chill in tweed and yellow tights, she is carrying a car seat at her side, limping along with its weight. When she enters the light of the room, she raises a finger to her lips for silence.

"She drives Bonny around to get her to sleep," Philip whispers.

"Shhhh," Nina says.

"And when she wakes up, it's . . . interesting," Philip says.

"What do you mean?" Maria says.

"There's a lot of screaming."

But without Philip or Nina's knowledge, Bonacieux has already awoken and is now staring at Maria in silence.

"Maria, this is Nina," Philip says.

Distracted, Maria takes her hand. It is smaller than Maria's and cold. Maria is ashamed of the note written on her hand in ballpoint pen. It reads: 403 FEDERAL STREET. 11 AM. In contrast, Nina's is manicured and pristine.

"Could you watch her while we get the groceries?" Nina whispers. Maria nods and waves them on.

After they exit the room, Maria kneels before Bonacieux. She cannot believe her ploy has landed her here. She touches Bonacieux's toe. The child is not cherubic. There are no rolls. But her cheeks are rosy and full, and Maria cannot help but think she is the loveliest child she has ever seen. She understands there is a trickery of genes at work, but refuses to acknowledge any bias. Who can deny Bonacieux's beauty?

She emerged from Maria's own flesh. These facts together astound Maria and fill her with an energy unfamiliar and huge. This is what brings people to church, she thinks, curiosity about the unknowable. For her, that magical quandary is rising to the surface again, like it did in earnest at the quickening, those first early movements of Bonacieux within Maria's startled womb. Again she feels like she is touching the unknown—or instead, it is she who is being touched by it.

"Hi," Maria says. Her voice sounds unlike any she has ever before used in seriousness. It is coy and high and sweet and she is not embarrassed. "It's OK," she says, and rubs Bonacieux's cheek. The child turns to her hand as if it might be food and begins to cry softly. Maria unclasps the seat straps and gently lifts her daughter to her chest where Bonacieux becomes silent and still. Maria thinks she may have even fallen asleep again but is not sure. She is afraid to chance a look. When Philip and Nina return, Bonacieux lifts her head and turns, silent and calm and curious. They stop, stunned, just inside the room.

"She woke up," Maria says.

CHAPTER 10

Across the cracked concrete of Ann Street, Maria pushes a blue pram. Inside, Bonacieux lies within its cushioned womb, watching shadows play across the sunshade. An old station wagon creeps toward them across the hardtop, and in a panic, Maria rushes to the curb. She is unaccustomed to being aware of such danger. It is the third day Maria has watched Bonacieux.

She is paid eight dollars an hour and is filled with a constant dread that Bonacieux is going to either die or be abducted on her watch. If the child sleeps more than ten minutes longer than her usual length of nap, Maria cannot help but enter the nursery and place her ear close to Bonacieux's lips in an effort to confirm that she still breathes. Maria has not yet grown comfortable eating food from Philip and Nina's kitchen and still packs her own lunch, despite the fact that they insist she not do so.

At the top of Karen's driveway, Maria gently lifts her daughter and carries her inside.

"Mom?" Maria calls, placing Bonacieux gently atop a small quilt on the floor.

"One second," her mother says. She has had a hard time getting out of bed the past few days.

"It's OK," Maria says, "we can come in there," but already her mother is rustling down the hallway.

"Coming, coming," her mother says, and then appears in the doorway resplendent in silk pajamas printed with newspaper headlines. Maria does not know where these clothes have been purchased, but her mother has been spending time late at night shopping on odd Japanese websites. She now also owns several brightly colored clogs. Today she is wearing neon green ones. It is as if her clothes have become some battle flag sent up as a warning to any personal threat—even sickness—lest it think her lines are not still well formed and standing.

"Well, well, well," Maria's mother says, sitting gingerly in a tall wooden chair at the table. She smiles at Bonacieux. "That thing's just plain cute. No getting around it."

"That's her," Maria says. "Little Bonny Price."

Her mother wiggles her fingers at the child, but there is no recognition here—at one day old, Bonacieux looked little like she does now. Maria's mother has no clue who this child is. But Maria knows this cannot last. The Prices live five blocks away. Karen will learn the child's full name through social osmosis if she doesn't already know it, and somehow it will pass to her mother. And Bonacieux is no one else's name anywhere, save old books and bad movies. It's only a matter of time. So Maria understands she must disclose the truth. All morning she has been preparing herself to do so, and unsure of how long her will might hold, she feels it must happen now.

"We have to talk," she says.

"Isn't that how you hate to start a conversation?" her mother says. "Isn't that the exact line?"

"It is."

"Do you hate to start this conversation?"

"I do."

"Oh, this sounds good," her mother says, pulling at the front of her pajama shirt, straightening the headline MAN WALKS ON MOON. She grins, thrilled with any life that might still course through her.

"Her name isn't Bonny, exactly," Maria says.

"What do you mean?"

"The baby. Her name isn't Bonny. It's just her nickname."

"So?"

"Her name is Bonacieux."

Maria's mother looks like she is about to laugh. Clearly she does not understand the obvious message Maria is trying to deliver. Maria feels the need to explain that this is not funny.

"What?" her mother says.

"It's Bonacieux."

"What are you saying?"

"That her name is Bonacieux. The name I named my daughter. That baby is named it. And it isn't a coincidence."

The message has now been received. Her mother stops smiling and turns to the child. Maria is not sure what her mother is thinking—she is clearly in shock, amazed that the child, who was a stranger only moments ago, has now suddenly become her granddaughter. Maria has not prepared any explanation beyond this point but now recognizes the obvious need for one. She is afraid of sounding crazy. But she isn't crazy, she tells herself, she's just in an odd situation, one in which few people have ever had the chance to find themselves.

"It's complicated, but not crazy," Maria says. "Even though I know it sounds that way. Last summer . . ." She places Bonacieux's bottle on the counter. "I used to see Philip like every day last summer, walking his dog. Here, in Beaufort. He's the husband . . ."

"I know who he is," her mother says.

"Well. I'd see him all the time. He doesn't know me; I'd just see him walking. So when I was looking at the adoption sites, I just happened to recognize his picture on one. It was like a sign. Like fate. That's why I picked them. Because I knew who they were." She gestures toward Bonacieux. "I just thought . . ."

"Do they know this?"

"Christ," Maria says. She shakes her head. "No, I just thought . . ." Bonacieux places one foot into her mouth. Maria feels the conversation slipping away from her control and regrets not having thought it out further. She is not sure what impact her news is going to have on her mother, or other people for that matter. She is now only a witness to its effect. "And then, when we went trick-or-treating on Halloween I saw her. And then Karen found the job listing. It's all like a miracle."

"You pick a person to adopt your daughter because you know where they live, then you go to that place," Maria's mother says. "It's not really a miracle at all."

"Well," Maria says. "OK."

Her mother runs her hands over the headline Dow Jones Collapses, then struggles out of her chair. In a series of jerky folds, she lands beside the child. Maria cannot tell if she is angry or amazed. Perhaps she is both. Her mother pets the down on Bonacieux's head. She kisses her nose. "Jesus Christ, Maria," she says, rolling a bit of Bonacieux's hair between her fingers.

"Yeah," Maria says, unsure of how to respond.

"Sweetie girl," her mother says, rolling onto her back on the floor. And then, with a feat of strength Maria did not know her mother was even capable of, she lifts Bonacieux, squealing, into the air. They are not going to discuss the dangers inherent in this situation, not today, Maria can tell. But she also knows from the look on her mother's face that no matter the risk, her mother is not going to let this child stay out of her arms for long.

CHAPTER 11

MORNINGS PHILIP AND Nina's house is skirted by fog. Maria approaches on foot. It is a five-block walk through roads empty and cracked by weeds. Gulls undulate atop gusts in the cold. Rain falls often, coming first with wind. A turning over of leaves. The first drops fall large and clumsy, then all of a sudden in a rush. The ocean seems no longer to reflect the light but to absorb it. It is a gray, heaving mat.

Philip works early, most often in a converted storage shed in the side yard. Inside is a wood-burning stove, a small oak table, and a wooden folding chair bought from a church yard sale. ZION LUTHERAN is stenciled onto a slat on the back. He has begun a new book about the history of adoption in the United States. He says he is starting at the end. That the last chapter is about Nina, Bonacieux, and him.

But when Maria arrives at eight each day, Philip has not yet begun work. He drinks chicory in the kitchen with Bonacieux. He makes Maria a cup. Nina wakes later, sometimes napping already by the time Maria even arrives. She sleeps in the guest room now because, she has told Maria, she does not want to wake Philip when she feeds Bonacieux at night. But Maria knows Philip wakes with the child too. She wonders if there is something else afoot. She sees them pass without speaking. Sometimes Philip will ask Nina a question and she will not even reply. They soften in Maria's company, but she has seen them when they did not know that she could. Nina is prone to long silences. She does not seem mean, but rather just a touch cold. It is, in fact, to her credit, Maria thinks. It complements Philip's warm sophistication. Still, Maria can feel Philip relax when Nina is not around. Maria feels the release as well. She has long conversations with Philip, but only when Nina has left the house. She eats their food now, answers their phone, and borrows Nina's raincoat from the closet without asking. Where before she was guarded and careful, she is now assured and at ease.

Each day Maria sketches Bonacieux. She works quickly with a heavy mechanical pencil, filling her ribbon-bound sketchbook with examinations of baby toes and her daughter's face while napping. Any rendering of the child produces nothing but soft curved lines, and it occurs to Maria that the innocence of Bonacieux's youth is part of what makes her so easy to draw. The more one lives, she thinks, the harder the lines become, the more they proliferate, the more difficult they are to capture. The curve of Bonacieux's cheek requires little more than a brief stroke, while the hollows of her mother's face demand labored shading, a network of acute angles, and prolonged study of the architecture of the skull. After a while, drawing Bonacieux's face seems like nothing more than transcribing a series of circles. The act is a simple sacrament, a silent worship of the flesh.

Bonacieux has no real difficulties of note. She is healthy. She has no allergies. She has no colic. Empirically she is adorable. Maria's early fears of the world around her child have abated and been replaced by a burgeoning confidence. She is surprised to discover of herself that she is a disciplinarian. She establishes a rigid schedule for the child's naps and meals. Straying from this timetable by even a quarter of an hour can throw off the schedule for days.

Philip and Nina trust Maria's instincts with Bonacieux more than their own. The guidelines she establishes are immediately sacred. Philip and Nina respect them with a religious awe. They do not wonder from where Maria's knowledge has come. They only strive to follow.

Maria makes Bonacieux's baby food by grinding cooked vegetables in a small food mill, then freezing it in serving sizes ready to be thawed for each meal. In a spiral-bound notebook, she maintains a record of the time and consistency of each of the child's bowel movements. She reports to Nina about this and has begun to get frustrated with Nina, who does not maintain the records well herself.

It is not motherhood of the child that has given Maria her skills. It is something else. An aptitude, innate. She is astonished by it and proud. It surges up inside of her, confident and aggressive. The neighborhood, the house, the weather—they all seem to allow it free range. Why not become sharp, hard, and loving all at once? She is in the home of Blackbeard, she is in the home of her daughter, she is on the edge of the continent. She imagines the strictest disciplinarians are those who do not foresee a long life for themselves. They must ensure the safety of the next. She is glad her mother was not sick until after she, Maria, had grown. Her own childhood was so lax. She feels she thrived in its flexibility and questions why, if that is the case, she does not strive to re-create it. She does not know, but trusts in the instinct to control.

Each afternoon, Maria wheels Bonacieux to Karen's house. She wants her mother to be in contact at every opportunity. It seems like, if her mother willed herself to live long enough to see Bonacieux be born, as Maria still believes, then the child's presence might just stretch her mother's remaining time further. After the initial shock of discovery, her mother has been only thrilled with all ensuing contact with her granddaughter. Maria wonders at any concerns her mother might harbor about the situation, but for now her mother is only enjoying each day.

And there is this: it cannot be doubted; her mother has begun to improve. To Maria the correlation seems direct: the chance to see her grandchild has given her another reason to live. Maria feels justified in her superstitions. It is as if the trajectory of her mother's life were that of a ball thrown high into the air. It has reached that magical point where the ball floats for a split second at its apex, but Maria is not sure this arc will now turn downward. She feels like it might just as well take off again and rise anew. She is trying to allow herself to believe this is a possibility. And why shouldn't she?

Her mother walks to the water every day. Her hair has begun to regrow. Some days she goes out without a hat. Some days she smokes a cigarette with Karen on the porch, telling life to go fuck itself. But the pinnacle of each day for Maria's mother is Bonacieux. Sometimes her mother will even come to Philip and Nina's house on her own, stopping to visit during a walk. Philip in particular enjoys her company. They talk academic shop. They share many mutual friends. Around her mother now, Maria feels the short arcs of time connecting. Life is stretching forward in small growths past where it should have already ended.

EVENING, EARLY DECEMBER. The day is dull and biting, filled with a damp chill that cuts through Maria's wool coat. The magnolia in Karen's yard glitters with cold white Christmas lights, hung two days prior by Christopherson and his lawn care partner. The cloud cover clears late in the day, and the last of the sun's light, fading and red, suddenly fills the sky. It's postcard material, so beautiful Maria feels it's too easy to enjoy. That she should resist it. But she cannot. Her heart, it seems, has expanded with pseudo-motherhood. In her art history class once, Maria's professor said that Diane Arbus's photographs of mentally disabled children in Halloween costumes wrought beauty from the grotesque. He said standard beauty in today's world had been rendered powerless. At the time it seemed profound. Now Maria wonders if the professor ever had children.

Her phone rings.

"I'm so sorry," Nina says. Bonacieux is crying in the background. "I know you're busy."

"I'm not busy," Maria says. She tosses Karen's *Architectural Digest* into a wicker basket beside the couch.

"I just can't get her to sleep," Nina says.

"OK," Maria says, her heart racing on the thrill of Nina's dependence. "You want me to come over?"

"Could you?"

Already Nina has found motherhood impossible without Maria. It is not that she is a bad mother at all; it is only that she is perhaps too willing to allow Maria to be the one to handle difficulties such as these. And Maria is only too eager to help. Without her, Nina would rise to the challenge, but Maria enjoys the cultivation of dependence. Together, the three of them—Nina, Maria, and Philip—seem to be building a house dependent on one trick joist, but Maria has decided to not think about structural integrity. She has chosen to ignore the future. Her prognostications have already turned out to be so wrong so often that she is now ceasing to make them. She is weaving a patchwork only of the smallest pieces of time here. Days, hours. Scenes.

Through the cold evening Maria drives the five blocks to Philip and Nina's house. It appears alit through a frame of trees as if it too were posing for a postcard, and in fact, Maria has seen several postcards for sale in town featuring an image of this house at this very time of day, in this very light.

Inside, Nina paces the kitchen, Bonacieux held tight to her chest. The child is wailing, whipping her head from side to side. Nina's eyes are red. Her face is wet. Paul Simon plays low on the stereo in the dimly lit living room.

"I'm losing it," Nina says. "I'm totally losing it."

"Sweetie," Maria says, touching Bonacieux's head. "When did you start bedtime?"

"Six thirty," Nina says, guilt bending the note in her voice.

"That's too late. You've got to start early, crazy early. Give it *hours*. She's overtired."

Maria takes Bonacieux. The child continues to cry, rising in volume as Maria takes her.

"My God," Nina says.

"It's fine," Maria says. The crying doesn't bother her like it does Nina. "Go for a walk."

The screen door bangs shut as Maria carries Bonacieux into the nursery. Within stands an antique wooden crib, once Philip's. One ornate red velvet loveseat. A marble-topped dresser. An old dry sink now filled with books buttressing one stuffed flamingo. Two original Albers prints, different colored rectangles, hang on the eastern wall. A tall rocking chair. Maria loves this room. She aspires to it.

She swaddles Bonacieux, still crying, then calmly kisses her daughter's forehead. Bonacieux strains against the blanket as Maria places her into the crib.

As Maria closes the door behind her, Bonacieux's cries continue to fill the house. Framed in the front hall window, Nina sits on the porch with her hands over her ears. She too is crying. A glass of wine stands untouched on the wicker table beside her.

Maria opens the door. "Go," she says. "Walk. This will end in . . ." Maria looks at her mother's Cartier wristwatch. "Six minutes. Maybe seven."

Nina flits across the freshly mown lawn, happy to take Maria's advice. She wears a sheepskin blanket over her shoulders like an elegant squab. With each step that she approaches the darkness at the edge of the lawn, it gradually erases her form.

In the kitchen, Maria watches the second hand. She believes in this process, certain that her daughter needs these private moments to learn how to work through the emotional turmoil of another day of learning how to live. But tonight Bonacieux will not stop crying. Things carry on long past when Maria expected them to cease. Like an addict, Nina returns to the lawn, only for Maria to wave her back into the darkness. Maria finds herself in new parental territory. She reenters Bonacieux's room, afraid something has truly gone wrong. The child is red-faced and lying at a strange angle in her crib, the swaddling blanket loose and kicked into one corner. Maria lifts her, checking the diaper. It is clean. Bonacieux sobs against Maria's breast. Sudden and alien and urgent, Maria feels her milk let down.

She tries to ignore it, hoping it will not stain her shirt. Bonacieux will not be consoled. Maria begins to feel panicky. She understands how babies are shaken. She kisses Bonacieux, whispers to her, rocks her, bounces from foot to foot, but nothing works. Finally, at a loss, feeling like she has reached some emotional valley, Maria sits on the loveseat and lifts her shirt.

Directed by an innate compass, Bonacieux attaches herself to Maria's glistening nipple. Tears well up from the pain as Bonacieux begins to suckle. Maria does not know what exactly is being produced. This long after childbirth, it doesn't seem possible that this is real breastfeeding, but maybe it is. Something is exiting her body and entering Bonacieux's. The child is now silent, consumed with the process of suckling. Dust wavers in the nightlight, making the air around it appear almost solid. The boundaries between things—people, air, light—seem to meld. Maria grits her teeth until the child finally rolls off. In her sleep, Bonacieux turns her face to Maria. A sacrament has been made and inner grace here bestowed, yet Maria is not its recipient. She swoons on the rush of transgression.

CHAPTER 12

FOUR SMALL WOODEN sailboats, each painted dark green, float down Taylor's Creek with their canvas sails aloft. Six men row a long wooden canoe behind them, in the center of which sits Santa Claus. Children line Front Street, most screaming "Santa!" some simply watching in silent awe. Bonacieux views it all high above the heads of the others, held aloft by Philip.

Nina shoots photos of her husband and daughter. The frames click off in such rapid succession that the camera ticks along like a clock. Sometimes she shoots hundreds in a day. Maria considers the promise made by the Children's Home Society of North Carolina, that her daughter's adoptive parents would supply her with a photo album once a year. Perhaps some of these very photos will be collected for delivery to her. She wonders if the images are screened by the employees of the adoption service, if Anne Vanstory will recognize Maria if she appears in any, which she is sure she will. It is foolish, she thinks. They have more than enough to keep them busy. Still, it is a reminder of the risks she is taking and the consequences she is unsure of.

Nina uses a gunmetal Leica with a huge lens that Maria covets. Maria looked into the model, desiring one for herself. The camera costs more than two thousand dollars. It is yet another confirmation for Maria that she has chosen the right family for her daughter, one that amasses the effects of life with precision. She is not afraid of extrapolating meaning from material. These items are proof of care, of taste, of an unabashed respect for elegance.

Maria retrieves candy from the pavement and hands it to a boy who crams it into his pocket. She is disappointed that he does not say thank you. She is uncomfortable in crowds and cannot remember ever having even been to a parade before. Her mother would never even consider doing anything other than avoiding civic celebration. But, Maria thinks, this is lovely. The cries of the children erase anything but thrill.

BACK AT THE house, Philip pours three glasses of brandy, which, like the parade, are a mystery to Maria. She does not even know exactly what brandy is. Is it wine, or is it liquor? To her it smells of both. She does not let on that she is unsure, though. She tries to exude confidence. With glass in hand, she takes Bonacieux to the nursery for a diaper change. There, while her child lies half naked atop the marble-top dresser, kicking the air with quiet and calm abandon, Maria hears Philip and Nina in the kitchen.

"Well, I had her all morning," Nina says.

"When?"

"That's not fair," Nina says. "Don't make me explain it."

"All I'm saying is that this is why we have help," Philip says.

"OK," Nina says. "But I have plans."

"By all means, go," he says.

Maria has heard these arguments before. Nina seems to have some built-in clock, marking all time spent with or away from the child. If there is any imbalance, she lets Philip know. Maria does not get the feeling Nina in fact cares so much about spending equal time with or away from the child—there is so much quality time to be had, what with their incredibly open schedules—it seems more like just a chance for her to fill an insatiable need to cry foul. By the time Maria returns, Nina has left. Already Philip's mood has lifted.

"Can I ask you a favor?" Philip says, taking Bonacieux into his arms.

"That's one of those lines," Maria says, and Philip laughs. She has told him about her list of distasteful conversation starters. Already he seems to know her as well as anyone. She sips the brandy. Drinking with adults in daylight is intoxicating on its own merits, and though Maria does not dislike Nina, she too feels a rise in mood at her absence. The day is quickly filling with simple pleasures. Brandy. A parade. She feels lifted, like Bonacieux above the heads of others.

"Can I interview you for my book?" Philip says.

"About Bonacieux?"

"No, no. About your own child."

Maria wipes her nose with the back of her hand, endeavoring to convey an unflappable nonchalance. She understands that Philip appreciates how comfortable she is in this house, how she is at times crude. She tries to not let her fear betray her now and sips the brandy slowly, trying to exude indifference.

"What do you want to know?" she says. She is pleased with her act.

"Let's see. What was the one most surprising thing about the whole process?" he says.

"That I had to sign over sixty pages of legal documents and that the father of the child only had to sign two, and they're about his health."

"Wait," Philip says, and unclips a ballpoint pen from Nina's cross-word. "That's good." He begins to make notes along the margin of the newspaper. "And when did you decide to give your child up for adoption?"

"Early."

"Why?"

"Uh. Well I'm pro-choice and everything."

"OK," he says, as if she's stating the obvious.

"I don't know. My mother was really sick, so."

"So . . . what? Did you want her to see the kid?"

Maria still does not know quite how to answer the question. "That was part of it, I guess. But I actually didn't even know if she'd still be alive. Mostly I just wanted, like while my mom was sick, it seemed right not to *not* make another person if I could. If that makes any sense. I don't know. That logic is probably illegal in China."

Philip writes rapidly.

"You know, at first," he says, "I couldn't believe that you'd had a kid."

"Why?"

"Because you're so not a screwup."

"Thanks, I guess."

"But so that's actually why you had the kid," he says. He looks up from the newspaper, and she feels the sudden power he must wield in a classroom. He is considerate and confident. He changes lives, she is sure of it.

"We don't have to do this," he says. "I'm sorry." He looks down at the newspaper now riddled with notes.

Maria is suddenly suspicious of her endeavor to remain so calm. What has given her away? She is surprised to be read so easily by Philip. Already he has come to know her so well. "It's fine," she says.

"No. No. I shouldn't involve you in this."

"Well, do you know anything about Bonacieux's mother?"

Philip shakes his head, folding the notes in half. "I know she didn't have any diseases."

MARIA PUSHES BONACIEUX through the neighborhood, passing the historic homes, many now empty for the winter. She considers how close she just came to her secret, how they were speaking right around it, how she can speak about it with no one other than her mother. This morning at the parade, life seemed so calm and safe. She felt as if she had carved out some previously uncharted region of sanctuary. But she has since been reminded of just how precarious her position with Philip and Nina really is. Has anyone before been in a similar situation? She does not know but feels that the only possibilities might be found in Lifetime movies and supermarket tabloids. The inability to converse about her life with someone else, to reveal herself to someone new, increases her anxiety. It seems the only way to gain any perspective. But she knows that even the idea is unwise. She must keep her information secret lest her life actually become some tabloid fodder.

At Karen's, Maria's mother has prepared the bed for naptime: one half for her, the other for Bonacieux. One pillow has been moved to the side to keep the child from rolling off the mattress. Her mother glows with expectation.

"I'll let you know when she wakes up," her mother says, tucking Bonacieux in. She lies beside the child. "It's time for me to recharge."

They have been sleeping together during afternoon nap like this, curled in seemingly untenable positions: arms crossed under bodies, legs dangling off the mattress. Time together only while awake is no longer enough for either of them.

Maria strolls slowly down the hall. The smell of salt water, of suntan lotion. It seems part of the wallpaper in Karen's house. Oranges. She feels it is her house now. Karen is happy with them here. Once again, their presence has eased something in her life. Maria's fear of imposition has passed.

In the kitchen Maria dries dishes while Karen rinses.

"Does she make you think of your own?" Karen says.

Maria understands that Karen is talking about Bonacieux two times over, both as her daughter and her charge. She longs to discuss this duplicity with Karen, certain it will ease her burden, but knows that she cannot.

"Sometimes," Maria says. "Yeah."

Karen nods while dipping a handful of silver forks into a depth of water. As she lifts them back out, soap strings off of them in rainbows. "You know," she says. "You're going to be a good mother."

Maria nods. She thinks, I already am a good mother. Or, am I a terrible one?

CHAPTER 13

IT IS FOUR days into January. Christmas lights still hang from the magnolia in Karen's yard. On the lawn across the street, an inflatable snowman nods softly along with the breeze. A holly wreath hangs on Karen's front door, but all celebrations here have ended. The holidays are over, and Beaufort seems colder than Chapel Hill this time of year. The salt water in the air creeps through even Maria's favorite wool sweater, a Fair Isle number Jack found in a Dumpster the previous March. The wind is brisk across the inlet. But despite the chill, Maria likes to sit on the porch after dinner bundled in a green plaid blanket. The fact that Bonacieux has been asleep already for an hour makes it feel like Maria has passed deep into the night. But it is only eight o'clock. She understands at last the conservative sleep schedule of parents.

Someone moves in the yard beside her. It is Christopherson. He wears a red plaid hunting jacket and is kicking a magnolia seedpod through the leaves in the early darkness, his skateboard dangling from one hand clasped tightly onto an orange wheel. Since Halloween, he has, for the most part, existed apart from Maria. Leaf removal has kept him busy. Their schedules rarely overlap, and for Maria it is a surprise to even see him.

"Jesus," Maria says, placing a hand to her chest. She startles him.

"Sorry," he says.

"What are you doing?"

"Going to the pier party."

"What's the pier party?" Maria says.

"It's at the pier. It's a party. They're gonna burn a boat. Want to go?"

Maria has a sudden desire to speak with people who are not parents, whose preoccupations are not the basics of life.

"Yeah," she says, and stands. "One second."

In the front hallway Maria catches herself in an antique oval mirror freckled with oxidized spots. Her bangs have curled in the humidity, her hair shortened and thickened. Her eyes, as always, are only barely visible. She likes what she sees and understands that she is playing with Christopherson's affections. Why not, she thinks. She has often thought of their Halloween episode and longed for another. What have her days been filled with but self-denial, she asks herself. Her needs are meager. The gravity of this situation is light. Objects in her orbit might float. She requires neither sex nor love—she only wants someone to take her to the pier.

In the living room, her mother paints her fingernails while watching *Antiques Roadshow*. Maria remembers her disavowal of this very show only a few months ago. Hers is not the only life that has changed so quickly over the weeks.

Maria says, "I'm going for a walk."

"I think they're having the pier party," her mother says, not looking up from her nails.

"OK," Maria says, unable for some reason to admit that this is indeed where she is going. How her mother knows what this is she is not sure, and she wonders for a moment if she has been trapped in some setup. Her mother has always thought of Christopherson as second-rate. He has not excelled in school and evinces no aptitude for the arts. But he is the son of her best friend, and her mother is nothing if not observant. A young man is in the house with a young woman. There need not be much detective work to extrapolate romance. Perhaps it is all by design, though Maria feels it is likely her mother has read too much into the situation. She cannot bring herself to care, one way or the other. She is simply ready to go.

Christopherson stands in the yard, spinning his skateboard by the wheel so rapidly that it is only a blur at his side. At Maria's approach, he ceases the motion and the board twirls to a stop.

"Take me to the river," Maria sings, but Christopherson is only confused. It's a Talking Heads reference that Jack would have caught. Of course Maria wasn't even alive when the song was written, but this is another reminder that she is older than Christopherson by years not marked by time.

The pier is lined with colored lights. Propped upright, in a decrepit fiberglass dinghy tied to the pilings, is one massive Christmas tree, slightly browned and hanging on to its last few strands of tinsel. A boy rolls into the light on a long skateboard. A girl plays Van Morrison on the guitar. These are the bodies that rose in silence to greet Maria in the graveyard, she is sure of it. There are a dozen or so people here already, all teenagers, high schoolers she guesses. But Maria cannot tell. Some of the girls look like they could be older than she. Maria thinks about her own high school years, a time in her life she is utterly surprised to look back upon fondly, as if it were an epoch of emotional simplicity.

"What is this?" Maria says.

"They light the Christmas tree on fire and send it out into the water," Christopherson says. "It's cool."

Like the Halloween spectacle of gravesite sit-ups, the goals of this teenage theater seem admirably low to Maria. They aim only for magic that will not fail. Why she cannot hem in the boundaries of her own life so wisely she does not know.

Something about the indifference in Christopherson's reply brings Jack to mind. Maria once again imagines Jack naked with Icy People, performing assorted sex things he had once done with her. She wonders if they are together at that very instant. The thought is both infuriating and strangely exciting. She is filled with an erotic energy she hasn't felt in months.

"Everything cool?" Christopherson says.

"Is everything cool?" Maria says. "I mean, no. What. My mom's sick and I'm a college dropout babysitting . . ." She looks at Christopherson, weighing her sudden compulsion to finish the thought. Christopherson's bottom lip juts out just a bit farther than the top. His face is long and slightly goofy. It is the first time Maria feels like she has really seen him. She cannot help but think again that this is a boy. He smiles mostly upper gum.

"What?" he says.

"My mom tell you to bring me here?" Maria says.

"No. Why?"

"I don't know," Maria says. "I worry that she worries about me too much." Maria's increasing certainty that her excursion with Christopherson is of her own design, and not her mother's, makes her feel more trusting. She senses she must not waste the opportunity to speak with someone freely. She has become so accustomed to living with a guard around her words, the chance to speak any truth to someone who might actually want to hear it has become irresistible. She says, "You know I had a kid this summer, right?"

"Yeah," Christopherson says, almost blushing with a desire to understand. His attempt for nonchalance is sweet and beguiling. Maria can tell that he so wants for her to be comfortable talking about this with him, even if he doesn't know how to play host to this moment. It is enough for Maria, though, that he is trying to put her at ease. She wants to reward him for his aspirations.

"Well and you know the baby I've been babysitting?" she says.

"The Price's kid. Bonny P. Yeah."

"That's my baby."

Christopherson keeps smiling. He even allows it to grow wider. More gum appears.

"What do you mean?" he says.

"I mean, that's actually my baby," Maria says. "That's the baby I had."

"How?" he says. "You know them?"

"No, I'd just seen them around last summer, when we were here. And I happened to recognize a photo of them on this adoption site. So I picked them. It was, like, fate."

"Picked them?"

"To adopt my daughter."

"Uh," Christopherson says. His smile fades, as if bending under duress. This conversation is folly, Maria realizes. Christopherson is fifteen years old. "You mean they adopted your kid?"

"Oh fuck," Maria says.

"What?"

"I mean, am I crazy?"

Christopherson's smile now fails completely. Maria has terrified the closest thing to a friend that she has in this town. She begins to cry. Christopherson squeezes their sweaty palms together. She can tell that he doesn't want anyone to see her tears, but already people are turning.

"What do you mean?" Christopherson says. "You're not crazy. Hey, it's going to be alright."

But this is just the platitude of a teenager who has seen situations be nothing but all right. This is not going to be all right, Maria thinks. She sees no ending that does not close upon tragedy. The death of her mother, the shaming of herself, the destruction of all families involved.

These streets, the houses. The light between them. The toys of the children, expensive, rarely played with. This is the landscape of Maria's dreams. She has not been raised in the mountains, on an island, or in the winding alleys of some Italian village. She has spent her years here, in the suburbs of North Carolina. She tries to allow this nightscape to touch her. The water of Taylor's Creek is as exotic an element as she feels she has any right to be near. It laps at the banks of the continent only a few feet away from her. She takes a deep breath and attempts to keep her mind from spinning out possibilities. She tells herself to be thankful for Christopherson's sweaty palm. Its grasp is simple but sincere.

"Just forget that I said anything, OK?" Maria says.

"OK," Christopherson says, and although she does not believe for a second that he actually will forget, she does, in fact, trust him with her secret.

A boy wearing a puffy down jacket and khaki shorts pours gasoline from a plastic canister onto the old Christmas tree. He unties the boat with one jerk of the knot, lights a twist of newspaper with a lighter, and, as the boat drifts into Taylor's Creek, tosses the flaming paper into it. A small mushroom of flame bursts into the darkness. The heat rushes across Maria's face and she reaches up to her eyebrows, afraid that they have been singed. Her face, however, is not only unscathed, her cheeks are even still wet. Not even the tears have burnt off.

CHAPTER 14

S PRING ARRIVES EARLY in Beaufort. Afternoons, Maria eats egg-salad sandwiches for lunch at the Royal James Café, a pool hall one block from the water. Most days, her mother accompanies her, buying a *USA Today* from the vending machine outside and complaining that there are no good newspapers in town. Her mother demands the news of the world, charmed by the feeling that this small town is not a part of its events, yet simultaneously frustrated by that fact. Over meals, she reads the paper in silence while Maria tends to Bonacieux. Families with young children eat shrimp burgers only feet away from sunburnt old men chalking cues under a blown-up photo of a great white shark captured close to shore. The jukebox is all country and Jimmy Buffet. The place is so exotic to Maria that its absolute otherness puts her at ease. Any neuroses of her own do not here apply. These days have been calm, passing in a bliss she resists considering the end of. The waitresses think Bonacieux is hers. Maria wants to tell them they are correct. But of course she does not. She smiles and says no, do you know the Prices? If they do, they know only Philip.

Today Nina comes to lunch with Maria and her mother. Though Nina is carrying Bonacieux, the child wants to be held by Maria. She pushes and whines, but Maria does not butt in. The wedge between mother and child has been of her own construction, she knows. And although she is proud of being wanted, Maria pities Nina because of it. She understands that it is her own fault that Nina is not as good a mother as she might otherwise be. Maria has taken every opportunity. Bathing, bedtime, feeding, and playtime have all become hers. She hides these events from Nina, greedy for their reward. She is not proud of her competitiveness, but she cannot deny it. Having never before enjoyed competition, Maria is not accustomed to this need for dominance. It is not a game she enjoys only because she is good at it, but rather because it is being played with her own daughter and she is winning.

Nina has owned a house in Beaufort for more than a decade but still seems out of place at the Royal James. She is too fragile and fine to enter without notice.

"M'elp you?" says the waitress.

Maria can roll her eyes at Southern role-playing but is still expert at the parts. "Tea, please," she says. "Sweet." She looks to Nina, who nods her consent. "And unsweet for her," she says, motioning to her mother.

"You still practice?" Maria's mother says to Nina. They've been discussing the role of career in parenting.

"I stopped when I was pregnant," Nina says, fixing Bonacieux's collar. "We lost one at eight months. About two years ago now."

The reminder of Nina's miscarriage comes as a shock to both Maria and her mother. It gives Nina sudden import. Maria's mother places her hand atop Nina's. "I cannot imagine," she says.

"So," Nina says. She is uncomfortable. She has not spent much time with Maria's mother. Philip has. He seems to adore Maria's mother. Where he is open and playful with her, though, Nina is restrained. It is as if she knows she is speaking with family.

"Nina collects antiques," Maria says, desperate for a new subject.

"Addictive, huh?" her mother says.

"My God," Nina says. "The mailman probably thinks I'm a freak. eBay. Almost every day."

"Fine art?"

"Miniatures."

"I used to go to the antique malls," her mother says. She leaves off the part about her new desire to deacquisition these purchases. She has been shedding the accumulations of her life, gifting anything anyone likes. Maria admires this development, with its notes of esthetic purity.

"So what I wanted to talk about," Nina says, turning to Maria, "is that I'm going to Durham next Tuesday."

"What for?" Maria says.

"I'm interviewing with a law firm."

"For what?"

"A job. They're interviewing me."

Maria feels blindsided by the news that Nina is already planning an exit from Beaufort. She understands it is inevitable—sabbaticals by definition last for only so long—but still it feels too soon. She tells herself that Duke, in Durham, is so very close to Chapel Hill. Not even fifteen miles. She too can return home and still be with them. She admits to herself that this is, in fact, what she wants. The desire is not only for access to her daughter and the chance to parlay that into contact between Bonacieux and her mother, it is also a craving for the home of Philip and Nina and all that it entails. Maria has become intoxicated by it.

"Philip will be home," Nina says, "but I'm just nervous about leaving her for the first time. You know how he is. He's so great with her, but he just doesn't know what he's doing. So I was thinking. Would it be possible for you to stay late? Maybe even put her to sleep before you leave?"

"Sure," Maria says. She feels nourished by the need in Nina's eyes.

"Really?"

Maria only smiles, as if, she seems to say, of course, because who else would ever be able to do anything well with Bonacieux? Nina smiles back, a true smile of relief. Again Maria pities her. Nina does not know how Maria has crippled her.

"How does she sleep?" Maria's mother says.

"Ugh," Nina says. "It's not so smooth."

"That'll pan out in the next eighteen years," Maria's mother says.

"It's still like every three hours."

"I'll stay the night, if you want," Maria says.

"Really?"

"Yeah."

Again Nina's eyes fill with relief. "You can have the guest room beside Bonny's," she says.

"Perfect," Maria says, and as she speaks, she is embarrassed for Nina, for not knowing what is going to happen in her house once she leaves it. It is like watching the launch of a firework into the night sky. How does she not know this will explode?

NINA LEAVES TUESDAY afternoon in the blue Mercedes. The night is warmer than any in recent memory, the first cicadas of the season beginning to sing out to the darkness. The windows are open, though in Philip and Nina's house, there seems always to be at least one window ajar despite any cold. Maria puts Bonacieux to sleep again by breastfeeding her, something that has now become routine.

When she emerges from the nursery, the living room is lit exclusively by the fireplace. The fact that a fire even burns during this warm night while windows are open, a soft breeze snaking inside, describes the house accurately—a location where things converge. Inside, outside. The past here seems present. No one in the house is afraid of seasonal change. If Philip wants a fire, he lights one.

He pours Maria a glass of pinot. They speak of Bonacieux. They are more at ease together without Nina. He refills her glass. They laugh. He tells stories of bad students and his strange family. His brother is married to an ex-girlfriend of Philip's, a half-sister is chasing oil money in Dubai. He gossips about neighbors. He asks Maria about her art, and she opens her sketchbook slowly and hands it to him, bashful yet certain of her skill. He turns page after page of drawings Maria has made of Bonacieux, visibly shocked by each image.

"This is real," Philip says, quieted by her skill. "Do people know you can do this? This is like, like you suddenly telling me you can sing opera. Can you sing opera?"

Maria laughs, pleased that he has found in her any expertise. She has kept so much of herself closed off from him, her secrets surrounding Bonacieux having compelled her to hide almost anything else of import. The effect of his recognition is so strong it's embarrassing—she feels suddenly stronger, more beautiful, more alive. She is pitiful, is what she is, she thinks, a small vegetable in such need of water.

Much later, after hours, she checks on the child. Bonacieux sleeps like she was dropped on the mattress from a small height—her limbs stretch away from her, each in its own direction. What has flung them there, Maria wonders—a dream? Or a need to fill more space? She feels as if she is doing both herself this evening, both dreaming and finding more purchase in this house. When she exits the nursery, having placed an extra blanket over the child's legs, Philip stands at the end of the hallway smoking by an open window. He was not there before, and Maria wonders if he has followed her or just been drawn to the view. It is a window at which he often stands, now framing a moonlit Atlantic, but Maria has seen him there only during daylight. She still feels emboldened by his attention to her art and the sense that it has increased her worth. In the darkness she surges with power.

The silence is enforced by the proximity of a sleeping baby. They have had so much wine. Maria is embarrassed to speak, afraid her words will slur. She does not want any slip to mar the image she has of herself at this moment. She approaches, and without looking at her, Philip takes the cigarette from his mouth and passes it to her. She smokes it knowing only the dampness of the filter; it is the mark of his mouth now in hers. She rests her head against his shoulder. She understands at contact that it cannot be undone.

Philip waits long minutes until he turns. When he does, he smiles and wraps an arm around her. He kisses her easily, as if it is not the first time. She aspires to his nonchalance. He leads her to his room. Maria is scared of the physical act of love, of doing this for the first time since giving birth to the child now sleeping on the other side of the wall. She is nervous about the pain. She undresses with her back to Philip and when she turns she giggles. She covers herself with her arms. Philip lays her on the bed. When he finally enters her he sighs like he's had a deep realization. At this, Maria senses the loss of all her perceived strength, that magical increase in power, her sudden surge in confidence. In its place come the truths of marriage, the imagined conversation with Nina in which she learns of this encounter. It does not decrease Maria's thrill, but replaces it with one more dangerous. The realm of secrets has only grown larger now, and she is happy to have another person with whom to share at least part of its mysterious new landscape.

MORNING. BONACIEUX IS still asleep. Maria sits on the edge of the bed. Philip stirs beside her. Maria is naked. They have slept this way. The morning sun has only just begun to lighten the sky. On the edge of the continent, first light here appears sooner than it does even blocks inland. Still they are silent, afraid any sound will wake Bonacieux and bring an end to this spell. Philip arranges Maria atop pillows and she follows his wordless commands. Her skin is cold, but only on the outside.

CHAPTER 15

O UTSIDE KAREN'S KITCHEN window stands an azalea bush pinking with bloom. Already heavy with blossoms, each branch droops even further under the weight of a visiting party of bees who, as they lift away from each foraged flower and look for the next one to pollinate, send the blossoms bouncing up toward the sun. Animated with the pressure of life, even the shrubbery in this town is shaky after contact.

Six days have passed since Philip and Maria spent the night together. Nina has returned, and they have not been alone since. Never before has Maria been with anyone other than Jack, and she is still surprised at how different the experience was from her previous episodes with him. She did not expect that someone could know so well what to do with her body, but Philip seemed to understand her needs even better than she did. Since the onset of her mother's illness, Maria has regarded the flesh a region of profound mystery, one interested in self-destruction and betrayal. It has since become even more surprising. With it Maria has borne a child. She has slept with an older man. Before making love to him, Maria was only enchanted. Since, she has been consumed by desire.

Maria feels certain that her mother, sorting mail at the kitchen table in a yellow sundress and leather sandals, knows the source of

Maria's elevated mood. They have not discussed what happened with
Philip, but they do not need to. Maria emerged from a night at his
house a changed woman.

"Mail from Yale," her mother says, and hands Maria a manila
envelope. "From the ivory tower to my flower. A note for my goat. A
. . ." she has stumped herself with rhyme. "What the hell?"

Maria never told her mother about last season's inspired application. She was afraid of any appearance that she is planning for life after
her mother's death. She expects nothing from Yale, least of all an envelope, and it is surprising to her that anyone would even use the postal
service and not just send an email. She wonders if she should remove
herself so that she can learn away from her mother's eyes the news this
letter carries. But her mother has already seen the return address, and
to her the word *Yale* is like some magnetic force. Maria decides she
might as well look here and now.

The envelope is heavy, and she thinks of the myth that heavy envelopes mean good news. She tries to remember if this is supposed to be
true or not. She decides to find out for herself. The first sentence of the
letter inside answers her question. She does not even know what words
she has read exactly, absorbing their mass in a sequence of jumble and
flash. The meaning is all that she gets. It is what she has dreamed of for
years. She has been accepted.

"Holy shit," Maria says, and Bonacieux begins to fuss. Her mother
approaches, afraid of what message has been received.

"What is it?" she says. She takes the letter into her mottled hands.
As she reads she flinches softly, as if a soft wind has blown into her
face. "Sweetheart," she says. "My God." She lowers the letter and
looks Maria in the eye. "How did this happen?"

"I applied this past fall," Maria says. "Rigby told me to."

"Why didn't you tell me?" her mother says, unable to restrain her pleasure. It is as if she can only believe the reality of this news incrementally, the enormity of it too much for her to grasp at once. She looks happier every second.

"I didn't think it was going to work," Maria says. Which is, of course, true, but also not the real reason she kept her effort a secret. She does not want to discuss the truth, which is that it was only a Hail Mary in the awkward process of trying to plan for a life without her mother.

"Go," her mother says. "Tell me you'll go."

"OK," Maria says.

"Say it."

"I'll go."

Her mother hugs her, and as she does, Maria realizes she never before considered that a plan for life alone might not weigh heavily on her mother. She now sees that it might, in fact, lighten her load. Because what does a parent want but to know that her child's future is filled with promise?

Maria retreats to her room. It so warm that she simply removes her shirt and bra. Bonacieux attaches herself to Maria's breast. The pain of this act has now, for the most part, ceased. Maria's nervousness about it has also receded. The practice has become a given, and she now looks forward to these daily moments with Bonacieux that no one but she can replicate.

Maria's love for Bonacieux, and that is what it is, has only increased over time. But, Maria wonders, as Bonacieux suckles, drowsy and serene, is she toiling to care for the child because Maria loves her, or does she love the child because of the hours she has spent caring for her? She is not sure. In the end it doesn't matter. Either has produced the same outcome. The problem. The love.

In the silent room, Maria can hear her own blood rush in her ears. The urgent hum has nothing to do with the feeding, though—it is only a response to the thrill and confusion into which Maria has been thrust. Over the whirr of her veins, she hears her mother in the hallway, calling for Karen, thrilled with the news. The future is so insistent, despite Maria's greatest efforts to keep it from being so. She thinks of Philip's face buried into her neck. She remembers his slow, heavy breath. With her daughter in her arms and the memory of Philip playing fast across her mind, Maria closes her eyes tightly, confident in the knowledge she will tell Yale that she cannot under any circumstances attend.

NEIGHBORS WAVE AS Maria and Bonacieux walk their return path to Philip and Nina's house. The Mercedes is gone. Philip enters the back door only a few minutes after Maria, attempting nonchalance, as if he always rushes out of his writing shed at the moment of Maria's return.

"Nina went to the beach with Naomi," he says.

"Who's Naomi?" Maria says.

Philip shakes his head. Naomi is not important. His glance lingers longer than usual. He grins. He says, "Has she napped?"

"Yeah," Maria says, amazed that he might think otherwise. It is well past any hour at which a nap might successfully start.

"Damn."

He leans on the counter and becomes serious, like a boy who might be punished. He lifts the hair from Maria's neck and kisses her just above the collar. She wants to tell him about Yale but is afraid of having to explain exactly why she is not going to go. She raises an arm to the leaf of a fern hanging from the sill above. Philip moves his lips to her ear and fills it with his warm breath. Maria has aspired to reach this new territory, one populated by her own child, Philip, and her mother, and in its sunlight, now slanting through the window, spinning orange webs across her closed eyelids, she is ecstatic and lost in it.

CHAPTER 16

I'S JUNE, HOT and crowded. Parking spots have reached a premium. Houses unpeopled for months now scream with children throwing water balloons from windows. Maria and her mother have moved on from their roles as mere visitors here in Beaufort and have now become some type of residents. They know when to avoid crossing the drawbridge. They know where not to park. And they know the neighbors, many of whom have come to take great interest in the improving health of Maria's mother. Over the last few months, Maria has undergone a general remove of desire. She wants exactly what she has. Her successful practice of not thinking much about the eventuality of things has continued. The shift in seasons comes as more of a surprise than an inevitability.

From a tourist shop on Front Street she buys three white dresses. They are all exactly the same, folded into the same white box, each crispy white cotton and so simple that Maria feels confident she could have sewn them herself, within minutes, had she the right materials. She wears one almost every day, cinching around her waist one of three belts purchased at the Salvation Army: a black-and-white checked New Wave number, one brown suede, the other yellow plastic. She divides her body into two hemispheres, each erogenous. She is pleased with such a simple equation. Her hair continues to thicken and curl in the salty humidity. Almost no one in town has seen her eyes. When not couched behind her bangs, Maria covers them with oversized green Oliver Peoples sunglasses purchased on a whim in Raleigh, wiping out a third of her bank account. She feels it was money well spent.

It is the twenty-ninth of the month. Already Philip and Nina's house has been overrun with workmen in preparation for the Fourth of July, the occasion for their famous party. It's a local standard, a yearly marker of the season, and Philip says he rarely knows more than half the attendees. Philip and Nina shoulder the burden like a civic charge. Maria considers the responsibility of it all and admires its largess.

Christopherson has spent the last two mornings preparing Philip and Nina's lawn. He now stands atop a ladder, hurling wet clumps of leaves from a gutter. Two large men, each with thick neck hair fuzzing orange above the collars of faded polyester work shirts, drive spikes into the sandy lawn. They anchor a white tent large enough to hold a hundred people. Rosa, an elderly Mexican woman, appears with a vacuum in each room in which Maria tries to settle. At last Maria surrenders and escapes with Bonacieux to the public library, a squat brick eyesore just south of the ancient courthouse. She is glad to be free of the party preparations, and the sight of familiar faces on the sidewalk on her way to the library fills her with an ease to which she is not accustomed. She waves at Megan, the waitress at the Royal James, Darrel from the post office, who lost his dog and pasted pink poodle flyers everywhere. Before, these local demi-celebrities would never have deemed Maria worthy of notice, but with Bonacieux, she has gained entry to their society. She has a reason to now be known, a reason to be a part of this town.

Inside the library, on an IBM monitor the size of a microwave oven, Maria checks her email. This is where, a few weeks before, she declined her admission to Yale. She has lied to her mother about it, saying that the option to attend is there when she wants it. That there is no rush. The truth is, she did not solicit any flexibility. She simply supplied an electronic decline.

In her inbox today she finds the usual empty type. There is a sale at Urban Outfitters. An update to her Etsy account. A video of a lemur sent to her by her mother. But this morning Maria has received something more. When she thinks back on this moment later, it still makes her nervous. It is the end of something. She has received a message from Jack.

Hey, he says.

I look at Isn't Bonny Bonny? *every day. I found that shit right after you left. And you're all over it. I don't even know how to start asking how this happened. But I'll just start: how'd this happen?*

Jacque

Maria's fingertips tingle as her stomach begins to knot. She considers the obvious first: Jack has changed the spelling of his name. This doesn't surprise her. She knows he'll change it back, or to something else again later. The rest is what matters: he knows.

Like some barometer of panic, Bonacieux begins to fuss. Other public computer users glance sidelong at Maria, annoyed. She says, "Shhh," and signs out of her library account. Without responding to Jack, she exits the building.

So many times Maria considered this possibility, this exact thing, the chance that Jack might find photos of her and Bonacieux online. There was a time when she wanted him to. But that time has passed.

And now, he hasn't written with an apology or out of some unrestrained desire, but instead with a demand. Maria is not concerned that Jack has plans to destroy her insulated world, but he doesn't need malice for the outcome to be disaster. His interest alone is enough to spell danger.

She tries to employ her newfound ability to not think about the future, but in this case it does not work. As she moves toward Philip and Nina's house through the streets in which only minutes before she found social refuge, she now feels paranoid, scanning all visible pavement for Jack. She is on the lookout for his black Scirocco, expecting at any moment an appearance.

What she fears more than the revelation of her secrets and ensuing dissolution of her position within the Price house is the ending of whatever spell has been cast upon her mother's health. Maria cannot cease ascribing mystical powers to Bonacieux and the child's effect upon her mother. Before Bonacieux's birth, her mother was dying. Since her birth, her mother has ceased that grim progression and has, in fact, reversed it. Without naps, without Bonacieux, and without playtime and the changing of clothes, Maria fears her mother might just wither away. She is like a balloon inflated only by the child's presence.

On the cracked leather couch in Philip and Nina's living room, Maria applies sunscreen to Bonacieux's fair legs. She packs bananas, frozen strawberries, two bottles on ice, an extra pacifier, and a baked sweet potato wrapped in tinfoil. Philip is taking them out on the boat. Maria is glad to board any vessel today that is charted away from land.

In the study, Philip asks Maria to apply sunscreen to his shoulders. They are strong and sprouted with sparse gray hairs. As she rubs the lotion onto his warm flesh, Philip checks his phone. He could not be more at ease. In the rectangle of light at the end of the hallway, Maria sees the form of Nina appear and pause to watch. Maria removes her hands, and Philip, who has not seen his wife, pulls his shirt back onto his shoulders without saying a word.

In the kitchen, Nina says, "Isn't the water too rough?" She has no plans to join them, ever ready to capitalize on a chance to be alone, but today she seems determined to keep Philip inside.

"Maybe," Philip says.

"Stay here," she says.

"If it's too rough, we'll come back."

"Maybe we should stay," Maria says, trying to act like she doesn't want to be alone with Philip. She cannot tell if it has worked or not, though. Nina is too reserved. She only kisses Bonacieux and says, "Please be safe."

Maria feels Nina's eyes on the back of her neck as they exit. She tells herself that this suspicion is only an effect of Jack's note, that everything is actually fine. But she does not believe it.

Philip steps into the street, three worn canvas bags dangling from one thick finger over his shoulder. He wears frayed khakis rolled high above old brown boat shoes. A stained white oxford flaps untucked at his waist. It is all effortless, this elegance. Tortoiseshell sunglasses hang from a shoelace around his neck. His face is like a piece of parchment removed from a fire, tanned unevenly and worn, peeling atop one ear. His beard seems to have grown more coarse. His hair twists into thick unruly curls, absorbing salt from the air like a sponge. She conjures against this image a memory of Jack and feels like she has aged ten years since she last saw him.

Maria again checks both ways on Ann Street. It has been only an hour since she read Jack's email, but he sent it the night before and Chapel Hill is only four hours away. He knows Karen's name, could easily find her address. Maria feels his presence like some malicious humidity, heavy and invisible and uncomfortable. But the only thing she finds in the road is a man pulling two boys in a Radio Flyer wagon and Christopherson whacking weeds.

PHILIP NAVIGATES SLOWLY out of the inlet, the small boat rocking in high, choppy swells. Cape Lookout Lighthouse glimmers distantly in the morning sun. Just as Nina foretold, the swells continue to increase until they reach the edge of the Atlantic proper, where they are whipping themselves into white-topped crests. It is indeed too rough to venture farther, and Philip turns back, dropping anchor twenty yards from the island closest to town.

They are planted in a cove hidden from view but still so close to shore that, if they were to dive into the gunmetal water, they could swim to Front Street within minutes. One wild horse dappled in browns grazes undisturbed as Philip wades ashore, Bonacieux held high above his head.

He plants a striped umbrella in the tiny beach, conjuring a long oval of shade in which he lays a bed of towels. Maria wades ashore through cold water that never reaches higher than her navel. Philip feeds Bonacieux a bottle, and as he does so, the child falls asleep. Raising his eyebrows, as if to say, can you believe this worked? Philip lays Bonacieux on the shady palette. From a cooler, he produces a bottle of Pimm's that he pours over ice in two cups. He opens a can of soda water and pours it in. He slices a cucumber with a pocketknife and lets each sliver drop into the glasses. He hands one to Maria. Bubbles tickle her nose. She feels nostalgic for the moment as it happens. These minutes feel suddenly endangered.

Beside her Philip reclines in the sand, propped up on a shoulder. He is so effortlessly tan. Maria is still almost as pale as she was in November. The only mark of the sun she can identify on herself is a constellation of freckles that appear on the bridge of her nose each day, only to then disappear within hours as the night approaches.

"Where are you?" Philip says.

"I'm here," she says.

"Barely."

Maria is afraid to break the spell of this perfect morning, but any chance to tell a truth is one she feels she must take. She knows she cannot reveal everything to Philip, so she settles for small pieces. It's like scratching an itch that will not go away.

"It's stupid," she says. "My ex-boyfriend emailed me."

"This a guy in Chapel Hill?"

Maria nods.

"And he's, was he the father of . . . ?"

Maria nods.

"What's he want?" Philip says.

"I don't know."

"Listen," Philip says. "Is he here right now?" He turns to the wisps of weed, the craggy trees, the horse head now just visible over the far dune. He kisses Maria's neck. No one is here to see them except Bonacieux, and even her eyes are closed.

"Do you think Nina knows anything?" Maria says.

"Shhhh," he says. "No."

Maria lets him convince her. She takes Philip's salty earlobe between her teeth. They undress beneath a large yellow towel. Below Philip Maria arranges herself so that she can see Bonacieux. He enters her and Maria considers the dangers of discovery. They thrill her. When a boat passes, distant yet still within view, she buries her face into Philip's chest and shudders.

THE FOLLOWING MORNING, fingering Karen's iPad in the bathroom, Maria reads another email. Jack sent it after midnight. *I want to see her too*, he says. *Please write back.*

Maria must respond. Her silence, she understands, will only make her more attractive. She types, *I'm not in a position to get you involved in my life right now. Please respect my privacy.* She types, *I'm sorry*, then deletes it. She types the sentence again. And sends.

FIVE DAYS LATER Maria is sitting on the Turkish rug in Karen's red living room with Bonacieux, stacking concentric rings on a padded pole, when Karen enters and says, "You have a friend here." Maria knows it is Jack before Karen even has a chance to raise her eyebrows and say, "His name is Jack?"

Bonacieux cries out in frustration, trying to reach a plastic hippo on the table, straining until red in the face. Maria lifts her, kissing her cheek, savoring the moment like it is the last of some kind. She gives Bonacieux the toy, and the child sighs softly into Maria's ear, relieved to cease her struggle against gravity.

Into the hallway Maria walks, wishing that instead of an appearance in the flesh, Jack could just slowly emerge from some mystic fog, that he could become a reality in her world again through gradual transition. But of course this is not how humans appear. There at the front of the hallway stands Jack, his hair cut, short, a trio of parallel lines etched into it close above his left ear. He looks more striated and veiny than ever. A new tattoo of an Alexander Calder mobile appears halfway out of his sleeve. He holds out both arms.

"My girls!" he says.

Maria is not sure where Karen is but feels confident the woman can hear them. Bonacieux hides her face against Maria's chest, and Maria raises a finger to her lips.

"Oh, she looks just like you," Jack says.

Maria twists her face in disgust and points down the hallway, as if to say, you must shut up.

Jack raises his hands in defense.

"Don't say anything," he says. "Nope. I just want to love you. Hot dog. My girls!"

"You need to zip it," Maria whispers, "right now."

His eyes climb up Maria's legs to her stomach, rising, stopping on her bangs. He nods approvingly and says, "You look hot."

"What are you doing here?" she says.

"Can I come in?"

"This isn't our house."

Karen enters the hallway as if on cue for either an introduction or an intervention. It confirms Maria's sense of having been eavesdropped upon.

"This is Jack," Maria says.

"I've heard about you," Karen says.

"'Bout how charming I am?" Jack says, throwing his arms out wide.

"No."

"You're a firecracker, you are," Jack says. Karen deploys her power smile.

"Would you excuse us?" Maria says, and leads Jack by the elbow down the hall, through the living room, and onto the side sunporch. She closes the door behind them.

"What do you want?" she says.

"Want want want," he says, wiggling his fingers at Bonacieux. "Just my girls."

Maria shakes her head. Bonacieux fusses, pulling at the buttons on Maria's shirt. Maria bats the tiny hand away.

"Oh, she knows her momma, don't she," Jack says.

"I don't have time for this," Maria says. "I need to feed her. Stay here."

Inside, Maria retrieves Bonacieux's bottle from the coffee table. As the child drinks, Maria pauses within the air-conditioned shade. She wants Jack to wait. He has brought danger and indiscretion into Karen's house. She needs to control him in as many ways as she can. She counts one hundred *Mississippi*s before returning.

When she does she finds Jack smoking a cigarette. "You mind?" he says. He gestures to a large orange ashtray on a wicker table, as if citing evidence that it's fine.

"Not around the baby," Maria says.

"Right. Jesus. Sorry," he says, truly surprised at his error. He eyes Bonacieux softly, then takes another drag. "B. Sweetie girl."

"Jack," Maria says. "*Now.*"

"Right right right," he says, crushing the butt into the tray with a tiny dance of the fingers. "Sorry. I don't know what I'm doing. But, so, before anything else, I'm gonna bottom-line it here. How'd you find her?"

"I wanted you to find me so badly," Maria says. "Did you know that? I cried for weeks. I was sick, literally sick to my stomach. You were horrible, horrible, and still, I'm embarrassed to even say it. I still wanted you to come find me."

"And I did!" he says.

"Too late, Jack. I don't want you here."

"Ouch, sweetie. Just give me a second."

"For what?"

"To talk about this!" he says, pointing at mother and child. "You knew, didn't you?"

"Yes," Maria says. She wants Jack to understand that her life exists completely separate from his. That she has her own secrets. "When we were looking for families, I recognized Philip in his picture online."

"You knew him?"

"I just recognized him from the last time I'd come down here. He walks his dog around here."

"And didn't tell me?"

"Nope."

"Why?"

"Because," Maria says, "you're not trustworthy."

Jack opens his mouth, bares his teeth, and inhales. He shakes his head and says, "Why you wanna break my heart? I'd kidnap that girl with you. You don't have to keep secrets."

"Jesus Christ," Maria says. "I'm not kidnapping anyone." She sits, Bonacieux settling into her lap, still working at the bottle. Maria gestures to the porch, as if it is the physical embodiment of all that now divides her life from Jack's. "We came down here to visit Karen, and then this job just popped up. I didn't ask for it. It just . . ."

Jack sits beside her and sighs upon their daughter's still bald head. His transparent interest in Bonacieux has dulled the edge of Maria's rage. She tries to imagine, just for a moment, what could have been. She and Jack conceived this child. What if they had kept her? The bottle loosens from Bonacieux's mouth and tumbles into Jack's lap. He lets it there lie. Their child has fallen asleep.

"We made that," Jack whispers.

Maria's minute fantasy of a nuclear family plays out for a few more seconds. She is impressed with Jack's fortitude to remain still for this long. Then the portable phone on the side table begins to ring and startles everyone. Bonacieux jerks herself awake.

"Oh no," Jack says, fumbling with the phone in an effort to silence it. "Stop!" It continues to ring. Maria bounces the child softly. "Here," Jack says, finally tucking the phone between cushions. "Come here. Let Daddy." He reaches for Bonacieux.

Bonacieux writhes away, crying, hiding in Maria's arms.

"Jack," Maria says.

"Sweet B."

"Jack," Maria says. She feels she must relinquish something to make him leave. "I'll text you," she says, hoping this is enough.

"You mean . . ."

"She's tired and hungry."

"It just sounds like she's sad."

"Trust me."

"OK," he says, breathless with inadequacy. "OK. Should I . . . ?"

Maria nods and points at the door.

"OK," he says again, rising. "OK."

He exits through the porch door. Maria is uncomfortable with the thought of any neighbors seeing him. She is worried about where he has parked. She is embarrassed at him here, in this neighborhood, back in her life.

Upstairs, Maria's mother stares at the ceiling. She does not even turn when Maria enters the room. Maria knows that she has already heard about their visitor. Karen has been here first.

"I didn't ask him to come," Maria says.

"He knows?" her mother says.

"Yeah," Maria says.

The direction of her mother's gaze, still upward, trained on the white stucco ceiling, is one Maria has seen before. It is where her mother looks in fear. She struck this pose in the days after her first diagnosis and often during her worst hours of nausea from the chemo. Maria understands she is not searching for a divine presence, but rather only avoiding looking at that which she cannot bear to see—the eyes of someone else who is just as afraid as she is.

"How?" her mother says, finally.

"Because Nina has this photo blog, and he found it online, and saw pictures of me."

"What's a photo blog?"

"Online pictures," Maria says. "You know."

"Can anyone see it?"

"Yes."

Again they fall silent. Maria is not sure what fear it is exactly that has now gripped them. Is it the possible loss of Bonacieux, or the ensuing mess that might play out if Maria's secret is revealed? It is, she thinks, both.

"Even if a bunch of people saw it," Maria says, "no one other than Jack would really know."

"I just don't want him to do anything stupid," her mother says. She finally looks at Maria. "He's a good soul, but he's also sort of a dimwit."

Maria leaves Karen's house embarrassed to have involved her mother in this affair and with the certainty she must act. Walking through the streets with Bonacieux, waving at neighbors, she phones Jack.

"Couldn't wait?" Jack says.

"Where are you staying?" Maria says.

"Morehead Motor Inn."

Maria knows where it is. It's on the other side of the bridge. She is glad it is not in town. "I'll come by after bedtime," she says.

"After you go to bed?" Jack says, confused.

"No, after I put Bonacieux to bed. After baby bedtime."

"What time is that?"

"Sevenish."

"She goes to bed at seven?"

"Yeah, that's when kids go to sleep," Maria says, again reminded of the gap between their daily lives. "I'll come by after that."

"Seven," he says, incredulous.

The rest of the day is long. The humidity thick. Bonacieux seems immune to the heat. She pees on her blanket while Maria changes her diaper, thrilled with the air across her flesh. Maria opens the freezer and leans as far as possible inside of it, watching her breath emerge. Before leaving, she tries on each of her belts. She stands before the mirror, then turns, looking over her shoulder. She rubs the fabric of her dress softly between her fingertips. Somehow in this hour of uncertainty, she feels beautiful and strong and tells herself to remember this feeling lest it never again return.

THE MOREHEAD MOTOR Inn is a two-story red brick building wrapped three-quarters of the way around a parking lot just on the other side of the bridge. In the middle of the lot stands a central office and dining area housed in what appears to be a crumbling greenhouse. Far from the beach, the motel is a rarely visited piece of land. It is softest in the early morning, when the promise of a day at the coast imparts a paltry hopefulness upon its shabby exterior. But now, in the neon lights of evening, it sits beneath a cloud of doom, the hours of night stacked long and tall against it. WELCOME LIONS, the marquee says against a glowing yellow backdrop. FREE HBO.

Room 424 smells of baking soda and cigarettes. The lights from the neon vacancy sign fall inside in dull orange stripes. Maria sits on the edge of a hard mattress as Jack paces, smoking. He is shirtless, his torso like shrink-wrap on ribs.

"Hanky dank, danky dank," Jack says.

"What?" Maria says.

"I don't know. I don't know what to say," Jack says, ceasing his pacing. He holds his cigarette between his thumb and forefinger like a dart. "What's she like?"

"Who?"

"B."

"She's a sweet girl," Maria says. "She's shy. She's very cautious. Alert."

"Guess those aren't my genes," he says. "Philip and Nina are cool?"

"Yeah."

"They're rich, right?"

Maria nods. She cannot understand exactly why he is so interested in this. It is the question of one accustomed to want, and Jack is anything but in need. It is a plus, though, she accedes. She too is glad they have money.

"Why'd you come down here?" Jack says.

"What do you mean?" Maria says. She looks around the shabby room. "Here?"

"No, the town," Jack says. "*Here.* The real reason."

"Because my mom wanted to," Maria says. "And because you were humping Icy People."

"Pssss," Jack says, slapping the air. "That shit is over. But I mean, last time we talked, you were all like, let's go kidnap her."

"I did not want to kidnap her, Jesus," Maria says, shaking her head. "Stop saying that."

Jack kneels on the carpet. "Marry me," he says.

"You're ridiculous."

"I'm serious!"

"Get up," Maria says, and he does. He sits on the bed beside her, surrender in his limp posture. He has finished his interrogation, it seems. Maria wonders what's next.

"Can we at least get it on?" he says, and she thinks, I should have known.

Without any secrets left to discover, he will go away, Maria thinks. She understands that she must satiate Jack in order to drive him home. And she is not unwilling. Despite it all, she can still find the desire for Jack. He has purchase on a piece of her that has not been revoked. She

reclines on the bed without saying a word. He jumps into the air, land-
ing beside her on his stomach, bouncing to a rest. These days have suddenly run over with love. There is no fidelity to guard, she tells herself.
She needs all the affection she can get. Jack runs one hand up her white
dress and lets it there pause, cold upon her stomach. She wants it to go
elsewhere, everywhere. She waits for him to move it. She knows it will
happen. He will touch her everywhere.

CHAPTER 17

I T IS THE Fourth of July. Philip and Nina's yard holds the music of the party as if within a bowl. The jangle of women exclaiming. A murmur of men. Languid bluegrass from a trio of young men in jeans and white shirts playing banjo and guitar at the edge of the tent's shade. Ice against thin glass.

Jack moves like a false note through this symphony. He wears a loose hot pink tank top, tight jeans, green high-tops, and black sunglasses. The tattoos. People turn to watch him pass. He drinks Sprite from a half-crushed can in one hand and carelessly sloshes champagne out of a flute in the other. Maria has brought him here in an effort to inundate him with the details of her life. She understands now that he will learn how she spends her days and with whom, one way or the other. She can only hope that, by orchestrating the disclosure of information herself, she can better control any ensuing damage.

Around him, the napes of necks flash, tanned, doodled upon by stray blond hairs. A brunette in a strapless dress places a cigarette between her lips, and two men offer matches. The smell of perfume and sunscreen. Sunglasses. A man in a blue suit dances with a young woman, his hands held aloft as if he's casting a spell. The food is all so light it seems to disappear as it passes across your tongue. Salmon sliced thin as a leaf. Watermelon. Prosciutto. Watercress under lemony shrimp. Oysters atop crushed ice, crunching as they shift against the melt.

"Why is he here?" Maria's mother says, watching Jack pass through the crowd. Bonacieux, in a red dress, reclines in her lap. Maria's mother sits like the queen of this party on a folding chair, hatless and radiant as friends from home stop to express delight with the life there suddenly so apparent. Many people from Chapel Hill are here today. They have come to the coast for the holiday. Several ask if Bonacieux is Maria's. Maria assures them she is not. She wonders if they ask just because she's with a baby, or because they remember her pregnant.

Jack pops back into view and Maria says, "I invited him."

"I don't think that was smart," her mother says.

"It's just to prove to him that he doesn't want to be here."

"He does, though," Maria's mother says. "You're the only thing in his life that isn't stupid."

Jack stops to talk to a small boy in a Batman shirt. He kneels, points at the boy's chest, and vigorously begins to explain something. The boy raises his hand to give Jack a high five, but Jack lowers the hand and continues his monologue. When finished he approaches Maria and her mother with his champagne held aloft, like a torch lighting his way.

"For you, m'lady," he says, presenting the drink to Maria's mother.

"I can't drink that stuff," she says.

"You can't *not* drink it," Jack says. "If these bubbles pop for anyone, they pop for you."

Despite herself, Maria's mother smiles. Maria cannot begrudge her mother for having missed this man in her life.

Last night, as they lay in Jack's bed, time indeed did seem to stop. There was only the moment at hand. Maria thought neither of the future, nor of their past. Jack was so clumsy, but it did not matter. The thrill came from the new ways in which she could now surprise him. The lessons she has learned from Philip have begun to pay new and surprising dividends. She was not led by Jack, she was not surprised by him—it was all the other way around.

"And I'm off for ham biscuits," Jack says, floating back into the stream of humanity.

"He makes you forget, doesn't he?" Maria's mother says.

He does, Maria thinks.

While Maria's mother greets another face from home, Christopherson approaches. He is handsome in a tuxedo and carries a platter half filled with triangular pimento-cheese sandwiches. He is a member of the catering crew this afternoon, consistently employed yet less preoccupied than anyone Maria knows.

"Dude your boyfriend?" Christopherson says.

"Philip?" Maria says, terrified.

"Come on," Christopherson says. "The *dude*."

"Oh. Yeah, used to be."

"So he's the . . ."

Maria nods.

"That why you're all weird?"

"No."

"Then why are you all weird?"

"You know what I want you to do?"

"What?"

Maria is silent.

"I don't know," she says. "Yeah, I guess that's why I'm all weird."

Bonacieux becomes restless in Maria's mother's lap. Maria lifts her and carries her to the edge of the lawn, where she spreads a small baby blanket and they sit. Bonacieux pulls clover into bits. Jack saunters toward them, and the eyes of the party turn.

"I met a guy who drives limos," Jack says, kneeling. "He was telling me stories about prom. Shit is hilarious. Can I hold her?"

Bonacieux cries as Maria passes her to Jack. It is the first time her father has held her since the day that she was born, and Maria is glad it is happening before an audience. Things feel safer with Jack in a crowd. Bonacieux strains to escape Jack's arms.

"It's not you," Maria says. "It's just any men at this point. Anyone except for Philip."

"Baby baby," Jack says, bouncing her. "This is all yours. All yours, little girl. You're a rich person living on a well-mown lawn."

He gently places Bonacieux on the blanket and lies there beside her. The child ceases to cry, reaches out and gently touches his chin. Jack says, "Ah."

Nina flits like a fish through the edge of the crowd. She wears a short yellow dress and white Converse low-tops. A coral necklace. She disappears within a group of guests, then reappears fifteen feet away, where she kneels, points her camera at Jack and Maria, and begins to shoot.

With Bonacieux's hand in his, Jack turns toward her and smiles the truest smile Maria has ever seen on him.

Philip follows Nina out of the crowd. His linen suit is wrinkled. The sleeves of his jacket are pushed up to his elbows. He has not shaved and does not even appear to have brushed his hair. He holds his hands into the air and says, "Daughter!"

Without rising, Jack—who is still lying on his back in the grass—raises one hand into the air.

"I love your little girl, sir," Jack says.

"Me too," Philip says, shaking Jack's hand. "Philip Price."

"Lebron James," Jack says.

"Always good to meet a basketball legend."

"That's Jack," Maria says. "He's a friend from home."

"You mind?" Philip says, and lifts Bonacieux. "I have to show her off."

"Let me come with you," Jack says, rising. "I need a hundred more miniature biscuits."

Together Jack and Philip cross the lawn. Already Philip is laughing at something Jack has said. Maria senses the folly of this risk but knows it is too late to avoid it.

When Jack finally departs that evening, it is in the limousine of his new friend. He is too drunk to drive. The car grinds loud and slow across the gravel driveway as it executes a multiple-point turn, the white stones beneath the wheels smaller than marbles. Jack stands, appearing out of the sunroof from the chest up, and waves, holding up a plastic flute of champagne like some Gatsby from a skate park.

Maria and Philip drink lukewarm chardonnay on the porch and watch him disappear behind the azaleas. The fireflies have amassed beneath the magnolia and hover over a scattering of wadded napkins and cracked plastic cups. Playing loose with Bonacieux's sleep schedule for once, Maria has wheeled her pram beside them, where, within its piled blankets, the child plays with a singing caterpillar. Inside, Nina prepares the nursery for bedtime.

"I was jealous of Lebron," Philip says.

Maria sips her drink in silence, afraid to touch Philip, to take his hand, to lay her head on his shoulder, all things she longs to do.

"And surprised," he says.

"Why?"

"Because. You're what a parent dreams their child will become. And he . . . isn't."

Two at a time, like stars sent up from the earth, fireworks lift off of a shrimp boat in the creek and rise into the sky. They blossom against the dark in bright oranges and blues. After the fire powder burns off, each burst leaves behind it a memory of smoke in the shape of a palm tree. Maria tries to draw Bonacieux's attention to the blasts, suddenly aware that fireworks might actually be exciting for someone. Never before has she understood people's attraction to them. They always bored her, seemed wasteful and a relic of some tradition she did not understand. But, as Bonacieux turns to the sky, Maria realizes they are an illustration of the magic not yet uncoded in the world. The mysteries of life, still intact. Bonacieux smiles, stilled by the sight above.

"Fireworks," Maria says, Bonacieux focused on the sparks now shattering the sky.

"How did you and him become a thing?" Philip says. It takes Maria a moment to realize that he's talking about Jack. When it does become clear, she resents it.

"You don't know him," she says, reluctant to discuss Jack with Philip. It seems the two should not even spend time together in conversation.

"We talked," Philip says. "I liked him, actually. He had a lot to say."

"Oh shit," Maria says. It is worse than she feared. "Like what?"

"He loves you, for one thing. And your mom."

"Please." She knows that Jack is nothing but sincere. That is not in doubt. But even the charms of his sincerity are not always benign.

"And he told me about Yale," Philip says, turning to look at her. She does not meet his gaze.

"How'd he know about Yale?" Maria says.

"Your mom."

"Crap." She should have managed this news herself, she thinks. The withholding of it has now given it extra import.

"Why didn't you tell me?" he says.

"What is there to tell?"

"That you're leaving the state. That you're going to one of the best universities in the world. That . . ." He is aghast.

Yale, Maria thinks. The name alone enacts such transformation on the minds of academics.

"I'm not going anywhere," she says, and as she does, she sees fear seep into Philip's face.

"Look," he says, clearly afraid of her attachment. It is as if he is, just now, realizing the possible dangers of making love to her, or bringing her into his house, of making her happy.

"This isn't about you," Maria says, striving to keep her voice from betraying the truth that so much of her decision is, in fact, because of him.

"'Cause, you can't stay for *this*."

"You think I don't know that?" she says. "I can go whenever I want."

Philip glances over his shoulder. "Don't make a scene," he says. "I'm not."

Philip lowers his voice. "I'm not going to lie to you. I want everything. I want you. I want Nina. I want Bonacieux. I want it all. But I'm just saying I know that's not realistic. I know it can't all last."

"Yeah, well, you're right. It can't," Maria says. She isn't sure what she means by this. She does not want Philip to leave Nina. She does not want him to leave Bonacieux. He has no idea how important the fidelity of their family is to her. But Maria does not want him to leave her either. She realizes that she too wants everything, but watching the smoke dissipate into a faint mist falling thin across the water, she knows everyone here cannot have everything all at once.

CHAPTER 18

THE MORNING AFTER the party, in the Morehead Motor Inn parking lot, an overweight woman flaps the back of her arms while trying to show a man how to pack a beach umbrella into an old station wagon. They argue, short of breath, while Maria lifts Bonacieux from her car seat. The asphalt reflects the sun back up at them as they cross the lot toward Jack, who, in tight yellow pants and cutoff black sweatshirt, waves from the balcony. The day seems thirty degrees warmer here, warmer even than it was on the other side of the bridge. There are no trees here, no shade, nothing but old cigarette butts and cracked asphalt with pieces of broken green glass glittering in the soft tar. Maria feels as if she has stepped into an ashtray inside of a tanning bed.

Past the door of Jack's room, where a sign on the doorknob says SILENCE PLEASE, PLEASE DO NOT DISTURB, Jack has moved the bed against the wall, under the window, and all the other furniture against the opposite wall. The floral comforter has been spread on the carpeted space between.

"It's so she'll have a play area," he says, gesturing to the floor with pride.

"They don't wash those things," Maria says.

Jack reluctantly sets Bonacieux on the bed. He hands her a phone book. She tears out a page and looks at it as if it might shift shape.

"She is too cute," he says. Maria does not remember him ever having used the word *cute* before and appreciates the softening effect their daughter has already had upon him. Bonacieux tears another page in half and begins to shake it. "My God! Is she always like this?"

"Pretty much," Maria says.

"Our girl," Jack says, swinging an arm over Maria's shoulders. He looks her in the eye and smiles. "You wanna massage my penis?"

"Jesus," Maria says.

"It just feels so tight. I think it's swelling up." It's a joke he's used so many times before. It has no capacity to shock, that is not what he's trying to do. Maria doesn't think he even really wants what he's saying, but rather is just trying to make the moment feel like it has been plucked from a memory of their past.

"Don't," Maria says, pushing him away. She points to their daughter and raises her eyebrows. His effort to re-create the repartee of days past is exactly what she doesn't want. It reminds her of her urgency in coming here. "You know what?" she says. "You need to leave."

"My own room?"

"No. This town."

"Why?"

"Because," Maria says, "whatever my mom and I have been doing, this whole setup down here, with Bonacieux and her and me and Philip and Nina and all of it, it's been working. She's getting better."

"Who is?"

"My mom!"

"OK," Jack says.

"Don't condescend to me," Maria says. "Not about this."

"What we need to do is go see a movie," Jack says. "And then we can practice kissing. And maybe some massage."

"Goddamn it," Maria says. "You really want to see me naked?"

"Uh."

Maria unbuttons her shirt. It is unceremonious. She lifts her bra above her breasts and simply leaves it there, crumpled awkwardly around her neck. She props Bonacieux in her lap and lets the child begin to nurse.

"Your life is all porn and video games or whatever," Maria says. "But this, this is mine."

Jack looks stunned, but he also looks thrilled. Maria is concerned that she has taken the wrong risk in her effort to shock, that this might in fact turn him on instead of stun.

"Actually, we'll do this later, sweetie," she says, removing Bonacieux from her breast. The child cries at the separation while Maria rebuttons her shirt. "I need to go."

She opens the door. A maid's cart is parked on the walkway. Bonacieux continues to fuss, rooting around for Maria's breast. Maria removes a shower cap from the maid's cart and hands it to the child.

Jack yanks it away.

"I don't need your help," Maria says.

"You just gave her a plastic bag to play with."

"It's a shower cap."

"Pudding cup," he says. "What are you doing? I was just joking about all the sex stuff."

Maria feels the need to break something. "Go fuck Icy People," she says. "The only person I have sex with is Philip."

Jack falls silent. In his shock he seems physically changed. Smaller.

"Yeah," Maria says. "That's what's going on. And you have nothing to do with it. You broke up with *me*."

"With Old Chub?" Jack says. "You doing it with Old Chub?"

"Yes."

"You want to ruin B's family?"

"Who are you to ask a question like that?"

Maria kicks the door closed.

The sun will set again here, the shrimp boats will dock, the drunk sorority sisters will dance to T-Pain with boys who they took Econ with at Wake Forest. And Jack will leave. Maria knows that the revelation about Philip will drive him away. He is confident but fragile. She knows the spots that break. The rhythms of this region will resume. Old fish will smell up the Dumpsters. Philip will tell her she's rare, she makes him young, she kills him. You are the best of us, the very best, he'll say. She will not be haunted by Jack in the house, Jack in the streets, Jack. The schedule that has kept her mother alive will not be threatened by Jack.

CHAPTER 19

MARIA AWAKENS TO a whistle in her nose that is the exact same frequency as Bonacieux's cry. She sits up in her bed, blocks away from the child, afraid something has gone wrong. Her mind spins on the possibilities. She tells herself it is only her own face making this cry, but cannot dispel an unease. Sleep will not return, even though it is her day off. Waking early has already become ingrained. She dresses quickly.

The streets of Beaufort are empty. The rising sun shines through the limbs of the old live oaks, the trees that have turned the streets into tunnels, lighting the leaves in a range of greens so rich it seems that the air has been whipped into some vernal froth. On the piers along Front Street three fishing boats rig out. Gulls peck the water at the bottom of sharp dives. Horses saunter through valleys of dunes. She crosses the drawbridge toward the Morehead Motor Inn. Jack's Scirocco is gone. The door to 424 is ajar, a maid carrying an armful of sheets through it.

At Philip and Nina's house, every window is open. The doors are open, even the screens. Instinctively Maria worries about mosquitoes entering and biting Bonacieux. In the yard stands Philip in his blue bathrobe. Water arcs sadly out of a hose in his hand and splashes atop the large scarlet blossoms of a rosebush.

Maria imagines a marriage. She imagines parking the family car, now a newer version of itself. It's been years. This is her home now. She puts her arms around Philip. He laughs. They are awkward with the respect of love. Each wants to know who will pick up Bonacieux from school, who will attend her ballet. They both will. This is all a dream.

Maria has no reason to be here, no employment responsibilities on this date. It is her day off. She should keep driving, but cannot. She parks, driven by the edge of a panic nebulous and confusing. Jack's departure has left her feeling as if a great danger has been averted, one that Philip needs to know about. She walks briskly across the lawn, and Philip turns, surprised, the hose shifting direction with him. Water gurgles into the grass at Maria's feet.

"Hey," he says, confused and curious.

"He left," Maria says.

"Who?"

"Jack."

"Oh, alright."

"And I've been thinking about what you said," Maria says, the words coming quickly, "about us. The other night. And I'll do whatever it takes so that nothing changes. I don't want anything to change."

"What's going to change?" Nina says. She is in the open window to Maria's right, sitting at the small kitchen table drinking coffee. Maria had not seen her. Philip is silent and alarmed. Maria knows she should say something, that it is this silence that is incriminating.

"My schedule," she finally says.

But the spell has broken. Nina has smelled the trace of a secret. Any knowledge at this point might be hazy and unattached—perhaps

Nina has only sensed the possibility of betrayal; perhaps she has feared it for weeks. It does not matter, though. Somehow Maria understands at once that it is only a matter of time before she knows everything.

"Why would your schedule change?" Nina says.

"That old boyfriend of hers was trying to get her to move home," Philip says.

"What old boyfriend?"

"That guy at the party. Jack. But she's not going to."

"Jack?" Nina says. "How do you know this guy?"

"It doesn't matter. He was the guy with the tattoos at the party. But he just . . ." Philip looks like he cannot believe he has become involved in explaining this.

"He wanted me to go home is all," Maria says. "I told Philip. But I'm not. I mean, I'm here to be with my mom."

"Yeah," Philip says. "So, I'm glad things are calming down for you. We don't want you going anywhere. I was worried. But no longer. Thanks for letting me know."

"OK," Maria says. "See you tomorrow!"

Maria is embarrassed to return to Karen's house and explain the tears that have started to fall in the car. Because what has happened exactly? Nothing. Still, she is confident that her despair is not unfounded. Nina knows, she knows, she will know. It will all unravel, of course, like it was always clear that it would. Maria can sense the end and cannot believe she has brought it upon herself.

She drives north on 70, the shrimpers swinging out into the Atlantic beside her, spreading away from each other like seeds cast off from a pod. From a galvanized tin lean-to under a live oak, she buys a damp paper bag of boiled peanuts. She smokes a cigarette on a stretch of public beach populated by two dead jellyfish. Another, still alive, floats through the waves. In each swell it glows dully, luminescent against the dark salt water. She listens to a cassette tape of the first movement of Wagner's *Ring Cycle* and imagines herself underwater, floating, watching the lights play on the surface high above.

In the early evening, the warm air filled with the cutting song of crickets, Maria returns to Karen's house. Karen and Maria's mother read magazines on the porch. At Maria's approach they smile and wave. Those are the faces that will stop smiling, she thinks, when the mess I've made comes to light. The pressure of responsibility feels physical. She even feels heavier and wonders if through an increase in concern alone she has managed to gain some type of psychic weight. She waves back, barely able to raise her hand into the air.

THE NEXT MORNING the Mercedes is gone. Maria opens the kitchen door. Dishes are piled in the sink. A wine bottle lies on its side on the floor. Philip's pipe is on the table, a plastic baggie of weed half open beside it. The room smells like vinegar.

"Hello?" she says.

"Yeah," Philip says. His voice is tired.

Maria follows it into the living room. He is slumped on the couch in his bathrobe, Bonacieux alert in his lap. *Curious George* plays on Philip's laptop. Bonacieux has never before watched TV in Maria's presence, and its appearance here is all the confirmation she needs to know that Nina has departed. Philip's eyes are framed with bags. His hair is flat and greasy. Bonacieux smells of poop.

Maria is worried about what her mother will say, what Karen will say. What will happen to Bonacieux. Like Jack predicted, Maria is the one who has ruined this, the perfect family for her daughter. She tells herself to not look forward, not to extrapolate, but she cannot keep the vista of the future from presenting itself to her, like some tragic drama she is doomed to watch, knowing it will end with a stage filled with bloodied actors.

"What happened?" Maria says, as if she doesn't know.

"She left."

"Who, Nina?"

Philip doesn't even bother to answer.

"Why?" she says.

He sighs, as if too tired to play this game.

"She knows?"

"Yeah," he says.

"How'd she find out?"

"She just did," Philip says.

"You told her."

He shrugs. "She already knew. She knew. That's all. She knew."

The wind through the open door is warm. Maria's lover and daughter sit on the worn leather couch before her. They need her, and she, she will give herself to them completely. But it will not be enough. The first piece of the family has now come apart. Maria understands that the only thing she can do to solve this problem is to leave their lives for good. But that is not something she is ready to do.

CHAPTER 20

L ATE AUGUST. THE heat has held for months. The sunrise shimmers off greasy asphalt and new sheets of galvanized tin roofing. A
confusion of birds still sings a daily mess of counterpoint, but the mosquitoes are thinning on the drought. The North Carolina coast is an
excess of scorched riches now, open stretches of beach devoid of vaca-
tioners, empty parking lots, post office windows shuttered. Rejected
hermit crabs tossed out car windows by teenagers who'd received them
for free at Wings burn solid to the hardtop. The weight of the old
heat shatters the will of gardeners on their hard and browning lawns.
Eighteen drownings have been stopped by Carteret County lifeguards,
but the danger has now passed. Those left behind in this town are all
natives, born attuned to the tide.

Maria flips through an old issue of *Vogue*, the pages rippled from
some long-past rainfall through an open window. The accouterments
of Nina hide in plain view everywhere. Earrings. Scarves. Spices Philip
doesn't know what to do with. The arrangement of artwork. There is
a drawing Maria made of Nina in June; she is seated on the sand, her
knees drawn up, her body folded into an *N*. In it she does not smile. It
is pinned above Nina's dresser. Even Maria has resisted moving anything once connected with Nina. It seems like, if she does, the sophistication of this life might evaporate. She realizes that Nina too was part

of what she fell in love with here and that she must do everything she can to maintain the shadows of her presence.

For the first time Maria has days where she tires of Bonacieux. She feels guilty at the joy that washes over her once the child falls asleep or when Philip takes Bonacieux along for a jog in his streamlined three-wheel stroller and leaves Maria alone at the house. She stays over most nights now and understands what sleep deprivation is. Both eyelids have begun to twitch intermittently during any daylight hours. She thinks about how Nina handled such challenges, with grace and silent exhaustion. She admires her in her absence.

Their lovemaking happens in a blur. Only memories of small things Philip has said linger. A certain way he touched her. You make me young, he says. You remind me I'm alive. He lowers his fingers into her underwear and stops before he touches her. Touch yourself, he says, and she does. They fall asleep entangled. She awakes on the floor of the nursery, on the couch. She falls asleep while nursing behind locked doors. She tells Philip that her breasts are sore. They hurt, she says. Gentle. He kisses them anyway and discovers milk on his lips. He looks up in surprise. "It's classic babysitter stuff," Maria says. "Happens even with fifteen-year-olds. It's like, even my body knows how much I love her."

Maria has told her mother and Karen much of the truth. She assumes they guess the rest. What she says is that Philip and Nina have been fighting, that Nina has gone home. Karen says this has happened before. "There was a student," she says. Maria wonders if this is the knowledge Anne Vanstory was so hesitant to share. The information is almost physically painful. Somehow the fact that Philip is married is nowhere near as troubling to Maria as the thought of him having an affair with another young woman.

The dream of what could be. Maria allows it to return again, to spread far into the future. At school plays in later years, at musicals, she and Philip laugh when told Bonacieux looks just like Maria. When the child is grown, much later in life, they are somewhere safe, a lake vacation maybe, when Maria finally tells Philip the truth. Her whole scheme of love. He is pleased by it. When Maria's mother dies, it is in her sleep, in her eighties. Maybe nineties. The memory of this early fear of mortality only a minor footnote on her history. Maria tries to see each of these things as a real possibility, but her dreams fail to truly convince her.

Though Nina has been absent for weeks, her absence has been only physical. She is in touch with Philip constantly, mostly via texts that chirp out of Philip's phone all day. And Maria is not afraid to read them. Philip leaves his phone on the table, the counter, anywhere but his pocket. He takes pride in his predilection for leaving the thing behind whenever he leaves the house. At first, the messages were exclusively about Bonacieux, and Philip replied dutifully.

How is she sleeping?

Still waking up about three times a night.

She said anything else lately, any other words?

Ferdy for the dog, paci for her pacifier, but mostly still just your name. All the time.

My mom can pick her up.

No, I'll just bring her.

But lately they've touched on marriage. Nina sent him a message recently that said *Can we talk?* And Maria assumes that they did, because the next message said *Because it's not only about us. I want a family. I have one. I will work for it. The question I was trying to get at is can you.*

Maria wonders if Philip wants her to read these messages, if he leaves his phone around on purpose. But Maria does not know what to do with any of the information the messages convey, whether Philip wants her to have it or not. She does not feel guilty having read them, no. But she does feel guilty for Nina. Bonacieux is Maria's biological daughter, but Philip and Bonacieux are Nina's family. Maria is not unaware of what she has done to it.

"I REMEMBER WATCHING you walk by every day last summer," Maria says. They are in bed. Bonacieux has been long asleep. It is after dark. The windows are open, and the sounds of water lapping ashore drift soft across the yard. Philip's arm lies heavy across her stomach. "I was in love without even speaking a word to you," she says. He says nothing. She hopes that he is asleep.

THESE DAYS PHILIP works long hours. The book is coming along, he says. It is more complicated than pirates, easier to write, less academic. "I'm so sick of pirates," he says, every time it comes up. "Blackbeard was a bad person. Being a parent has made me like him even less." With his new book, he says, he can apply his technique but not his expertise, and it's a combination that works. He has extended his sabbatical for another semester. In January he will move back to Durham, and Bonacieux with him. Maria knows it before he tells her. A sabbatical cannot last forever. She is surprised even at the extension.

"I know you think I can't do it without you," he says.

"Chapel Hill is like ten miles away."

"And you would be in it?" he says.

Maria shrugs. "Maybe."

"What about Yale?"

"If I go anywhere, it'll be back to Chapel Hill."

"Why?"

"What, you don't want me to?"

"I'm just saying, it's Yale. You should go."

"I know you think this is about you," Maria says. "But it isn't." She understands that she isn't convincing him, but it is enough for him to know she is trying. "So you can relax. I just like Chapel Hill. I want to be home. And if you still need someone to watch Bonacieux, I might be available."

"That would be nice," he says, and smiles, eyes averted.

They are lying to each other, each knowing what the other knows. It is a diplomacy of things unsaid. She has seen him on the roof, standing on the widow's walk, staring at the horizon. He is only watching the ships execute their slow maritime dance, but she feels like he's watching for Nina's return. Maria understands the math of a summer camp romance: the ending is built in. She does not know if that is what this even is, though. She feels like, if she loses Philip, there will never be a replacement. He has proven youth less interesting than that which comes after. With whom can she appreciate the riches she has come to expect from a life lived in Philip's domain? Not Jack, this much she knows. Not any of her leftover friends in Chapel Hill. Jane, counting her bad tattoos. Icy People, rapping in dirty underwear. For the first time Maria's own selfish concerns trump the voodoo appeal of Bonacieux. Her desire is larger even than romance or health or parenthood. She has a hunger for the entirety of a life with another family, and here is the feast to sate it.

CHAPTER 21

O N   T H E   M O R N I N G of Bonacieux's first birthday, Philip and
Bonacieux sit at the kitchen table, a marble slab atop twisted
iron legs. A cut crystal chandelier dangles above them, its dim light not
passing more than a few inches before the pink of the rising sun takes
over, casting the room in glowing pastels.

"The horses are gonna nuzzle your hand," Philip says, feeding
Bonacieux a forkful of scrambled egg. He's talking about her party,
which is to be held that afternoon at a farm. She doesn't follow, of
course, but is happy nonetheless. She eats well with him, better than
she did with Nina. He is softer, more willing to indulge. Their bond is
growing in Nina's absence. Bonacieux understands so much already—
allegiance, love, and mood. Maria wonders where her daughter's
understanding stops, though. She hopes the gap is large. Her actions,
she has come to realize, have been based on the child as a passive
observer. An object that cannot act upon knowledge. But now Maria
is beginning to understand that this arrangement will not last forever.
What will happen when Bonacieux can voice a desire to be breastfed?
What will happen when she grows up and continues to look more and
more like Maria? It is already happening. Bonacieux will not always be
a baby. Soon, very soon, she will become a girl.

Philip has cut his hair. Cropped at his temples, it is long on top and swept back in a damp dark dash to his left. Strands of gray highlight the grain. Almost handsome, deep uneven temples push his face just out of balance.

"And we'll have cupcakes," he says. "Sweet and messy, serious cake stuff. You want cupcakes?"

Bonacieux seems to want cupcakes, yes, but it is only that she wants anything Philip says in that tone of voice. Philip has never made a cupcake anyway. The kitchen is the kingdom of Nina. But she has maintained her distance, staying in Asheville with a sister. These days Philip cooks her recipes himself. They are the only ones he knows.

"Mom," Bonacieux says, unattached to a person. She looks around the room, and then, as if to confirm any doubt, says it again. "Mom."

There is nothing surprising about this. Neither Maria nor Philip even really reacts. Words appear like sparks off a fire from the child these days, small and portentous and glimmering. Not that Bonacieux doesn't understand what the word *mom* means, but she uses it all the time, rolling it on her tongue like a candy. It is her favorite word, but Maria knows she is not using it for her. To Bonacieux, Maria is Mary, Ma, or Mar. Mom is only Nina, and Nina permeates everything.

Just that morning, she sent several messages to Philip, and Maria has already read them.

Is she having a party? Nina said.

We're going to see the animals at David's farm. Bryce and Liz are bringing their kids. Darren and Debora too. Doing a pony ride.

I wish I was there. Does she even remember me?

Nina. She says your name all the time.

Do you miss me?

Nina.

You can. You can miss me, and you can tell me that you do if you do. You have done everything that you've done, and I am still not afraid to say I miss you. Because I do.

I miss you.

THE CUPCAKES HAVE been baked. The potato salad made. Hot dogs purchased, buns. Paper plates. Two cases of Pacifico chill atop ice in a blue cooler. Before they leave, Maria pops the plastic lids on two containers of confetti and stuffs handfuls of the glittering shards into her pockets. She has been to more parties in her time in Beaufort than in all the years of her life leading up to this point and now feels the desire to be armed with the weapons of joy any time she attends one. The corner of one plastic star of confetti pierces her finger, and a bulb of blood pushes into the light like a small balloon just filling with air.

The farm is a pasture that belongs to Philip's neighbor, David Hughes. Lavishly watered, the fields are a surprise of green velvet in a county of withering husk. Down the gravel drive they pass two banded cows, a horse, and a goat standing atop a doghouse.

"Today is the last day of summer," Philip says. The anniversary of Bonacieux's birth has, for the first time in weeks, lightened his mood. He reaches into the backseat and pats down her hair, but there is no order for it to regain. It stands back up like a memorial to static electricity. "You ever wait for it and then miss it when it happens?"

It is a quote from *Gatsby*. Maria makes no response, savoring this life with a man who trusts her to catch his allusions. She has shifted her repertoire from Jack's pop culture amalgam to Philip's refined quips.

At the house, Anna Hughes, David's wife, stands on the porch in a short khaki dress. Each strand of her black crop of hair is somehow distinct and gleaming. Her dark eyes are shadowed by thick eyebrows. She seems unbearably chic.

"So lovely!" Anna says, as Philip removes Bonacieux from the car. Then softer, "So beautiful."

"Genes," Philip says, and they laugh.

Four families arrive in a parade of European machinery. Maria does not know them. Nina's exit has complicated friendships. Allegiances have not yet been determined.

Freed from car seats, children huddle in twitchy pods around animal noses pressed through wire. The women are competitive in their beauty, the men broad-shouldered and sure. David's stable manager, a single reed of a young woman, saddles an old horse speckled with gray. With Bonacieux in her lap, the woman circles the arena, weaving between three large orange barrels. Maria can barely watch. She senses an imminent fall, an accident possible everywhere. But there is no accident, just a slow lap of the yard before the rider hands Bonacieux to Anna. The other women gather around, cooing.

"And now it's all yours," the rider says, handing the reins to Maria. "Philip says you're good with them."

She is impressed that Philip even remembers the stories of her days as a sunburnt horse counselor at Camp Celo. She glances over at him. He stands with the other parents, all of whom hold sweating glasses in the shade of a looming old Osage orange tree at the edge of the yard, where chairs have been set around a table now covered in presents. Philip does not see her, though. He is laughing at the joke of a woman in knee-high leather boots. Someone Maria does not know. Someone who looks like she has spent thousands of dollars on the clothes she is wearing. Someone who, when Maria was introduced to her earlier, looked past Maria to a couple behind her, waving while she shook Maria's hand.

Maria does not feel like riding the horse. What she feels like is telling them all that the child is hers. But instead she says, "OK," to no one in particular, and mounts.

The animal is old, at least twenty-five, but still powerful beneath her. In the shade with their cocktails, the parents seem impervious to sweat. Maria cannot imagine a way to enter the conversation they are now having, but as she trots past them, she is overcome with the desire to impress. She is aware she occupies some space between the two groups here—not child, not adult, not quite servant, not quite master. Her position is so qualified: she names for herself what she is—a nanny and a mistress.

She passes one of the large orange barrels in the corral and kicks it over. It is an old show trick she learned at camp. The barrel rolls onto its side. At the edge of the paddock Maria turns, the children now gathered into a tight knot of anticipation. She has caught the attention of the parents too. One of the mothers is pointing. Maria reaches into her pocket and loads her fist with a handful of spiky confetti, then gives the horse a kick. "Hya!" she says, and the beast takes off. Maria drives him directly toward the barrel. At its edge he jumps, and, in air, Maria releases the confetti. Sunlight breaks into pieces on the twisting spangles above.

The children scream in delight as Maria lands in the shimmering cloud.

"Again!" a boy yells, as Maria brings the horse to a stop. She rushes on the thrill. The only recent chances she has taken with her body have been in bed with Philip.

Across the yard, Maria looks for Philip's reaction. But he is on his phone, preoccupied and unnerved. He has not even seen. The last piece of sparkling plastic falls to the hoof-trampled yard.

Maria spurs the horse into another trot, turns, and kicks over another barrel. She wants Philip to witness. This ancient beast has only so many days left to shine. She rounds the bend and drives hard back toward the orange canister, reloading her palm with confetti before half standing in the stirrups. Again she releases a handful of confetti as the horse lifts into the air. But this time, as they rise over the barrel, the horse's front hooves hit the top of it and crumple. His legs fold into the ground. Maria slides down his neck, and as she does, the horse flicks his head, tossing her off like a fly. She rolls across the hoof-hardened dirt and comes to a stop a yard away, looking up into a sky now filled with bright confetti sprinkling down upon her.

"You OK?" the trainer says, suddenly above her. She is angry and concerned. "Hey!"

There is shouting. The horse rises slowly and walks away, annoyed. Maria says nothing.

"She's hurt!" the trainer says.

"Nothing's wrong with me," Maria says, and sits up, glitter falling off of her.

AT HOME, LATER, Maria closes her eyes and imagines herself beneath a guillotine. Any conversation she had with the other adults at the party had been only about the fall. The embarrassment she feels is so potent that it makes the whole lining of her insides ache. But Bonacieux does not care that Maria fell from a horse. She is nuzzled against Maria's breast in the shady nursery, suckling, while one small fan rotates in the corner. Each time its breeze passes over them, Bonacieux looks up briefly, her eyelids fluttering in the wind.

The child falls asleep. It is another victory. Maria allows herself to cherish each day now, each nap, each bedtime. The ability to appreciate these moments makes Maria feel like, before she was a mother, she never understood anything about anything. She had the knowledge that her own mother had toiled at the task of raising her, but she never before understood it. Of course she didn't. She had not yet had the eventual epiphany of any new mother—an appreciation of her own.

Philip too is asleep, he in the living room. On the floor beside him is a plastic jar of beads, a stuffed giraffe, and a wooden cart carrying an elephant that can bob his trunk as he rolls. These are only a few of the presents Bonacieux has received. His cell phone buzzes in the kitchen. Glancing at Philip's closed eyes, Maria opens the phone. There is a new message from Nina. It is in response to others, seemingly a continuation of some other conversation. Maria feels confident that Nina is the person whom Philip was speaking with when he took the call at the farm. What she sees now is this:

Not while Maria is here, Philip has written.

Then from Nina, *How is it that she trumps me in my own house?*

I don't want a scene in front of Bonny.

Your life is a scene in front of Bonny.

Maria feels sick. She puts the phone back on the counter and places the monitor by Philip's head. They are conspiring against her, around her. And why shouldn't they, she thinks? Nina is right, this is her own house. And Philip is right, Bonacieux should come first. The embarrassment from before swells up again, feeling this time like a confirmation of something true.

SHE DRIVES BACK to Karen's house, walks into the living room, and stops in the middle of the carpet.

"What?" her mother says, knitting on the couch. CNN is muted on the television. "Come here. What."

Maria sits on the white leather couch. It is cool to the touch. Her mother presses Maria's head to her shoulder and caresses her hair.

"What happened?" she says.

"It's all already happened!" Maria says. She does not know if she has the fortitude to explain, but her mother waits it out. She seems to understand that more is forthcoming, and of course, she is right. Maria can't stand to not talk about it any longer. "The family that adopted my daughter is all screwed up."

"Whose isn't?"

"But, and I know this is going to sound super dramatic, but the problem about this one is that it's all my fault. I picked them for my daughter, and now . . . I'm ruining it."

"It's not your fault," her mother says.

"Philip and I," Maria says. They are silent for a moment. Obama plays basketball on the news.

"Oh," her mother says, unsurprised. Maria is sure she has suspected as much for months.

"We . . ."

"Yeah, I get it."

"So I mean."

"Yeah," her mother says, petting her head in long slow strokes. She sighs. "OK."

"Ughhh," Maria says. Long moments pass. Her mother's caresses give her strength. "And today we had Bonacieux's party, and I tried to show off and jump a barrel on a horse but then I fell off the horse and everyone treated me like a child servant. Oh my God."

"Oh, sweetie," her mother says.

"I just mean, I never wanted a family. I don't care about having a ring. Rich friends. Anything like that. I just want you to not be dying and to have someone smart who likes me and wants to be with me only. And that's fine. But I also want to be able to see my daughter whenever I want to and still not have to be her mother. And I know that's impossible, really. I mean, I've sort of made it possible, but it can't last. It's all completely selfish and destructive, and I get that, and I've been reading Philip's texts too, and he and Nina have been talking, and, like, the only reason they're not working their problems out is because of me."

"You're being melodramatic," her mother says.

"I'm not. Look, Nina is living in her sister's basement. And this is her family! The ones I picked because they were perfect!"

"You're not the only person in this situation with agency," her mother says. "And nobody's perfect."

"With agency?" Maria says. "I don't even know what that means. Don't use professor-speak."

"I mean that it takes two to tango."

"This is like a three-way tango. I feel like I invented this tango."

"You didn't invent anything," her mother says.

Maria feels a growing measure of clarity, a sensation new for her in relation to anything concerning Philip or Bonacieux. She is finally discussing both of them with another human being. Such a basic need—companionship in the face of confusion. Such basic reward. For the first time she begins to realize what she actually is considering.

"I can't keep doing this," she says.

"Then don't," her mother says.

"Just quit?"

"Sure."

"But you won't see Bonacieux anymore," Maria says.

Her mother laughs. "You're sweet to be thinking of me here."

"She was making you so much better."

Her mother sits up straight, as if shocked.

"Look," she says, "I don't know what healthy people think this is all like, but being sick isn't something you just suffer. It's a job. And if I wanted to submit my resignation I would have done so long ago. Hey, listen to me now. I've got more to live for than just Bonacieux. She's not making me better."

Maria is embarrassed at such bald emotion. It is potent and thrilling. It gives her the feeling that she has just survived a terrible accident, that she can see the world in a more vital way, can appreciate the mundane. Everything is suddenly heightened. The light in the room calls attention to the composite bans of its spectrum. She can feel every bump of the pebbled leather of the couch. It is as if she has just emerged from years within a prison. She understands that this amplified receptivity will only be fleeting. Now is the moment to act.

MARIA RETURNS TO Philip's house. At the curb she parks. She has never parked here. Before, it has always been in the driveway. She approaches the front door, a door she has never before entered. She has not changed clothes, has not washed her face. She is worn and raw. Her eyes burn. She rings the doorbell.

"What are you doing?" Philip says, and waves Maria in.

"We need to talk," Maria says, remaining on the porch. She loves how Philip looks, how he is flawed, how his face is asymmetric. Has she ever noticed that his nose was clearly once broken? She imagines what broke it, savoring the possibilities. A bar fight. An accident at sea. The map of life is laid out across his flesh. She is seeing it for the first time.

"Isn't that one of those lines you hate?" he says.

"We have a problem," Maria says.

"With what?"

"With what?" Maria says, and tries to think of the answer. "Um . . ." It is almost too big for words. "Our lives."

Philip squints, as if Maria is not in focus. She had not meant to put it this way, but the hyperbole of the statement surprisingly puts her at ease. It has set the bar so high she might not even meet it.

"There's a problem with our *lives*?" he says. "Isn't that a bit dramatic?"

"I'm not sure it is, actually."

"It is," he says, and his confidence inspires Maria to prove him wrong. She feels as if she has a secret weapon, one she has longed to reveal to him for months.

"You're wrong," she says. "And not only are you wrong. I'm right."

"Well, OK then," Philip says. "If this is a lecture, please, by all means, carry on."

This is the closest they have ever come to having an argument, and Maria is surprised to find it so satisfying. It is the first time she has felt truly equal to Philip.

"First of all, you think I don't think about Nina?" she says. "That I don't see all those texts she sends? She's right, you know. This isn't fair. Not to her."

Philip makes a face, dismissive, as if to say let *me* worry about her.

"Yeah, but I think about her too," Maria says. "And you know what, and this is the more important thing. What we're doing isn't fair to Bonacieux."

"Maria," Philip says.

Maria senses a sad relief in his eyes. She is embarrassed to only now understand that he has probably been waiting for her to do this. That she is solving his problems for him.

"You want this, don't you?" she says. She is suddenly angry that he is not trying to stop her.

"I've said it before, and I'll say it again," Philip says. "I want everything. But I'm not going to claim that I can have it."

"You made this mess," Maria says.

"Is this a mess?" he says. "This is just . . ." He waves a hand in the air, as if softly backhanding a fly.

"You have no idea what kind of mess this is."

"I have no idea, huh," Philip says.

"Don't talk to me like that. You don't even know."

"OK. OK."

She feels the truth close to revealing itself and recognizes the danger at hand. Bonacieux has begun to cry in the living room behind Philip. Her daughter's wails are like lines attached to Maria, reeling her in. But Maria resists the pull and turns her back on Philip. She knows that if she sees Bonacieux for even one second, there will be no escape.

"Maria," Philip says. But she can tell that this is not a true protest. He wants her to go. He is letting her float away without even a fight. It is so much easier for him this way. Maria feels as if he has disrespected her. If only he knew the actual situation in which she has been living, that he would give her the respect that she deserves. The continued cries of her child push her to the edge of panic. "I understand," he says. "I do."

"No you don't," Maria says.

"OK."

Maria turns, furious at the condescension in his voice. Bonacieux cries even harder behind him. "That," she says. "That person crying? She's my child."

"I know she is, I understand that too," Philip says, nodding. But it is clear he is only trying to placate her and that he has not understood at all what she is trying to say.

"No, I mean for real," Maria says. "She's the child I gave birth to."

"She is not, Maria. She is not. I know this must be so difficult, but you're talking about two different things."

"I recognized you in the photos online, on the adoption site," Maria says.

Philip squints in confusion. "For the adoption of who?" he says.

"Of Bonacieux," Maria says. "I recognized you. I saw your picture and recognized you, from when I'd see you around last summer. And I picked you because you looked nice and I knew you lived in a town that I love."

Philip turns his head like a puppy to a whistle.

"You're serious," he says.

Maria nods and Philip seems to flush. The satisfaction Maria had been enjoying from this argument ceases. It is as if a door has now closed behind her, locking, leaving her in a new and foreign land. Philip's face has undergone a transformation. His lips have thinned, his eyes narrowed. A crease now stands vertically on his forehead above his nose. Maria's confidence in being his equal disappears. In its place she finds fear.

"How'd you find us?" Philip says. His voice is flat and direct.

"Online, like I said. And then later trick-or-treating," Maria says. She can tell he does not know exactly what she means. "Look, I didn't plan any of this."

Bonacieux continues her wailing. It is not her cry of boredom—it is one of need. Something is required. Food, a changing. Something. The sound fills the air with pressure.

"We need to go check on her," Maria says, pointing to the hallway behind him.

"You need to leave," Philip says. He is directing, as if managing a dangerous animal. Never before has Maria seen him like this. There is no room left for maneuver.

Maria's will is gone. All she wants is to do now is soothe her daughter. She steps forward.

"Just . . ." she says.

"Go," Philip says. The danger of finality fills the air. Maria wonders, for a moment, if Philip might hurt her. "Right now. Go."

He blocks the door. And so this is it. Maria has played her last card. For the second time she is losing Bonacieux for good. She wills herself to turn, but she can still hear Bonacieux, even as she crosses the lawn. It is the last of her daughter's voice that she will ever hear, she thinks. And so Maria herself begins to cry so hard that she is afraid she will not be able to drive safely. She thinks, how does one find a way to physically move during times like these? But she has made it this far, at least, and now, thank God, she can entrust a machine. She spins the car away in a rush, leaving Philip on the stoop. It is all she can do to steer. Even inside the car, she can hear Bonacieux.

AFTER HER MOTHER goes to bed that night, Maria fights the urge to return to Philip's house. In her room she still cries, blowing her nose into an old bandana of Philip's. She cannot be alone. She dries her face and walks down the hall. At Christopherson's closed door she knocks.

Like some prototype for the Southern young man, Christopherson appears in moccasins, Levis, and a polo shirt. These sartorial decisions soothe Maria at sight.

"Hey," he says. She can tell that he is unsure of how to act around her, unaccustomed to being with another person so clearly in emotional turmoil.

"Oh God," Maria says.

"You want to come in?"

"You have any cigarettes?"

Christopherson shakes his head.

"Anything to drink?"

"No."

"I feel like passing out."

"OK," Christopherson says, confused, as if making yourself pass out is already part of different person's past.

"Like doing that trick you taught me."

Maria tosses the wet bandana on the glass coffee table in Christopherson's room. Against the wall, she begins to hyperventilate. The sound of the air rushing in and out of her lungs scares her, but she wants the escape, if only for the seconds of reprieve it might grant. She does not care that Christopherson seems scared as he counts her passing breaths. She trusts him to be polite and follow her direction. When Maria stands, her legs wobble loopy beneath. The room presents itself at an angle. Before Christopherson can even press her chest she falls.

She dreams of Philip holding her hand, singing with her. Together they run over gravel that flies up at their heels, rising toward the sky behind them. She carries Bonacieux with her as they run. She laughs at the scene, embarrassed by her own visions even while in them. It is so ludicrous that, even if it were to be real, she would still have to laugh.

When she awakens, shards of glass glitter around her. The frame of the table lies under her lower back. She has fallen through it. A splatter of blood stains the carpet beside her. Christopherson is screaming. Maria raises her voice to join him.

CHAPTER 22

I T IS EARLY September. Fourteen sutures hold together the flesh of Maria's left arm. Her back, punctured in dozens of places, is marked by a diagonal bruise stretching from her left shoulder blade all the way to her right hip. It was left there by the frame of the glass table on which she fell. Nine days have since passed. Nine days in which Maria has been confined to her bed, a soft prison for which she is thankful, as she has never before longed so much for Bonacieux, and if she were not otherwise confined, she feels confident that she would have already found herself back on Philip's doorstep, which, she understands, is not something that can occur. She does not know if there are legal ramifications for what she has done. Twice she has heard sirens and feared they were sounding for her.

"It's Pirate Invasion day," her mother says, setting an orange plastic plate at Maria's bedside.

Through the window come the intermittent yelps of cartoonish piratese. Someone addresses their matey. Someone's timbers have shivered.

This is a yearly civic fete during which hundreds of costumed enthusiasts descend upon Beaufort for days of invasion reenactment and excessive drinking of rum. The odd cultural obsessions of Maria's generation have begun to fill her with disgust, and these yells entering her room make her long to have lived in a different time, perhaps one in which pirates were actually real.

Maria's mother stands at the window. Topped by a chic gray crop, her head bears no trace of its former baldness. A rich tan has replaced the pallor of the past. For the last nine days she has delivered medicine and food to Maria. She has petted her good arm and, on the first night after the fall, even slept in the rocking chair beside her. Their roles as caretakers have reversed. Maria has savored these hours. They have reminded her that she is a daughter. She wonders if the physical pain has helped distract her from thinking of Philip and Bonacieux even further, if it all would have been even more intense without. She has explained everything to her mother, including how she fell. She is exhilarated by revelation now, after so many months of living so hemmed in by secrecy. It seems like there is nothing they cannot now share.

"Isn't it time the pirate fad ends?" her mother says. Maria enjoys the unity of their shared contempt. "And why are pirate women supposed to be sexy? Pirate women didn't exist."

As the cries of the pirates continue to sound, Maria is sure Philip is delivering a lecture somewhere to a room full of confederate Blackbeard fanatics. She is also confident that he is embarrassed by them. It is an understanding she will never be able to share with him.

"I have to go back to Chapel Hill," Maria says.

"This will end," her mother says. "It's only two days long."

"I don't mean because of the pirates," she says.

Her mother turns to her, elegant in her waste. Her face is so creased that it seems to have been folded in on itself and just now reopened. The effects of the disease upon her flesh have rendered a body seemingly more true to her personality. Over the phone, Dr. Jeanette has said that remission is not a realistic possibility, but that each case is different. Every body has its own mysteries. "Apparently people can live in the Dakotas permanently," her mother said after one call, reprising her code name for life after cancer. "Reports are there's even electricity there." Maria shifts gently, moving from one set of sores to another. It is not only her wounds that ache, however. Without a child to nurse them, Maria's breasts have become engorged and even more tender than some of her bruises.

"I just can't stay here," she says.

"But you can in Chapel Hill?" her mother says.

"Absolutely."

"Even with . . ."

"I don't care about Jack."

"He cares about you."

"How long are you going to stay here?" Maria says.

"Without you?"

Maria does not point out that her mother no longer seems to need her. It is something she has yet to truly convince herself of. How the tables have turned, she thinks. It is what for so long she has wished for, to again be the one to be mothered. To cease taking care. But now that the change has come, she wonders if she is being foolish for leaving. Perhaps this is a time she should capitalize on, milking as much as she can out of what time she has left.

"I have to leave," Maria says.

"My scheduling conflicts disappeared long ago," her mother says. "I might be here awhile."

When her mother leaves the room, Maria slowly gets out of bed, proving to herself that she too can operate without assistance. It feels nice to stretch her legs. In the street a man in a tricorn hat and leather vest shares a cigarette with a second man wearing a braided beard. When a third in a captain's uniform turns the corner, they all brandish sabers, which seem to have been forged from actual steel. Maria is again reminded of Philip and wonders if he is now as disgusted with her as he surely is with men like these.

TWO DAYS LATER, Maria waves to her mother and Karen with her right arm—her left is held close to her chest in a sling—while she rolls the Volvo away from the curb. She drives in the direction of the drawbridge, then, once out of sight, circles back. She cannot help herself. She nears Philip and Nina's house. The rosebushes along the hedge sag in the late heat. The grass needs to be mown, the yard watered. Maria can't help feeling this failure of nature as her own fault. Philip has not maintained Christopherson's schedule of yard maintenance; that was Nina's chore. If Maria had not entered Philip's life, the yard would now be green, the bushes buoyant and blooming. She can only extrapolate what dying roses might foretell in regard to care for Bonacieux. She wheels forward just a touch and comes in sight of the driveway. The Mercedes is parked in the gravel. Nina has returned. Maria knows now that the grass will regain its color. She knows now that she must continue driving.

Through the open window the wind rushes in. Highway 70 is almost devoid of all other traffic. From time to time, a car passes in the other direction, and once, as Maria becomes stuck behind a slow-moving Caprice, she passes it in the face of an oncoming truck. As she enters the closing aperture between them, the truck honking its horn, she savors the rush of survival. The sun, still low in the eastern sky, burns brightly in the rearview mirror. Squinting in the light, the road shimmers on the horizon, as if it is flooded at that future spot, a pond of cool water she can follow but of course never reach. Maria adjusts the angle of the mirror so that the sun shines somewhere other than in her eyes, and then she is not sure the bear is even a bear until she is almost upon him. He is walking slowly north across the fast lane, and as she approaches, Maria slows to a halt. The beast has the same white markings on his head as those on the bear Maria sighted that day almost a year ago when she first drove to Beaufort. She cannot believe this thing is still alive and, in an instant, wonders what happened to the little girl standing beside it that day last year. Was she eaten alive? Perhaps all bears in these woods have similar markings, Maria thinks. Who is she to simplify the minutiae of nature? She presses her hand on the horn and sustains a wavering squonk. The bear stops and turns to her, flinging open his mouth as if it has been hung from a broken hinge. He joins her alarm with a cartoonish roar of his own and together their warnings float high into the sky, dissipating into a place where they can scare no one.

Maria takes her hand off the horn. The bear ceases his roar as well, then lumbers quickly into the pines. Maria is left alone, her fingertips tingling, desperate to tell someone about what she has seen. She can think of no one to call, though. Only her mother, but this story would merely instigate panic, and Maria has done enough of that already.

THE FRIENDS MARIA grew up with have, in the years since graduation, spread across the country. All children of professors, lawyers, and doctors, they viewed it a failure to stay in town. They now populate Hanover, Berkeley, Ithaca, Williamstown. All that remain in Chapel

Hill are the girls Maria used to cruise with: Icy People, Jane at Whole
Foods, Dotty who works at Caffé Driade. She does not know quite
what else she is returning to.

   Maria takes the exit for Chapel Hill, passing a strip mall with a
tanning salon and large Chevron that could be anywhere. She does
not feel yet that this is a homecoming. Not until she enters Chapel
Hill proper does the feeling of home return. She is surprised to find
the sensation a pleasant one. The storefronts here are each attached
to childhood memories. University Mall, where she would see Santa
Claus and where her mother would remind her that the man in the
suit was not in fact Santa Claus, but rather just a man in a costume.
The Wendy's where she used to park in high school. Whole Foods,
where she worked for so long. Jane who still works there. She tries to
imagine what locations in Beaufort might trigger such future memories
for Bonacieux, then realizes that there will be none. Nothing that has
happened in her daughter's life thus far will linger in her memory.
All recollections have yet to be formed. They will be attached to the
geography of Durham, perhaps, or maybe another town with which
Maria is not familiar. Whatever they will be, though, Maria will not
be in them.

   The house, maintained by neighbors and a couple who was hired
to check in two times a week, is a time capsule from another life. The
photos of Maria as a baby that line the hallway upstairs and that she
always passed without a glance now cause her to stop and marvel at
how much she looked like Bonacieux. Her mother's room is that of
an invalid. A seated bedpan still stands beside the mattress. A small
metal cart, holding a box of tissues and one large container of lotion,
stands tucked into a corner. The tableau reminds Maria of just how

sick her mother actually was. Like the memory of pain, it has, in the
months since, become hazy and abstract. She is glad, of course, and
tries to remind herself that this was the endgame all along. To make
her mother well. She is not sure if her mother is in fact well, but she is
not worse. Of that Maria is sure. But she is afraid of what will happen
to her now. Without Maria. Without Bonacieux.

On the chest of drawers in Maria's bedroom is a copy of *Ina May's
Guide to Childbirth*. The coffee tin filled with her vintage sunglasses
rests atop the notepad in which, during labor, Jack marked off time
between contractions. It all seems drawn from history.

She unclasps her black-and-white checked belt, flings it into a corner, and lifts over her head the white dress she is wearing. She spreads
it atop her bedspread, marveling at how worn it has become. Outside
Beaufort, the ghosts of baby food and spit-up suddenly now appear
as stains across the fabric. There, it was all invisible. She drops the
dress into the dirty-clothes bin, in which she is surprised to find an old
pair of the large medical underwear given to her to wear in the days
after giving birth. Her closet is filled with vintage dresses bought from
Time after Time, the tiny thrift store on Franklin Street. She runs her
hand across their fabric, each shoulder stiff with a wire hanger. She is
thrilled with this new old wardrobe.

She zips on a yellow dress with blood-red trim. She buckles an old
leather belt around her waist. It feels odd to have the freedom to be
away from a house for hours at a time. Afternoon naptime approaches,
and she feels the responsibility to stay inside, to get Bonacieux to sleep.
To put her in bed with her mother. She wonders who is putting the
child to sleep right now. Her breasts strain at their flesh, filled with
milk. She begins to think that perhaps she should email Philip, let him

know that she has left, ask him if they are still interested in open adoption. It was Philip and Nina, after all, who first floated that idea, in the very first letter Maria read. She was the one who opted out. Perhaps it might still be an option, she thinks. It's a desire untethered to reality, but it has momentum nonetheless. Afraid to allow herself to indulge it any further, she leaves the house in a rush.

She returns to Whole Foods and finds Jane behind the deli counter. In her late twenties, an early streak of gray in her bangs, Jane is a lifer. Her boxy white jacket is folded over a soft little body scattered with tattoos, almost all of which Jane says she now regrets. Her only goals in life seem to be to find a boyfriend and to keep this job. She is serially successful at both.

"Little Mama!" Jane says, seeing Maria approach. "Tim!"

Tim, the fish guy in rubber overalls and fluffy muttonchops, looks up and waves grimly from a display of cod on ice.

"My God!" Jane says. "You're tan!"

A stooped old man wearing shorts, white socks, sandals, and a safari hat approaches. His basket is filled with supplements.

"I'll be with you in one second, Mr. Vollmer," Jane says. "What happened to your arm?"

"I made myself pass out and then fell through a glass table," Maria says. The man with the supplements glances sidelong at Maria and quickly shuffles away.

"Jesus, girl," Jane says. "I'm taking you out."

"No," Maria says. She does not want to go out. Already she feels like she's reliving an episode from her youth, something she has moved beyond.

"Trust me," Jane says.

Despite her misgivings, Maria suspects there might be some truth in Jane's advice. Interaction with anyone other than Philip, her mother, or Bonacieux seems necessary at this point for her to achieve something that might approximate good mental health. And so at nine Maria returns to Whole Foods. Jane has changed into oversized grandma glasses and a dashiki. Maria feels like she has missed a fashion epoch in her year away. Without explaining where the Dodge Diplomat has gone—it is not here—Jane follows Maria to the Volvo.

"How's your mom?" Jane says.

The fact that Jane even remembers Maria or her mother surprises Maria and moves her. Her expectations of friendship have fallen so low.

"She's a lot better," Maria says.

"Better better?"

"Her hair's back."

"Great. That's great, right?"

"Yeah," Maria says, laughing, thinking how nice it is to talk with someone her own age. She had forgotten the feel of easy rapport. The confidence inspired by speaking in a shared rhythm. The night swells with sudden promise: a memory of joy.

"What the hell have you been doing?" Jane says. "Surfing?"

"Yeah, right. Babysitting."

"Good lord. For real?"

"For real."

"Wasn't that weird?"

"You have no idea," Maria says. She wants to talk about Bonacieux, but still the secret feels so radioactive, even now, even after the people from whom it had to be kept have already learned it all. "But it was great, too," she says. "I miss the little girl. A lot."

They drive west on Franklin Street, past the college bars and into the realm of the townies. Parked cars line the streets. Maria cannot find a spot. It feels like years since she has seen so much nightlife. The search for a parking place brings the sudden progress of Maria's excitement to a halt. Stopping and starting, cutting tight crowded corners, Maria pines for the quiet of Philip and Nina's porch. What she cannot believe is that there are this many people with no one to tend to at night.

"Hopie's bartending at Orange County," Jane says, as if in consolation. Maria does not know who Hopie is but takes the information to mean that it will not matter that Maria is still three months shy of her twenty-first birthday.

When they finally do step out of the car in the gravel lot behind the Bank of America, the air feels strangely flat as it snakes into Maria's nose. After the salted humidity of the coast, even taking a breath here seems both easier and less interesting. Young people leaning against the wall of the bank smoke cigarettes. One man with a cowboy shirt only half buttoned scratches a leg with the foot of another. His black pants are rolled high, revealing ankles mottled with scabs. A woman beside him has a magnolia tree tattooed across her chest. It blossoms out of a T-shirt with the collar cut off. Maria does not make eye contact. She feels she might have outgrown life as a single townie before she is even of legal age to experience it.

Inside the dark confines of the Orange County Social Club, the jukebox pumps Culture Club atop the raised voices of people Maria longs to look like, people she is simultaneously compelled to make fun of. Bodies swell within the room as if floating in a few feet of dark water—shifting slightly against each other, seemingly unable to guide the subtle movements of their own flesh.

"Is Jack gonna be here?" she shouts over the din.

Jane shrugs. "What's the deal with you two?"

"You probably have a better idea than I do."

"That whole thing with Icy People," Jane says. "What a cluster-fuck."

In the back of the bar stands the very Icy People in question. She leans over the red felt of a pool table in the light of the low-hanging lantern, illuminated as if by a spotlight. She is the brightest object in the room. Maria imagines Icy People as a baby: crying for her mother, loving a stuffed rabbit, having flesh so soft it feels dangerous to tickle. And Maria is filled with understanding and forgiveness. She has, of course, imagined herself as the mother.

Maria and Jane drink whiskey on ice. It is past ten o'clock. Bonacieux has been asleep for hours. Karen is watching CNN. Her mother is tucked in. Philip glows in the light of the fire. Nina flips through *Vanity Fair*. So many lives continue right now without Maria—she wonders if anyone now imagines her. If they do, they do not envision her here. She wishes she could be listening to Bach with Philip and yet even this fills her with guilt. Not because of her transgressions, but because she feels like she should be longing for her mother instead. Her mother is the one, after all, who is sick.

Icy People steps up to the bar, and Maria touches her arm. Icy People has not seen Maria, and when she turns, she sneers. She looks ready to fight. She would appreciate the performance of it, Maria thinks. It would be an asset to her persona.

"Everything's cool," Maria says.

"OK," Icy People says, unconvinced.

"I'm serious."

"OK."

"I love that song about having things and stuff. It's been stuck in my head for like months."

"Thanks," Icy People says, thawing in the warmth of Maria's praise. "What'd you do to your arm?"

"Fell through a glass table."

"Damn, girl."

"Yeah," Maria says. "It hurts."

LATER, IN THE car, Maria lays her head back and watches the rain slide like melted light down the windshield. She knows she should not drive. But Jane has gone home with a bartender named Johnny, and Maria has never before called a cab. She starts the car and cruises east, slowly exiting Carrboro. Around her, barhoppers hold hands, laughing on the sides of the streets. She stops and rubs her eyes, only to start again and then stop two blocks later. She comes close to running two stop signs and once jumps a curb, sending pedestrians screaming into a lawn. The danger in this enterprise is palpable, but part of Maria wants to be caught. She passes a young police officer and waves, but he only waves back and smiles.

When she gets home, she cannot stop herself. She opens her computer and begins a message to Philip. *Is there any way I can see Bonacieux again?* she says. *It is all that I want. However it can happen. I'll do what you say.*

CHAPTER 23

MARIA AWAKENS TO the tritone doorbell. She has slept in her clothes. The quilt her mother made for her tenth birthday slides off the bed and settles onto the floor as she rises. She moves her tongue around her dry mouth, remembering in terror the email she sent the night before, positive that this is now Nina or Philip standing on the stoop, or maybe even the handsome police officer from the night before who has returned to finally arrest her. Her head throbs. As she stumbles down the hallway she says "Hello hello hello" aloud, trying to rid her voice of any trace of sleep before she must face whatever actual human awaits. She opens the door, and there, backlit by a painful morning sun, stands Jack.

"You were spotted by my spies," he says.

There is nothing Maria wants less than Jack right now. She wants French press coffee in Karen's kitchen. She wants Nina's silk robe. She wants Bonacieux against her. Croissants. Grapefruit. But something animal comes over her and she finds a reason to not close the door, because in one hand, Jack holds a greasy paper bag from Weaver Street Market, and in the other, two Styrofoam coffee cups. Maria's desire is carnal. She longs for the contents of that bag. Its appearance keeps her from thinking about all other complications so near at hand.

Behind Jack, Maria's Volvo is parked with its back wheels in the driveway and its front two in the yard. "Jesus Christ," she says, rubbing her eyes.

Jack hands her the bag, heavy with promise, and finds her car keys on the front hall table. He backs the Volvo out of the grass and straightens it in the driveway. Maria knows it is too late, though. The neighbors have all already retrieved newspapers and gone to work. The Copelands have probably already padlocked their hot tub. The smoke signals have surely gone up: Maria has returned. There was a time when no child on the block was more quiet, more invisible, more sought after to babysit than she. Now Maria is the girl who climbs nude into cold hot tubs and parks in the grass. She is the one who got pregnant at age nineteen. She is the one whose mother is sick. Pity her and beware. That's what the smoke signals say.

"Eat," Jack says.

An egg and cheese biscuit. Cheese grits. Coffee. Maria feels better with each bite. Jack bends to his toes, then holds his arms out wide till his sternum pops. In silence he washes dishes. He rubs Maria's shoulders.

"Ow," Maria says. "Stop."

"What happened to your arm?" Jack says.

"Ugh," Maria says, and fans the air.

Jack seems to sense that this injury has been the result of something more than just an accident. He softly rubs his thumbs across the skin at the base of her neck.

"I told them everything," Maria says.

Jack continues his caress.

"You hear me?" Maria says.

Jack comes around the table. He leans on it and looks her in the eye. He is older now, Maria realizes, older than his years. Like her.

"They aren't our family," he says. "That's the whole point."

Our family. Maria considers what her family is. Does it now include Jack? She is not sure. The definition has become blurry. It is a classic question of the modern age, Maria thinks. She has read too many essays about it in her mother's subscriptions. But why shouldn't her family now include Jack? The roster is anything but crowded. What she does know is that they had a child together, and that this child would look up at Maria from her breast, more satisfied than Maria can remember ever having been. Bonacieux longed for Maria's arms. It seemed she actually needed Maria's proximity to live. But Maria is now gone, and the child is surely still alive. Maria holds her face in both hands and wonders at the half-life of memory, certain that Bonacieux will never leave Maria's own memories but that Maria is already disappearing from hers.

SHE CROSSES CAMPUS that evening and enters the Ackland Art Museum. In the renaissance gallery, she sits on a maroon bench before an expansive portrait of Saint John the Evangelist. She feels as if some refinement is required to lift the last of her lingering hangover. The museum is empty, with the exception of three security guards, each of whom it seems would like to speak to her. She, however, does not want to talk. Her days have undergone a simultaneous narrowing and expansion, their focus on Bonacieux and Philip and her mother somehow removing all other social interest while at the same time making the world larger, more filled with magic, unknowable, beautiful and scary. Now that this focus is gone, she feels her world again shrinking, filling with the mundane.

CHAPTER 24

MARIA DRINKS TEA while paging through an old *New Yorker*. It is the following morning. She enjoys the way this house feels removed from the present, how she can enjoy articles several months old and have no thought for the news of the day. She has turned on no lights, letting the flat gray light of the overcast morning permeate the house like a fog. She wears her old red robe, the one she got on her sixteenth Christmas. She closes the magazine, and as she rubs the terry cloth between her fingers, Bonacieux returns to her. There are so many triggers for this. Bathing. Sleeping. Cooking. But now this too, the feel of terry cloth. With its touch Maria is there, kissing the back of her daughter's neck, nuzzling her cheek. She is breastfeeding her, a soft blanket tossed over her shoulder. She can hear her soft breath.

Maria is snapped out of her reverie by the phone. It is her mother.

"I'm coming home," her mother says. Her voice is all business, leaving little room for conversation.

"Are you OK?" Maria says.

"No, I'm sick. I need to see Dr. Jeanette."

Maria measures her breath. Already she is telling herself that all is as expected. Not yet two weeks away from Bonacieux, and her mother has started to fail. It is her fault, Maria thinks. Her chest seems to contract under a sudden insidious pressure.

"What can I do?" Maria says. "I can come get you."

"Calm down," her mother says. "Karen'll bring me."

"I love you," Maria says. It is something she rarely says on the phone. She cannot, in fact, even remember the last time she said this to her mother, but she is afraid and feels the need to let her mother know it. It is like the bell announcing that an elevator has reached the ground floor, that now is the time to step out and see exactly where you've landed.

IT IS EVENING. From Karen's car, Maria's mother walks across the fallen leaves slowly, as if very sore. She is wrapped in the same red plaid blanket in which she hid on her trip to Beaufort one year earlier. Her face no longer appears to have been creased by a life well lived; it is now just skin across bone. The ephemeral blossom of life that had returned no longer fills her cheeks with color.

Maria does not rush out to see her. At the kitchen window, she fiddles with a banana peel. This is yet another woman she does not know, another iteration of what she longs to be unchanging.

"Love," her mother says as she enters. "Oh, sweetie. I need to lie down."

Karen follows in a cacophony of door banging, clumsy with bags and a basket filled with seashells and assorted flora and fauna. A wasp nest, dead beetles. Bird feathers. From somewhere a turtle shell. Maria's mother has reacquainted herself with the wonders of nature. She has become a connoisseur of biological minutiae. Karen gingerly sets the collection beneath the back hall table.

"It just started yesterday," Karen says, as her mother disappears down the hallway.

"What is it?" Maria says.

"Fever. Vomit."

Karen fetches more bags while Maria enters her mother's room. Already her mother is under the sheets, her clothes folded into a neat pile atop the dresser.

"I don't even know if those sheets are clean," Maria says.

"Ugh."

"Want me to call Dr. Jeanette?"

"I'm going in the morning."

"Can I get you anything?"

"A bucket."

Maria laughs, glad that her mother's sense of humor is still buoyant.

"I'm not joking," her mother says.

Maria finds the bucket in the laundry room, removing from it a mop and one dead moth. By the time she places it beside her mother's bed, her mother is already asleep. She walks the hall to her room, closes the door, and, in the hushed shadows, dials Christopherson.

"How's your mom?" he says.

"Sick."

"Man."

"And I know this is going to sound crazy, but I was calling to ask you a favor."

"OK."

"Can you maybe help me figure out a way that maybe we could get Bonacieux up here?"

"To Chapel Hill?"

"Yeah."

Christopherson is silent for a moment before he says, "Are you OK?"

"I know, I know," Maria says, "but I'm serious, Mom gets better around the baby."

"Maria," Christopherson says, afraid. His fear makes Maria cease. She can hear herself now, through his ear. This is crazy talk.

"OK," she says. "Nevermind. Nevermind."

"Is my mom there?"

"Yeah."

"She can help," Christopherson says. He has such faith in Karen, positive of her ability to fix. Maria even smiles. It is so simple. There is no reason Karen will be able to do anything more to help this situation, she thinks, yet Christopherson's confidence is sound in the logic of love. She is, after all, his mother.

THAT EVENING, MARIA joins Karen in the living room. Karen cups a large glass of red wine, swirling it slowly in the space before her. Maria knows there was no wine in the house before her arrival. She is impressed with Karen's foresight. Karen almost always presents an optimistic facade, but her habits reveal the truth. Maria has left a message for Jack but does not know where he is. She does not want to be alone and is glad to have Karen here in the house with her.

"You left quite a wake behind you," Karen says.

"Oh God," Maria says.

"Well, we don't get a lot of good gossip."

"Happy to oblige."

"I saw them out at dinner the other night." Maria understands by Karen's tone that she is talking about Philip and Nina.

"I wonder who was watching Bonacieux."

"She was with them."

"At what time?"

"Eight o'clock."

"She should have been in bed," Maria says, haunted by the disregard of Bonacieux's sleep schedule. "Was it a mess?"

"What do you mean?"

"Bonacieux. Was she melting down? At that hour . . ."

Maria can tell that Karen is struggling with her answer. "No," she says. "It was fine."

"Really?"

"Yeah. They looked . . ." Again she searches for the words. "Happy."

Maria considers this possibility. The news that they can carry on without her, in blatant disregard of her scheduling, is a disappointment.

"So you know everything about it?" Maria says.

"About?"

"Me. And Philip, and all that." She still has a hard time putting in words the fact that Bonacieux is her biological daughter, the memory of its secret status still giving it a hint a danger.

"I think so."

Maria sighs. "I'm sorry."

"For what? It was the most exciting thing that's happened since the Cheathams' mailbox got blown up by an M-80 last Easter."

Maria considers the milestones of Karen's life and wonders at the circumstances surrounding her divorce. Maybe the neighbors were all aflutter about that too. To have her own public humiliation aligned with the explosion of a mailbox is soothing to Maria. She envisions the smoke from her own blast dissipating.

ON HER BED, Maria listens to Joan Armatrading on her mother's old turntable. The rest of the house has fallen asleep. The music plays quietly, and so, when there is a tap at the window, Maria thinks first that it is a malfunction of the record player. She rises and sees at the glass the faces of Jack and Jane. A third person moves ghostly and indistinct behind them. It takes Maria a few steps before she recognizes Icy People. Maria tells herself to remain careful here, at least for appearances, but is in fact thrilled to see each one of these faces. This, her middle school fantasy of friends sneaking up to her window, has finally come true. She pushes up the frame.

"Hey," she says. "What are you doing?"

Jack turns to the girls and gestures to the window. They begin to climb in. First Jane, then Icy People, then Jack. They are in their pajamas. Jane carries a plastic grocery bag. Once in the room, she removes from it an assortment of dried fruit. Jack says, "I got your message. We thought we'd . . ."

He cannot find the words to finish the sentence. Maria knows what he wants to say, though. That they don't want Maria to have to be alone while her mother is sick. That this might be the last time she is sick. Her throat tightens as tears press against her eyes.

The fruit they have brought has been selected from the most expensive bins in the bulk foods aisle: mango, papaya, dates, and figs. These are the delicacies Maria is always afraid to purchase lest she deplete her meager checking account. Even with her mother sick in the house at that very moment, Maria's spirits rise. She smokes Jack's pipe and lies with her friends on the bed and the minutes pass like hours. Maria is glad the time has become so stretched out. She does not want to be alone with her mother's sickness ever again. And then, as if window tapping has been optioned for the whole night, there comes another tap at the pane. Again Maria rises, as does each of her friends. At the glass, she sees yet another familiar face: Christopherson.

"I called him," Maria says, as if this might explain it. She is terrified he has brought Bonacieux with him. But she sees that he is alone, and a wave of relief washes over her.

"I was worried about you," Christopherson says as she opens the window again. Before a crowd, he seems ashamed of this sympathy.

"So were we!" Jack says.

Maria, incredulous at this outpouring of concern, motions for him to enter.

"No," he says, but does so anyway.

"I can't believe all of you," Maria says, feeling as if she is making an acceptance speech.

Behind her the door opens. She turns. In the frame stands her haggard mother. The room falls silent with horror.

"What's happening?" her mother says.

"We're just hanging out," Jack says.

Maria's mother closes her eyes.

"Do you need us to be quiet?" Jane says.

"No, no," she says. "I need you to do just what you're doing. Stay with her forever. I'm fine." Maria can tell her mother is somewhere in the midst of a drug-induced sleep and wonders if she even realizes what is happening. "You're good friends," she says. "All of you."

THE NEXT MORNING, Karen, Maria, and her mother all climb into Karen's BMW, silent and efficient and clean. Jack and Jane and Icy People and Christopherson all slept in Maria's room, the boys on the floor. Christopherson snuck off before his mother awoke. Maria's mother has made no mention of the night before, but its effects have lingered for Maria. She feels buoyed by friendship and filled with a fortitude missing from her life even a dozen hours earlier. During the drive to Dr. Jeanette's office, they do not speak. Maria's mother shivers within a gray sweat suit and blue down coat.

In the waiting room, Maria and Karen read old *People* magazines. Maria skims the celebrity obituaries. When Dr. Jeanette emerges, he is without Maria's mother. He resembles Andy Griffith, though is humorless. They have known him for decades. Maria is confident that whatever news he carries with him will concern the schedule of fatality. He stops to rub the head of a toddler, then approaches.

"It's the flu," he says.

"The flu?" Maria says.

"Have you had the flu vaccine?"

"No," Maria says, unsure of why they are discussing her vaccination schedule.

"They still have some at Walgreens," he says.

"Just like the regular flu?" Maria is incredulous that this is all it could have been. She waits for further diagnosis.

"Well, it's a nasty one," Dr. Jeanette says.

"This doesn't have anything to do with cancer?"

"Her white blood cell count could be better," he says, and writes out a prescription.

The past hours were so filled with such expectation of bad news that now, in its place, Maria feels a strange disappointment. There is no room to really hope, she understands. But what does it mean to find hidden a wish for it all to end? There will be relief, she knows. It is the rest she is scared of. She has mothered a child; she is an adult. Soon she will also be an orphan. Like tracing a map before a journey, she has been over it all before. What scares her is the knowledge that the voyage will resemble little of the map.

AT HOME HER mother lies on the couch while Maria, shaky with relief, searches in vain for the remote control. The minutes have become less precious and more filled with air. Everything feels trivial. Light. Objects seem like they might begin to float.

"After chemo, this so isn't fair," her mother says. "It's bringing back too many memories of being sick on this couch."

"Yeah, but that was a different sick," Maria says.

"Either way, it's cold here in the Dakotas," her mother says. "Can you bring me a blanket?"

And so, for today, her mother is still alive, but in the minor places from which the fear of her death has receded, the impulse to see Bonacieux only strengthens, as if expanding to fill any available space.

CHAPTER 25

J ACK, WHO HAS endeavored to return to the graces of both Maria and her mother, buys three tickets to the North Carolina Symphony's *Rite of Spring* centennial celebration at Memorial Hall. He has noted Maria's lack of interest in the bar scene, in clubs, in going out with others their age. He does not press it. In fact, he seems invigorated by the challenge to sophisticate. And tonight, Maria is impressed. He even knows what he has done. These tickets were no blind purchase. He knows the piece well, knows its history, talks about how he wishes he could have seen its premier as they walk across campus, the warm evening chirping in the darkness around them. It is three weeks after Maria's mother came down with the flu, and though her mother is still very slow, her footsteps fall faster than before.

Maria and her mother giggle as they see people they have known for years enter the theater in their finest costumes. They have never before attended a concert together, and the novelty of it all keeps them at the bubbling edge of laughter.

"Shut up!" Jack says. "This is going to be awesome!"

Jack is not even being ironic, at least not completely. He is ready for any experience and perpetually prepared to enjoy. It is his most endearing quality.

"Show me the man who don't love Igor Stravinsky," he says. "Here they come!"

Onstage, a man in a tuxedo appears, shaking his sleeves. He arranges sheet music, aware of the eyes on his back. For some reason, Maria finds herself scanning the room for Philip and Nina. They are not here, but they could be. In a region like this, with the lives that they live, their paths are all made to cross. She wonders if Philip and Nina will decide to move away from the state, if only to be free of this hazard.

The music begins heavy and thick. Maria is made happy less by the performance itself, but more by the obvious fact that both Jack and her mother are enjoying it. During the quiet brought into the room by the opening of the second movement, Jack puts his arm around Maria and whispers into her ear, "I want to have your children," and Maria can tell that as he says it Jack does not, for one second, realize he has already had her child. She envies his ability to so absolutely leave the past behind. She has not told him of her email to Philip. She has not even shared with him her desire to keep Bonacieux in her life. Jack, for his part, has avoided the subject altogether, seemingly content to let the issue rise on Maria's terms.

As the final, violent sequence of the sacrificial dance presses dense against them, Jack squeezes Maria's hand as if he is falling off a cliff. Maria's mother grins like she's never before heard music. It is the fact that they have come through the trials of the past several months together. It's the volume. The lighting, the crowd. Maria cannot believe that there is not an option for such joy to continue forever. But Maria's mother is well for now. The night is magical; there can still be others.

If things are not touched, if all is kept safe, quiet, this small region of safety can be theirs. This time it is Maria, not circumstance, who is moving to bring it to an end.

CHAPTER 26

MARIA'S MOTHER ENTERS her bedroom, where Maria is unpinning posters from the wall. She is determined to remove the ephemera of her childhood and, if she is to sleep in this room, make it a space for someone who is no longer interested in *The Great Mouse Detective*.

Her mother sits on the bed. "I just got off the phone with Karen," she says.

This is not news. She talks to Karen daily. But there is more, Maria can tell.

"Yes?" Maria says, taking the last thumbtack from her Outstanding Student Art in 2008 merit award. It goes on the pile, atop Outstanding Student Art in 2009 and Outstanding Student Art in 2010. "And?"

"Philip and Nina moved," her mother says.

Maria paper-clips the awards together.

"OK," she says. "And what am I supposed to do with this information?"

"I just thought it'd be good for you to know. Maybe to help move things along, just knowing that their house is empty."

"Move things along?"

"Maria," her mother says, but Maria understands. She has been moody, distracted, preoccupied with memories of her daughter. Her mother knows what has been on her mind.

"So they sold it?" Maria says.

"I don't know. Probably not, but they left."

"OK," she says. "Thank you." She is not in the mood to get into this right now.

"You OK?" her mother says. Since Maria's fall, her mother has been solicitous of Maria's well-being, something that before she seemed to avoid on principle, as if her silence on the subject was a sign of respect for any causalities on the battleground of teenage emotion.

"I'm fine," Maria says.

"Look at all this," her mother says. She gazes around the room, its walls now almost completely empty. Some of the posters Maria has removed had hung for so long that the paint beneath them now shines out in a ghostly rectangle more bright than the faded space around it. That very morning, this room could have been the same one Maria slept in at age nine. It is now not much more than a guest room in need of paint.

"What?" Maria says, but she knows.

"I remember when you hung all these," her mother says.

Maria would have rolled her eyes at this only so long ago. But now she sits beside her mother, leaning her head onto her shoulder. She understands the sting caused by the passage of time, how its markers can be difficult to witness. Even when Bonacieux began to crawl, Maria missed the days of immobility. The passage of each stage was both exciting and an end.

"Mom," she says, "I can't have Disney posters up anymore."

"There are no Disney posters here."

Maria points to *The Great Mouse Detective*.

"Well, that doesn't count," her mother says. "There're no princesses in that."

IT IS EASY to find out where Philip and Nina have gone. There is so much information online. On Duke University's website Maria finds Philip's office hours, the listing for his spring courses, his office mailing address. The new proximity of her daughter—Durham only a dozen miles east—begins to work on Maria's mind. It would be so easy to just drive over there and find her. But Maria will not. There are guidelines she draws up to govern her own conduct. She will not find Philip and Nina's house. She will not spy on them. She will not surprise their family by showing up on the door or dining at the next table over. She will allow no scene to play out in front of Bonacieux. But in addition to the information about Philip's classes online, Maria also reads on Duke's events calendar that a panel discussion about adoption has been scheduled, its focus on transracial pairings in the South. It is being held at the law school. One of the experts is Philip.

She understands she should not under any circumstances attend the event, but while removing her childhood clothes from her closet, Maria finds herself in Bonacieux's bedroom. She is picking out a dress for her to wear to Easter brunch, and Bonacieux is on the floor below, pulling at Maria's leg. Maria picks her up and her daughter's arms go around her neck. And Maria begins to cry, because she knows she is not actually in Philip's house with her daughter, even though she can smell her, she can feel her soft flesh and hear her sighing into her ear. She knows that when she turns around, she will not see the nursery in which she spent so many hours, but rather the empty walls of her own childhood bedroom.

The event at Duke is open to the public. Anyone can go. And if she did, she would not cause a scene. She would not even speak with Philip if it seemed inappropriate. And though there is no reason why Nina or Bonacieux should be there, perhaps they would be. Maria wouldn't want anything more than a glance—something to help her reattach her daughter's image, because it keeps receding from memory. At night, in bed, Maria conjures Bonacieux's face, but it only rises to the surface in pieces. The curve of her neck, the roll of her chin, the small bags beneath her eyes, how her nose curls. These she remembers from having sketched them so many times, the act of putting pencil to paper itself a type of dance with which Maria could more soundly commit her daughter to memory. But even the sketches she no longer has, the book left behind in Philip and Nina's house. It is the relic of all her attention. All she has left are photos taken on her cell phone, but these seem incredibly inadequate. They don't look like her child. Bonacieux has become a cloud.

She dresses in one of her vintage dresses, one that Philip has never seen. She looks at herself in the mirror, gazes over her shoulder. Smooths the fabric across her stomach. He would be surprised if he saw me in this, she thinks. I look new.

FIVE DAYS LATER she puts the dress back on. Maria has been to Duke before, dozens of times. More. It is only twenty minutes east on 15-501. She usually enters its faux Gothic landscape with a joke, knowing that its splendor has so little to do with the rest of the city, but today her awareness of civic division is dulled by a growing anxiety.

There has been some local cobranding of the event with the *News & Observer*, as the topic has political relevance to three different state house races, and so it has drawn a large crowd in which Maria may hide. It is a good turnout for this type of thing, something Maria can appreciate after having sat through so many of her own mother's sparsely attended events. She finds a seat in the rear of the small auditorium, in shadows, among students. She wonders if she too looks like a student. She is not sure. She doesn't understand exactly how people see her nowadays.

She scans the crowd for Nina or Bonacieux, but does not see either. She tries to temper her expectations, telling herself there is no reason they would attend, but as the seats continue to fill, she keeps her eyes peeled. There is an undercurrent of disgust with herself as she does so. She has seen herself as a character on film before, the crazed spurned woman. But she is here only to catch a glimpse. She reminds herself that the event is for the public, that she is just part of the crowd. In truth she knows that she is not there for legal discourse.

Philip appears on the small stage, setting a soft leather briefcase on the table. Maria has never before seen him in a proper suit. He exudes the same casual elegance as always, now elevated by performance. His tie is a green polka-dot foulard, the thin wool suit navy blue. He sits behind a table with three other professors, all women. He arranges papers before him, chatting with his colleagues, then points emphatically to a part of the crowd far away from Maria. Along with Philip's fellow speakers, Maria follows the line of his finger and finds, to her astonishment, Nina and Bonacieux. They have entered without Maria's knowledge and are now encircled by a small group of admirers. Maria catches her breath. Her neighbor turns in curiosity, and Maria tells herself to remain calm. This is their debut, she thinks. Philip and Nina have only just returned to town. He is not even teaching this semester. This is the first time his colleagues have ever even seen Bonacieux. But the child is having none of it. Her face is buried in Nina's shoulder. Her hair has grown, a small lick of gold now swinging onto her neck.

Nina pets it as she talks to their friends. Maria is glad Nina is not forc-
ing Bonacieux to reveal herself. She simply allows the child to keep her
face hidden, which Bonacieux does, until Nina takes her seat. Then
Bonacieux opens her eyes and points them directly at Maria. Maria
smiles instantly and almost waves, but there is no sign of recognition.
A sea of faces fills the seats between her and her daughter. Maria is
simply lost in the swells.

The discussion begins, though Maria barely notes it. She watches
the movement of Nina and Bonacieux. From time to time she even
hears her daughter's voice, squealing across the room. At one point,
Bonacieux begins to fuss. It is a new act, one Maria has not yet seen.
She cries out, pushing against Nina. People in surrounding seats look
at them, annoyed. Students whisper. Maria wonders for a moment if
something is actually wrong, but it soon becomes obvious nothing is
truly amiss. This is just a young child trying to sit through an academic
roundtable. The child has every right to cry. Nina should not have
brought her here, Maria thinks, even though she is glad that she has.
The cries continue until even the moderator pauses in her discourse.
Nina rises and, bouncing Bonacieux on her chest, exits through a side
door as the child continues to scream. The discussion resumes, but
Maria can hear her daughter in the hallway.

She has a longing to rise from her seat, find Bonacieux, and take
her into her own arms. She is confident she could soothe her. At the
same time, though, Maria feels a strong and surprising surge of relief
that Nina is the one who now has the task of actually doing so. This
appreciation of Maria's freedom comes as a shock, and it occurs to
her that her dreams of Bonacieux have all been about moments that
require no real work. Napping together, feeding, walking, the first few

moments of waking. So quickly she has forgotten the hours of toil, of unbroken attention, of the inability to even shower for some days or the act of scheduling a nap several days in advance. She is blindsided by the discovery that a part of her has been growing in the child's absence, a part of her that wants nothing to do with being a mother. It is as if the time away from her child has poisoned the purity of Maria's emotion. Even the flap of hair growing on the back of Bonacieux's head seems to Maria less lovely than its absence. Maria is both disappointed with this discovery and, in a way, relieved. The realization that her desire points not only in the direction of Bonacieux, but also along a path directly away from her, carries with it a breath of freedom.

Eventually Bonacieux falls silent and Nina returns with her to her seat. Nina is flushed and clearly mortified. Maria savors the comfort of her hard plastic seat and is, for the first time, truly glad that she has come here.

Onstage, Philip has almost nothing to say. It is not until well into the discussion that he finally speaks, and only then it is after the moderator, a modish Indian woman who is so lovely that Maria can barely hear her over the mute of her beauty, turns to him and asks directly about his own experience.

"Yeah, my wife and I have been through it," Philip says. "Not a transracial adoption, exactly, but we would have. We were just so ready. It was the child who first became available that we adopted. It's a complicated process, whatever the ethnicity of the child, and I don't mean bureaucracy. What I mean is, it's just hard having a child." He laughs. A few audience members chuckle along with him. Maria glances around—they are the older ones, the other parents. Those who understand.

They discuss Philip's firsthand experience of process, a recitation of timeline and fall-throughs, all of which Maria has heard before. And then the moderator says, "Were the parents involved at all?"

"Of our daughter?" he says. "Birth parents?" He looks toward Nina. "No. Not at first."

"What do you mean?"

Holding his gaze on Nina and Bonacieux, Philip considers his words carefully. He says, "The mother found us."

People gasp. They are the same ones who moments before had been laughing. The same with whom Maria thought she had shared an understanding. Her face flushes. She should have expected as much, she thinks. She begins to feel the error of her attendance.

"She found you?" the moderator says, bewildered.

"Yes."

"How?"

"It's not hard these days, not with the internet, I guess. It didn't come from a bad place, I don't think. But it made things pretty difficult for us, for a while."

"Did she try to take the child?"

"No, no. Nothing like that," he says. "I'm not going to get into it, but it's all settled down now anyway. And in any case, our daughter . . ." He places his hand on his chest, unable to even find the words for a moment. He looks toward Bonacieux in the crowd. "Everything's worth it for her. In a way it's been good for us."

They move past Philip's account, but Maria can think of nothing else. He was generous to her, is what she thinks. Already she understands it was folly to ever think she could again be involved in Bonacieux's life. Just being here, seeing Philip and Nina outside of Beaufort, it is clear that the pressures of the world would be too great. At least she can leave this room with the kernel of hope that she is not hated, she thinks. The discussion ends and Maria rises with the crowd. But there is a bottleneck on the steps. Students are speaking to each other, pausing in the aisles and on the stairs. Maria looks over her shoulder. She feels an urgency to escape immediately, to exit before being seen. Never before has she felt such a need to flee from her own child. Nina and Bonacieux have approached Philip onstage. They are laughing. Philip is kissing Bonacieux's head. Nina's back is to Maria, who is inching her way to the door, but too slowly. Bonacieux turns from Philip and looks directly at Maria. Maria does not expect to be seen, again banking on the crowd to keep her hidden, but this is only barely a crowd now, and her cover is quickly thinning.

"Mar," Bonacieux says. "Mar!"

Maria pushes at the students before her, but there is nowhere for them to go. They push back, annoyed. Again she looks over her shoulder. Philip and Nina know Bonacieux's vocabulary well. They know what she means by Mar. They scan the room, but not with much interest. It is as if they cannot imagine Maria might actually be here. But she is, and Nina sees her first. Her mouth draws into a thin line as if pulled from either side. She wraps both arms around Bonacieux and turns the child so she cannot be seen. Clearly terrified, Nina says something to Philip. Maria watches his mouth. "Go," he says. There is an exit by the side of the stage.

"Mar!" Bonacieux says again, straining to look over Nina's shoulder as she rushes to the door. "Mar!"

The door opens, a bright sliver of sunlight swallowing Nina and Bonacieux, before narrowing back to darkness.

Maria, during all of this, has stood frozen on the steps, as if caught in a spell. She cannot believe she has come here, that she is the one causing terror and the need for flight.

Philip remains at the lectern. The lights have been brightened. The crowd, unaware of the drama playing out in their midst, has begun a more steady stream out through the exits. Philip lifts his briefcase and calmly places his papers inside it. He maintains a visage of taut focus. Businesslike, he steps down from the stage and approaches. He stops a half dozen steps below her.

"Is this going to happen often?" he says, his voice flat.

"No," Maria says, surprised to find herself breathless.

"What do you want?"

"I don't want anything," Maria says.

"Yes you do. Tell me."

"I don't!" she says. "I actually just realized, just here today, that I don't want anything. Just now. I'm serious."

"You wrote me an email. You show up here. You frighten my wife. I took the gamble that you wouldn't do any of this," Philip says. "But if I'm wrong, I'll make this serious. You can't mess with my family anymore."

"I don't want to mess with you. I'm . . ."

"You had every means to keep that child," Philip says, cutting her off. "Your family has money. The father is still around. I'm so embarrassed to think of what I did with you. What I put my family through."

"I only wanted . . ." Maria says. She does not know how to finish the sentence.

"It doesn't matter what you want," he says.

The room has now emptied completely. Maria collapses into a plastic seat still warm from its previous occupant. Philip continues past her up the stairs and exits the room without looking back. As he does, Maria understands that coming here was a colossal mistake. She is ashamed for what she should have known, which is that her exit in Beaufort was as good an end as could be. There is nothing she can improve on here. She had wondered earlier if Philip and Nina would be the ones to leave the whole region, fleeing any landscape filled with the possibility of Maria. But now she realizes it is she who must leave. That they are a greater risk to her than she could ever be to them.

CHAPTER 27

THE MAPLES GLOW in the afternoon sunlight. Autumn has transformed the North Carolina foliage into a lantern of reds, oranges, and yellows. The air smells of decay and reminds Maria of the playgrounds of her youth. Why, she wonders, did they all smell of rot? The wet mulch, decomposing in the shadows, of course. But it seems like something more, as if that decomposition was the actual smell of youth. Alive, so alive, yet marked for a certain transformation. An end. A new confederacy with the earth.

Maria's mother wears a dress that she has not worn in years. It is blue linen, a tan leather belt around her waist. Brown flats. Her hair has recently been trimmed. She is haggard but more elegant than ever. The fight with mortality has gifted her this. She is going to a reception at the home of the English department director. She goes out often now, determined to spend what capital is left. People are still unsure of how to react to her presence. Some don't know she was ever sick. Some think she has already died. Still others venture questions about her health, questions she is happy to field. Some shriek with joy at her presence. She kisses Maria on the top of her head and says, "Wash your hair."

Maria waits until her mother exits the driveway. Her mother has begun to drive again and has purchased a new blue Audi. Once it passes the window, Maria lifts the phone. She looks out the window again, assuring herself that she will have the house to herself, and then begins to dial the phone number written onto the back of her hand. It is for the Yale admissions office.

She inquires about reapplication. For several minutes, the young woman who takes Maria's phone call considers whether Maria might need to take the SATs again. "OK," Maria says, trying to hide her terror. But this is not an admissions counselor. Maria has the feeling it is a work-study student, probably someone her own age. Maria does not, it turns out, have to retake the SAT. She asks about what needs to be resubmitted and what might still be on file. They'll call her back, the young woman says, and Maria is happy to ring off.

There is a freedom to Maria's situation, one that she has engineered, one she has now begun to acknowledge. She understands how it happens, hundreds of times a day, how parents give their children away. Like Philip said, she has given up her child not because she couldn't keep it, not because of hardship, but for fear of hardship. Yes, she wants to feed Bonacieux. To lie with her and watch her, be with her as she learns to say each word blooming with promise inside of her mouth. To love her, yes. But since her epiphany at Duke, Maria has had to admit she desires only the moments of parental ease removed from the stretches of labor between. And those stretches, Maria thinks, are the miles where people become parents. She does not want to run them. Is this a weakness? Is youth an excuse? Both, she thinks. And neither. All of it. And yes, her own mother had a good year, but was it because of Bonacieux? Dr. Jeanette would think not. Her mother has stayed alive because of time and medicine. Maria wonders if she too needs medicine, because she feels certain that time alone will not make her well.

What she desires now is escape, an option possible only because Bonacieux is not in her life. And so her dreams have returned to Yale, which would be, of course, so much more than only an escape. It seems almost unbelievable to her that she turned it down just in April. She had dreamed for so long of leaving the South, of studying art within the Gothic archways she has as of yet seen only in photos, of being part of something she would take pride in. Because almost everything Maria has pursued thus far she has been embarrassed to discuss in Chapel Hill. Now she is embarrassed to even think of her own logic, only four months past, that led her to decline an acceptance to Yale. She hopes she has not lost her chance. She tells herself to stay sane.

Her phone rings three days later, in the late afternoon, when Maria is at Caffé Driade reading *The New York Times* at a wrought-iron table in the garden. An older couple is seated near her, also reading newspapers. They know her mother. The call is from New Haven.

"Hello, Maria?" says a woman on the phone.

"Yes," Maria says, just above a whisper.

"This is Susan Rollins, from Yale University."

The name of the school makes Maria's stomach drop. It is august and huge in the ear.

"Hi," Maria says weakly, unsure if she should address the woman as Susan or Ms. Rollins. She decides to not address her directly at all.

"I received your inquiry from Monday."

"Yes."

"You know, transfer applications are accepted even less frequently here than standard entry. Only twenty-three total last year."

"Yes," Maria says, afraid of sounding like a robot. She needs to say something else, but she does indeed already know this information.

Not the actual number, but something like it. She has read Yale's website closely.

"So I remember your package from last year," Susan Rollins says. "We were disappointed that you couldn't come."

"I had some family complications," Maria says.

"I remember that your mother had been sick."

Maria allows a moment of silence to pass, afraid to clarify that her mother is in fact still alive. She feels the assumption of death on the line and lets it linger there, sensing it might work to her advantage.

"And I'm very sorry about that," Susan Rollins says. "So, circumstances do change things, and we understand this, and last year I tagged your file with a note saying as much."

"Thank you," Maria says, though she is unsure of what she is thanking Susan Rollins for. She does not understand how or if a tagged file might positively affect her. "Does that mean . . . ?"

"Yes," Susan Rollins says. "It does. We have a spot."

"So . . ."

"You can come in the spring if you'd like."

Maria turns away from the couple beside her. She wants her joy to be tempered by no one else's gaze. This isn't what she expected. It is almost too easy. She is unused to good news and does not know how to contain herself. She says, "Yes, I would like to. Very much." She is not ashamed to let Susan Rollins hear her cry.

SOMEWHERE IN MARIA'S house, a Mozart piano concerto plays low on a clock radio. Leaves collect on the steps outside, across the grass, coloring the ground orange. Jack crosses the lawn. He looks shrunken.

His clothes have become less torn of late. He wears black Dickies and a black work shirt tucked into them. He has removed the large plugs from his ears. He seems to be aspiring to a quieter place in life. Once inside he does not speak. Maria waits for him on the couch, where she has watched his approach through the cold bay window. He sits beside her and takes her hand. She leans her head against his shoulder, her forehead touching his neck. As always, she can feel his heartbeat. Maria has told him over the phone of her plans.

"It's not for another three months," she says.

Jack waits a long moment before he says, "Why wait?"

"This semester's already started."

"I mean me. Why drag this out?"

"It's not about you," she says, almost intoxicated with her sudden power. She is aware that this feeling is not one she could ever maintain, that it is a product of only this moment, one that, by design, is meant to burn out. It is the heightened receptivity that surrounds an ending.

"It's about that you don't want to be with me," Jack says, the evocation of pity a rare note in his voice.

"Jack, I can't say no to this again."

"You did for Old Chub."

"No," Maria says, determined not to let the conversation slip into accusation. "For my mom. For Bonny."

Jack watches the leaves fall for another long moment before saying, "We were the three musketeers."

"Jack," Maria says. She feels, in this moment, a new love for Jack. Everything before was teen magic. He has done so much with her. Conceived a child. Prepared for the death of her mother. Watched sunrises and driven across the state. He has brought her despair as well as joy. None of it is enough, though, to convince her that she should not take the opportunity to leave him.

MARIA STANDS OUTSIDE her mother's bedroom. It is 10:20 AM, November 7. Three weeks have passed since she spoke with Susan Rollins. She squeezes her eyes tightly shut, grimaces, and tells herself to be fierce. She nods her head, trying to pump herself up. There has been no sound from her mother's room since Maria awoke at seven. Breakfast for both of them waits downstairs. The eggs are cold. Maria has already had her coffee. Checked her email. For a few moments, she went outside and kicked a spider web off the drain spout. Now she has come back in. Her mother has not slept this late in years. In a rush, as if diving into cold water, Maria opens the door.

The window in Maria's mother's bedroom is open, and as Maria pushes the door into the room, the pressure changes and the yellow curtain sucks tight against the window screen. Through the fabric, the sunlight colors much of the room a soft yellow. It plays across the worn red rug, an antique Persian that Maria and her mother found listed on Craigslist. Maria is afraid to move her eyes off the pattern in its weave. She remembers the plumber from whom they purchased the rug, how he had said, when they rolled it up to put in the back of the car, to keep the fringe all facing the same direction. Not to roll it too tightly. How her mother had said, "Are you serious?" and the plumber seemed offended. Maria is baffled as to why this memory has chosen this moment to surface. She raises her eyes to the bed. Her mother lies on her side, facing away.

She would already have moved. She would have already turned, already said, "Morning, sweetheart." This is how Maria knows. But of course, she already knew. Everything was known, everything foretold. It was only a question of when. The question has now been answered.

Maria puts a hand on her mother's shoulder. There is no response. A Nancy Drew novel lies on the floor. Of all things, this is what her mother had been reading. Maria sits on the edge of the mattress.

There is nothing gruesome here. The scariest changes that occurred to her mother's body all happened while she was alive. An odd euphoria charges the air. Maria is surprised to realize she has felt this way before, at her high school graduation. The knowledge of a chapter closing and the relief and sadness it brought with it seemed to make her even smell the same things as she does now. The warmth of the sunlight, the dust. Fabric softener. Cut grass. She begins to cry.

In the bedside drawer is a pack of cigarettes. It has always been there. Maria's mother would smoke a cigarette from time to time, at night, on the front stoop. It was a fake secret. She knew Maria knew. Now Maria opens the drawer and removes the pack. She puts a cigarette into her mouth and raises the red lighter, hidden within the cardboard, to its tip. But she cannot bring herself to light it. She is afraid to burn any relic of her mother's life. Immediately she is aware that everything from here will dwindle. It is too soon to urge on that progress. She suddenly understands the plumber's concern about the rug's fringe. Part of his life had been lived on that tasseled edge. The cigarette still in her lips, Maria reclines beside her mother. She can

CHAPTER 28

JANUARY. MARIA STANDS under an archway, the shadows of a
bare low-limbed linden falling across her feet. Above her a gilded
hexagonal lamp hangs from a thick black chain. She is in New Haven.
Dark shutters frame windows in red brick dormitories along a trio
of low buildings before her. The quad is populated by a handful of
teenagers tended to by parents. It is orientation for off-season arriv-
als. One young woman is crying, ashamed of her break. Others try to
ignore their parents, carrying multicolored folders of information several steps ahead of them. Maria's mother had joked that she was even
more excited about Yale than Maria. Maria wishes she could have
been here with her, but today Maria is alone.

She watches young men. Part of her understands that they are at
their most appealing like this—seen across leaf-littered gray sidewalks,
wrapped in nylon and wool, book laden, dreamed-of only. They shuffle past. Maria is quiet, still behind her bangs, but she is not meek. A
confidence new to her has filled these first few days in New Haven.
She is comfortable in the sight of strangers now. When she meets their
gaze, she does not feel the need to smile and nod. She can just look
right back. She thinks she is perhaps less kind these days, more stingy
with her emotion.

With several dark blue envelopes containing information about university enrollment, Maria skips all orientation events and instead returns to her new apartment. It is on the third floor of a large old house off Bristol Street, where the ceilings fall at sharp, odd angles in tandem with the heavily gabled roof. Holes in the plaster mark where the artwork of former tenants once hung. It does not feel like a home. It is a vessel for long-term passengers.

Her roommate, Jennifer, is a sophomore whom Maria found on Facebook. Jennifer's mother accompanied her from New Jersey to help with the move and has, since they arrived, been sleeping on Jennifer's floor. No one has said when or if Jennifer's mother is going to leave, or why she is even staying. Maria has yet to ask. The woman keeps her white hair in a bun and wears large wire-rimmed glasses, white running shoes, and the same floral dress every day. That morning in the kitchen, she retrieved an empty glass jar from the trash and gave Maria a detailed description of how she makes bath salts and uses "these containers" to hold them. "It's good for Christmas," she said. Maria does not know if this woman has anywhere else to go. She exudes desperation. Something, Maria is sure, is not right.

Soon after Maria enters her bedroom, Jennifer knocks on the door.

The roommate wipes at her eyes, which are red. Jennifer is a kind, very pale cellist from Basking Ridge. "Fuck," she says.

"What?" Maria says. "It's alright."

"I know you're probably wondering when my mom is going to leave."

"It's OK."

"She's between houses," Jennifer says. Her voice cracks as she speaks. She is clearly mortified. Overwhelmed. "There's, um . . . It's hard to explain . . ."

"She can stay here as long as she wants," Maria says. "As far as I'm concerned."

"Seriously?"

"You don't have to explain. Yeah."

"Oh my God," Jennifer says. She is blindsided with relief. She begins to cry. "I'm sorry. Oh my God."

TWO DAYS LATER, on the sidewalk returning from class, Maria finds Jennifer at the mailbox.

"This came," she says, holding out a padded envelope. It has been forwarded to Maria from her address in Chapel Hill.

Within, Maria feels the edges and heft of a book. The return address is the Children's Home Society of North Carolina. She knows what this is. Adoption service guidelines require it be submitted to birth parents once every year. It's a photo album of Bonacieux.

She is unsure about whether or not she even wants to look. For the first time in months, she can feel the promise of new days. Enrollment in her studio art classes has made her stomach ache with excitement. The café near her apartment appears to teem with unlimited mystery. She recognized the name of one of her professors in the *Times*. She is nervous of it all, so potent and fragile and scary. But she cannot resist the urge to see new photos of Bonacieux. Jennifer has already started up the icy steps. Maria peels the package open.

Inside she does not find a photo album. Instead it is Maria's blue sketchbook, the one in which she had drawn so many portraits of Bonacieux while in Beaufort. There is nothing else, no note. Maria unties the blue ribbon and looks inside. Her drawings. Strapped to Philip's chest in a sling, Bonacieux faces forward, reaching toward

Maria. She drinks a bottle in Nina's lap, wearing nothing but a diaper. She sleeps in her car seat. Her face is in shadow, the sun falling just below her chin. In a baby pool, she is sketched from behind. She wears a flowered sun hat that glows against the background. She is laughing, staring straight up. Her mouth open in glee. Gums. She is asleep, holding her bear. That flesh. Again, Maria is lifting her daughter from the crib, arms and legs going around her. She is kissing her. She is holding her up to be seen. The light falls on her. The child doesn't look like Maria. She doesn't look like Jack. She looks only like herself.

Here, alone, Maria will tie shut her sketchbook. She will wash her chapped hands in the apartment's cracked sink. See a matinee by herself. She will buy the coat hangers that she has forgotten to pack. There is a student from her painting class who will pass her on the street and nod, silently; it will please her to be recognized. The lights in her apartment will appear from the street below, windows glowing on the top floor there like the cabin of a slow-moving ship. There is ice on the steps, but she is not afraid. Maria starts up them, running, leaping from one icy step to another.

ACKNOWLEDGMENTS

THE AUTHOR WOULD like to acknowledge the assistance of the University of Mississippi and John and Renee Grisham for providing the support, time, and space to finish this novel.

A portion of this work was originally published in the spring 2013 issue of *Glimmer Train*, under the title "Life Drawing."

Nat Jacks, Jack Shoemaker, Daniel Wallace, Chris Offutt, Rosecrans Baldwin, Kevin Moffett, Eli Horowitz, Edan Lepucki, Leslie Jamison, Danielle Evans, Tom Franklin, Mathew Vollmer, Jess Walter, Winburne and Joan King, Patty Boyd, and Abby Brown each provided essential support.

This novel is a work of the imagination. Parts of the geography of Beaufort, Chapel Hill, and Durham have been altered or simply imagined, and much of what happens in this book resembles nothing about the reality of these places.